The Jew
And Other Stories

Ivan Turgenev

Contents

THE JEW
AND OTHER STORIES

BY

Ivan Turgenev

INTRODUCTION

In studying the Russian novel it is amusing to note the childish attitude of certain English men of letters to the novel in general, their depreciation of its influence and of the public's 'inordinate' love of fiction. Many men of letters to-day look on the novel as a mere story-book, as a series of light-coloured, amusing pictures for their 'idle hours,' and on memoirs, biographies, histories, criticism, and poetry as the age's *serious* contribution to literature. Whereas the reverse is the case. The most serious and significant of all literary forms the modern world has evolved is the novel; and brought to its highest development, the novel shares with poetry to-day the honour of being the supreme instrument of the great artist's literary skill.

To survey the field of the novel as a mere pleasure-garden marked out for the crowd's diversion--a field of recreation adorned here and there by the masterpieces of a few great men--argues in the modern critic either an academical attitude to literature and life, or a one-eyed obtuseness, or merely the usual insensitive taste. The drama in all but two countries has been willy-nilly abandoned by artists as a coarse playground for the great public's romps and frolics, but the novel can be preserved exactly so long as the critics understand that to exercise a delicate art is the one *serious* duty of the artistic life. It is no more an argument against the vital significance of the novel that tens of thousands of people--that everybody, in fact--should to-day essay that form of art, than it is an argument against poetry that for all the centuries droves and flocks of versifiers and scribblers and rhymesters have succeeded in making the name of poet a little foolish in worldly eyes. The true function of poetry! That can only be vindicated in common opinion by the severity and enthusiasm of critics in stripping bare the false, and in hailing as the true all that is animated by the living breath of beauty. The true function of the novel! That can only be supported by those who understand that the adequate representation and criticism of human life would be impossible for modern men were the novel to go the way of the drama, and be abandoned to the mass of vulgar standards. That the novel is the most insidious means of mirroring human society Cervantes in his great classic revealed to seventeenth-century Europe. Richardson and Fielding and Sterne in their turn, as great realists and impressionists, proved to the eighteenth century that the novel is as flexible as life itself. And from their days to the days of Henry James the form of the novel has been adapted by European genius to the exact needs, outlook, and attitude to life of each successive generation. To the French, especially to Flaubert and Maupassant, must be given the credit of so perfecting the novel's technique that it has become the great means of cosmopolitan culture. It was, however, reserved for the youngest of European literatures, for the Russian school, to raise the novel to being the absolute and triumphant expression by the national genius of the national soul.

Turgenev's place in modern European literature is best defined by saying that while he stands as a great classic in the ranks of the great novelists, along with Richardson, Fielding, Scott, Balzac, Dickens, Thackeray, Meredith, Tolstoi, Flaubert, Maupassant, he is the greatest of them all, in the sense that he is the supreme artist. As has been recognised by the best French critics, Turgenev's art is both wider in its range and more beautiful in its form than the work of any modern European artist. The novel modelled by Turgenev's hands, the Russian novel, became *the* great modern instrument for showing 'the very age and body of the time his form and pressure.' To reproduce human life in all its subtlety as it moves and breathes before us, and at the same time to assess its values by the great poetic insight that reveals man's relations to the universe around him,--that is an art only transcended by Shakespeare's own in its unique creation of a universe of great human types. And, comparing Turgenev with the European masters, we see that if he has made the novel both more delicate and more powerful than their example shows it, it is because as the supreme artist he filled it with the breath of poetry where others in general spoke the word of prose. Turgenev's horizon always broadens before our eyes: where Fielding and Richardson speak for the country and the town, Turgenev speaks for the nation. While Balzac makes defile before us an endless stream of human figures, Turgenev's characters reveal themselves as wider apart in the range of their spirit, as more mysteriously alive in their inevitable essence, than do Meredith's or Flaubert's, than do Thackeray's or Maupassant's. Where Tolstoi uses an immense canvas in *War and Peace*, wherein Europe may see the march of a whole generation, Turgenev in *Fathers and Children* concentrates in the few words of a single character, Bazarov, the essence of modern science's attitude to life, that scientific spirit which has transformed both European life and thought. It is, however, superfluous to draw further parallels between Turgenev and his great rivals. In England alone, perhaps, is it necessary to say to the young novelist that the novel can become anything, can be anything, according to the hands that use it. In its application to life, its future development can by no means be gauged. It is the most complex of all literary instruments, the chief method to-day of analysing the complexities of modern life. If you love your art, if you would exalt it, treat it absolutely seriously. If you would study it in its highest form, the form the greatest artist of our time has perfected--remember Turgenev.

EDWARD GARNETT.
November 1899.

THE JEW

...'Tell us a story, colonel,' we said at last to Nikolai Ilyitch.

The colonel smiled, puffed out a coil of tobacco smoke between his moustaches, passed his hand over his grey hair, looked at us and considered. We all had the greatest liking and respect for Nikolai Ilyitch, for his good-heartedness, common sense, and kindly indulgence to us young fellows. He was a tall, broad-shouldered, stoutly-built man; his dark face, 'one of the splendid Russian faces,'[1] straight-forward, clever glance, gentle smile, manly and mellow voice--everything about him pleased and attracted one.

'All right, listen then,' he began.

It happened in 1813, before Dantzig. I was then in the E---- regiment of cuirassiers, and had just, I recollect, been promoted to be a cornet. It is an exhilarating occupation--fighting; and marching too is good enough in its way, but it is fearfully slow in a besieging army. There one sits the whole blessed day within some sort of entrenchment, under a tent, on mud or straw, playing cards from morning till night. Perhaps, from simple boredom, one goes out to watch the bombs and redhot bullets flying.

At first the French kept us amused with sorties, but they quickly subsided. We soon got sick of foraging expeditions too; we were overcome, in fact, by such deadly dulness that we were ready to howl for sheer **ennui**. I was not more than nineteen then; I was a healthy young fellow, fresh as a daisy, thought of nothing but getting all the fun I could out of the French... and in other ways too... you understand what I mean... and this is what happened. Having nothing to do, I fell to gambling. All of a sudden, after dreadful losses, my luck turned, and towards morning (we used to play at night) I had won an immense amount. Exhausted and sleepy, I came out into

---

1   Lermontov in the *Treasurer's Wife*.--AUTHOR'S NOTE.

the fresh air, and sat down on a mound. It was a splendid, calm morning; the long lines of our fortifications were lost in the mist; I gazed till I was weary, and then began to doze where I was sitting.

A discreet cough waked me: I opened my eyes, and saw standing before me a Jew, a man of forty, wearing a long-skirted grey wrapper, slippers, and a black smoking-cap. This Jew, whose name was Girshel, was continually hanging about our camp, offering his services as an agent, getting us wine, provisions, and other such trifles. He was a thinnish, red-haired, little man, marked with smallpox; he blinked incessantly with his diminutive little eyes, which were reddish too; he had a long crooked nose, and was always coughing.

He began fidgeting about me, bowing obsequiously.

'Well, what do you want?' I asked him at last.

'Oh, I only--I've only come, sir, to know if I can't be of use to your honour in some way...'

'I don't want you; you can go.'

'At your honour's service, as you desire.... I thought there might be, sir, something....'

'You bother me; go along, I tell you.'

'Certainly, sir, certainly. But your honour must permit me to congratulate you on your success....'

'Why, how did you know?'

'Oh, I know, to be sure I do.... An immense sum... immense....Oh! how immense....'

Girshel spread out his fingers and wagged his head.

'But what's the use of talking,' I said peevishly; 'what the devil's the good of money here?'

'Oh! don't say that, your honour; ay, ay, don't say so. Money's a capital thing; always of use; you can get anything for money, your honour; anything! anything! Only say the word to the agent, he'll get you anything, your honour, anything! anything!'

'Don't tell lies, Jew.'

'Ay! ay!' repeated Girshel, shaking his side-locks. 'Your honour doesn't believe me.... Ay... ay....' The Jew closed his eyes and slowly wagged his head to right and to left.... 'Oh, I know what his honour the officer would like.... I know,... to be sure I do!'

The Jew assumed an exceedingly knowing leer.

'Really!'

The Jew glanced round timorously, then bent over to me.

'Such a lovely creature, your honour, lovely!...' Girshel again closed his eyes and shot out his lips.

'Your honour, you've only to say the word... you shall see for yourself... whatever I say now, you'll hear... but you won't believe... better tell me to show you... that's the thing, that's the thing!'

I did not speak; I gazed at the Jew.

'Well, all right then; well then, very good; so I'll show you then....'

Thereupon Girshel laughed and slapped me lightly on the shoulder, but skipped back at once as though he had been scalded.

'But, your honour, how about a trifle in advance?'

'But you 're taking me in, and will show me some scarecrow?'

'Ay, ay, what a thing to say!' the Jew pronounced with unusual warmth, waving his hands about. 'How can you! Why... if so, your honour, you order me to be given five hundred... four hundred and fifty lashes,' he added hurriedly....' You give orders--'

At that moment one of my comrades lifted the edge of his tent and called me by name. I got up hurriedly and flung the Jew a gold coin.

'This evening, this evening,' he muttered after me.

I must confess, my friends, I looked forward to the evening with some impatience. That very day the French made a sortie; our regiment marched to the attack. The evening came on; we sat round the fires... the soldiers cooked porridge. My comrades talked. I lay on my cloak, drank tea, and listened to my comrades' stories. They suggested a game of cards--I refused to take part in it. I felt excited. Gradually the officers dispersed to their tents; the fires began to die down; the soldiers too dispersed, or went to sleep on the spot; everything was still. I did not get up. My orderly squatted on his heels before the fire, and was beginning to nod. I sent him away. Soon the whole camp was hushed. The sentries were relieved. I still lay there, as it were waiting for something. The stars peeped out. The night came on. A long while I watched the dying flame.... The last fire went out. 'The damned Jew was taking me in,' I thought angrily, and was just going to get up.

'Your honour,'... a trembling voice whispered close to my ear.

I looked round: Girshel. He was very pale, he stammered, and whispered something.

'Let's go to your tent, sir.' I got up and followed him. The Jew shrank into himself, and stepped warily over the short, damp grass. I observed on one side a motionless, muffled-up figure. The Jew beckoned to her--she went up to him. He whispered to her, turned to me, nodded his head several times, and we all three went into the tent. Ridiculous to relate, I was breathless.

'You see, your honour,' the Jew whispered with an effort, 'you see. She's a little frightened at the moment, she's frightened; but I've told her his honour the officer's a good man, a splendid man.... Don't be frightened, don't be frightened,' he went on--'don't be frightened....'

The muffled-up figure did not stir. I was myself in a state of dreadful confusion, and didn't know what to say. Girshel too was fidgeting restlessly, and gesticulating in a strange way....

'Any way,' I said to him, 'you get out....' Unwillingly, as it seemed, Girshel obeyed.

I went up to the muffled-up figure, and gently took the dark hood off her head. There was a conflagration in Dantzig: by the faint, reddish, flickering glow of the distant fire I saw the pale face of a young Jewess. Her beauty astounded me. I stood facing her, and gazed at her in silence. She did not raise her eyes. A slight rustle made me look round. Girshel was cautiously poking his head in under the edge of the tent. I waved my hand at him angrily,... he vanished.

'What's your name?' I said at last.

'Sara,' she answered, and for one instant I caught in the darkness the gleam of the whites of her large, long-shaped eyes and little, even, flashing teeth.

I snatched up two leather cushions, flung them on the ground, and asked her to sit down. She slipped off her shawl, and sat down. She was wearing a short Cossack jacket, open in front, with round, chased silver buttons, and full sleeves. Her thick black hair was coiled twice round her little head. I sat down beside her and took her dark, slender hand. She resisted a little, but seemed afraid to look at me, and there was a catch in her breath. I admired her Oriental profile, and timidly pressed her cold, shaking fingers.

'Do you know Russian?'

'Yes... a little.'

'And do you like Russians?'

'Yes, I like them.'

'Then, you like me too?'

'Yes, I like you.'

I tried to put my arm round her, but she moved away quickly....

'No, no, please, sir, please...'

'Oh, all right; look at me, any way.'

She let her black, piercing eyes rest upon me, and at once turned away with a smile, and blushed.

I kissed her hand ardently. She peeped at me from under her eyelids and softly laughed.

'What is it?'

She hid her face in her sleeve and laughed more than before.

Girshel showed himself at the entrance of the tent and shook his finger at her. She ceased laughing.

'Go away!' I whispered to him through my teeth; 'you make me sick!'

Girshel did not go away.

I took a handful of gold pieces out of my trunk, stuffed them in his hand and pushed him out.

'Your honour, me too....' she said.

I dropped several gold coins on her lap; she pounced on them like a cat.

'Well, now I must have a kiss.'

'No, please, please,' she faltered in a frightened and beseeching voice.

'What are you frightened of?'

'I'm afraid.'

'Oh, nonsense....'

'No, please.'

She looked timidly at me, put her head a little on one side and clasped her hands. I let her alone.

'If you like... here,' she said after a brief silence, and she raised her hand to my lips. With no great eagerness, I kissed it. Sara laughed again.

My blood was boiling. I was annoyed with myself and did not know what to do. Really, I thought at last, what a fool I am.

I turned to her again.

'Sara, listen, I'm in love with you.'

'I know.'

'You know? And you're not angry? And do you like me too?'

Sara shook her head.

'No, answer me properly.'

'Well, show yourself,' she said.

I bent down to her. Sara laid her hands on my shoulders, began scrutinising my face, frowned, smiled.... I could not contain myself, and gave her a rapid kiss on her cheek. She jumped up and in one bound was at the entrance of the tent.

'Come, what a shy thing you are!'

She did not speak and did not stir.

'Come here to me....'

'No, sir, good-bye. Another time.'

Girshel again thrust in his curly head, and said a couple of words to her; she bent down and glided away, like a snake.

I ran out of the tent in pursuit of her, but could not get another glimpse of her nor of Girshel.

The whole night long I could not sleep a wink.

The next night we were sitting in the tent of our captain; I was playing, but with no great zest. My orderly came in.

'Some one's asking for you, your honour.'

'Who is it?'

'A Jew.'

'Can it be Girshel?' I wondered. I waited till the end of the rubber, got up and went out. Yes, it was so; I saw Girshel.

'Well,' he questioned me with an ingratiating smile, 'your honour, are you satisfied?'

'Ah, you------!' (Here the colonel glanced round. 'No ladies present, I believe....

Well, never mind, any way.') 'Ah, bless you!' I responded, 'so you're making fun of me, are you?'

'How so?'

'How so, indeed! What a question!'

'Ay, ay, your honour, you 're too bad,' Girshel said reproachfully, but never ceasing smiling. 'The girl is young and modest.... You frightened her, indeed, you did.'

'Queer sort of modesty! why did she take money, then?'

'Why, what then? If one's given money, why not take it, sir?'

'I say, Girshel, let her come again, and I '11 let you off... only, please, don't show your stupid phiz inside my tent, and leave us in peace; do you hear?'

Girshel's eyes sparkled.

'What do you say? You like her?'

'Well, yes.'

'She's a lovely creature! there's not another such anywhere. And have you something for me now?'

'Yes, here, only listen; fair play is better than gold. Bring her and then go to the devil. I'll escort her home myself.'

'Oh, no, sir, no, that's impossible, sir,' the Jew rejoined hurriedly. 'Ay, ay, that's impossible. I'll walk about near the tent, your honour, if you like; I'll... I'll go away, your honour, if you like, a little.... I'm ready to do your honour a service.... I'll move away... to be sure, I will.'

'Well, mind you do.... And bring her, do you hear?'

'Eh, but she's a beauty, your honour, eh? your honour, a beauty, eh?'

Girshel bent down and peeped into my eyes.

'She's good-looking.'

'Well, then, give me another gold piece.'

I threw him a coin; we parted.

The day passed at last. The night came on. I had been sitting for a long while alone in my tent. It was dark outside. It struck two in the town. I was beginning to curse the Jew.... Suddenly Sara came in, alone. I jumped up took her in my arms... put my lips to her face.... It was cold as ice. I could scarcely distinguish her features.... I made her sit down, knelt down before her, took her hands, touched her waist.... She did not speak, did not stir, and suddenly she broke into loud, convulsive sobbing. I tried in vain to soothe her, to persuade her.... She wept in torrents.... I caressed her, wiped her tears; as before, she did not resist, made no answer to my questions and wept--wept, like a waterfall. I felt a pang at my heart; I got up and went out of the tent.

Girshel seemed to pop up out of the earth before me.

'Girshel,' I said to him, 'here's the money I promised you. Take Sara away.'

The Jew at once rushed up to her. She left off weeping, and clutched hold of him.

'Good-bye, Sara,'I said to her. 'God bless you, good-bye. We'll see each other again some other time.'

Girshel was silent and bowed humbly. Sara bent down, took my hand and pressed it to her lips; I turned away....

For five or six days, my friends, I kept thinking of my Jewess. Girshel did not make his appearance, and no one had seen him in the camp. I slept rather badly at nights; I was continually haunted by wet, black eyes, and long eyelashes; my lips could not forget the touch of her cheek, smooth and fresh as a downy plum. I was sent out with a foraging party to a village some distance away. While my soldiers were ransacking the houses, I remained in the street, and did not dismount from my horse. Suddenly some one caught hold of my foot....

'Mercy on us, Sara!'

She was pale and excited.

'Your honour... help us, save us, your soldiers are insulting us.... Your honour....'

She recognised me and flushed red.

'Why, do you live here?'

'Yes.'

'Where?'

Sara pointed to a little, old house. I set spurs to my horse and galloped up. In the yard of the little house an ugly and tattered Jewess was trying to tear out of the hands of my long sergeant, Siliavka, three hens and a duck. He was holding his booty above his head, laughing; the hens clucked and the duck quacked.... Two other cuirassiers were loading their horses with hay, straw, and sacks of flour. Inside the house I heard shouts and oaths in Little-Russian.... I called to my men and told them to leave the Jews alone, not to take anything from them. The soldiers obeyed, the sergeant got on his grey mare, Proserpina, or, as he called her, 'Prozherpila,' and rode after me into the street.

'Well,' I said to Sara, 'are you pleased with me?'

She looked at me with a smile.

'What has become of you all this time?'

She dropped her eyes.

'I will come to you to-morrow.'

'In the evening?'

'No, sir, in the morning.'

'Mind you do, don't deceive me.'

'No... no, I won't.'

I looked greedily at her. By daylight she seemed to me handsomer than ever. I remember I was particularly struck by the even, amber tint of her face and the bluish lights in her black hair.... I bent down from my horse and warmly pressed her little hand.

'Good-bye, Sara... mind you come.'

'Yes.'

She went home; I told the sergeant to follow me with the party, and galloped off.

The next day I got up very early, dressed, and went out of the tent. It was a glorious morning; the sun had just risen and every blade of grass was sparkling in the dew and the crimson glow. I clambered on to a high breastwork, and sat down on the edge of an embrasure. Below me a stout, cast-iron cannon stuck out its black muzzle towards the open country. I looked carelessly about me... and all at once caught sight of a bent figure in a grey wrapper, a hundred paces from me. I recognised Girshel. He stood without moving for a long while in one place, then suddenly ran a little on one side, looked hurriedly and furtively round... uttered a cry, squatted down, cautiously craned his neck and began looking round again and listening. I could see all his actions very clearly. He put his hand into his bosom, took out a scrap of paper and a pencil, and began writing or drawing something. Girshel continually stopped, started like a hare, attentively scrutinised everything around him, and seemed to be sketching our camp. More than once he hid his scrap of paper, half closed his eyes, sniffed at the air, and again set to work. At last, the Jew squatted down on the grass, took off his slipper, and stuffed the paper in it; but he had not time to regain his legs, when suddenly, ten steps from him, there appeared from behind the slope of an earthwork the whiskered countenance of the sergeant Siliavka, and gradually the whole of his long clumsy figure rose up from the ground. The Jew stood with his back to him. Siliavka went quickly up to him and laid his heavy paw on his shoulder. Girshel seemed to shrink into himself. He shook like a leaf and uttered a feeble cry, like a hare's. Siliavka addressed him threateningly, and seized him by the collar. I could not hear their conversation, but from the despairing gestures of the Jew, and his supplicating appearance, I began to guess what it was. The Jew twice flung himself at the sergeant's feet, put his hand in his pocket, pulled out a torn check handkerchief, untied a knot, and took out gold coins.... Siliavka took his offering with great dignity, but did not leave off dragging the Jew by the collar. Girshel made a sudden bound and rushed away; the sergeant sped after him in pursuit. The Jew ran exceedingly well; his legs, clad in blue stockings, flashed by, really very rapidly; but Siliavka after a short run caught the crouching Jew, made him stand up, and carried him in his arms straight to the camp. I got up and went to meet him.

'Ah! your honour!' bawled Siliavka,--'it's a spy I'm bringing you--a spy!...' The sturdy Little-Russian was streaming with perspiration. 'Stop that wriggling, devilish Jew--now then... you wretch! you'd better look out, I'll throttle you!'

The luckless Girshel was feebly prodding his elbows into Siliavka's chest, and feebly kicking.... His eyes were rolling convulsively....

'What's the matter?' I questioned Siliavka.

'If your honour'll be so good as to take the slipper off his right foot,--I can't get at it.' He was still holding the Jew in his arms.

I took off the slipper, took out of it a carefully folded piece of paper, unfolded it, and found an accurate map of our camp. On the margin were a number of notes written in a fine hand in the Jews' language.

Meanwhile Siliavka had set Girshel on his legs. The Jew opened his eyes, saw me, and flung himself on his knees before me.

Without speaking, I showed him the paper.

'What's this?'

'It's---nothing, your honour. I was only....' His voice broke.

'Are you a spy?'

He did not understand me, muttered disconnected words, pressed my knees in terror....

'Are you a spy?'

'I!' he cried faintly, and shook his head. 'How could I? I never did; I'm not at all. It's not possible; utterly impossible. I'm ready--I'll--this minute--I've money to give... I'll pay for it,' he whispered, and closed his eyes.

The smoking-cap had slipped back on to his neck; his reddish hair was soaked with cold sweat, and hung in tails; his lips were blue, and working convulsively; his brows were contracted painfully; his face was drawn....

Soldiers came up round us. I had at first meant to give Girshel a good fright, and to tell Siliavka to hold his tongue, but now the affair had become public, and could not escape 'the cognisance of the authorities.'

'Take him to the general,' I said to the sergeant.

'Your honour, your honour!' the Jew shrieked in a voice of despair. 'I am not guilty... not guilty.... Tell him to let me go, tell him...'

'His Excellency will decide about that,' said Siliavka. 'Come along.'

'Your honour!' the Jew shrieked after me--'tell him! have mercy!'

His shriek tortured me; I hastened my pace. Our general was a man of German extraction, honest and good-hearted, but strict in his adherence to military discipline. I went into the little house that had been hastily put up for him, and in a few words explained the reason of my visit. I knew the severity of the military regulations, and so I did not even pronounce the word 'spy,' but tried to put the whole affair before him as something quite trifling and not worth attention. But, unhappily for Girshel, the general put doing his duty higher than pity.

'You, young man,' he said to me in his broken Russian, 'inexperienced are. You in military matters yet inexperienced are. The matter, of which you to me reported have, is important, very important.... And where is this man who taken was? this Jew? where is he?'

I went out and told them to bring in the Jew. They brought in the Jew. The wretched creature could scarcely stand up.

'Yes,' pronounced the general, turning to me; 'and where's the plan which on this man found was?'

I handed him the paper. The general opened it, turned away again, screwed up his eyes, frowned....

'This is most as-ton-ish-ing...' he said slowly. 'Who arrested him?'

'I, your Excellency!' Siliavka jerked out sharply.

'Ah! good! good!... Well, my good man, what do you say in your defence?'

'Your... your... your Excellency,' stammered Girshel, 'I... indeed,... your Excellency... I'm not guilty... your Excellency; ask his honour the officer.... I'm an agent, your Excellency, an honest agent.'

'He ought to be cross-examined,' the general murmured in an undertone, wagging his head gravely. 'Come, how do you explain this, my friend?' 'I'm not guilty, your Excellency, I'm not guilty.'

'That is not probable, however. You were--how is it said in Russian?--taken on the fact, that is, in the very facts!'

'Hear me, your Excellency; I am not guilty.'

'You drew the plan? you are a spy of the enemy?'

'It wasn't me!' Girshel shrieked suddenly; 'not I, your Excellency!'

The general looked at Siliavka.

'Why, he's raving, your Excellency. His honour the officer here took the plan out of his slipper.'

The general looked at me. I was obliged to nod assent.

'You are a spy from the enemy, my good man....'

'Not I... not I...' whispered the distracted Jew.

'You have the enemy with similar information before provided? Confess....'

'How could I?'

'You will not deceive me, my good man. Are you a spy?'

The Jew closed his eyes, shook his head, and lifted the skirts of his gown.

'Hang him,' the general pronounced expressively after a brief silence, 'according to the law. Where is Mr. Fiodor Schliekelmann?'

They ran to fetch Schliekelmann, the general's adjutant. Girshel began to turn greenish, his mouth fell open, his eyes seemed starting out of his head. The adjutant came in. The general gave him the requisite instructions. The secretary showed his sickly, pock-marked face for an instant. Two or three officers peeped into the room inquisitively.

'Have pity, your Excellency,' I said to the general in German as best I could; 'let him off....'

'You, young man,' he answered me in Russian, 'I was saying to you, are inexperienced, and therefore I beg you silent to be, and me no more to trouble.'

Girshel with a shriek dropped at the general's feet.

'Your Excellency, have mercy; I will never again, I will not, your Excellency; I have a wife... your Excellency, a daughter... have mercy....'

'It's no use!'

'Truly, your Excellency, I am guilty... it's the first time, your Excellency, the first time, believe me!'

'You furnished no other documents?'

'The first time, your Excellency,... my wife... my children... have mercy....'

'But you are a spy.'

'My wife... your Excellency... my children....'

The general felt a twinge, but there was no getting out of it.

'According to the law, hang the Hebrew,' he said constrainedly, with the air of a man forced to do violence to his heart, and sacrifice his better feelings to inexorable duty--'hang him! Fiodor Karlitch, I beg you to draw up a report of the occurrence....'

A horrible change suddenly came over Girshel. Instead of the ordinary timorous alarm peculiar to the Jewish nature, in his face was reflected the horrible agony that comes before death. He writhed like a wild beast trapped, his mouth stood open, there was a hoarse rattle in his throat, he positively leapt up and down, convulsively moving his elbows. He had on only one slipper; they had forgotten to put the other on again... his gown fell open... his cap had fallen off....

We all shuddered; the general stopped speaking.

'Your Excellency,' I began again, 'pardon this wretched creature.'

'Impossible! It is the law,' the general replied abruptly, and not without emotion, 'for a warning to others.'

'For pity's sake....'

'Mr. Cornet, be so good as to return to your post,' said the general, and he motioned me imperiously to the door.

I bowed and went out. But seeing that in reality I had no post anywhere, I remained at no great distance from the general's house.

Two minutes later Girshel made his appearance, conducted by Siliavka and three soldiers. The poor Jew was in a state of stupefaction, and could hardly move his legs. Siliavka went by me to the camp, and soon returned with a rope in his hands. His coarse but not ill-natured face wore a look of strange, exasperated commiseration. At the sight of the rope the Jew flung up his arms, sat down, and burst into sobs. The soldiers stood silently about him, and stared grimly at the earth. I went up to Girshel, addressed him; he sobbed like a baby, and did not even look at me. With a hopeless gesture I went to my tent, flung myself on a rug, and closed my eyes....

Suddenly some one ran hastily and noisily into my tent. I raised my head and saw Sara; she looked beside herself. She rushed up to me, and clutched at my hands.

'Come along, come along,' she insisted breathlessly.

'Where? what for? let us stop here.'

'To father, to father, quick... save him... save him!'

'To what father?'

'My father; they are going to hang him....'

'What! is Girshel...?'

'My father... I '11 tell you all about it later,' she added, wringing her hands in despair: 'only come... come....'

We ran out of the tent. In the open ground, on the way to a solitary birch-tree, we could see a group of soldiers.... Sara pointed to them without speaking....

'Stop,' I said to her suddenly: 'where are we running to? The soldiers won't obey me.'

Sara still pulled me after her.... I must confess, my head was going round.

'But listen, Sara,' I said to her; 'what sense is there in running here? It would be better for me to go to the general again; let's go together; who knows, we may persuade him.'

Sara suddenly stood still and gazed at me, as though she were crazy.

'Understand me, Sara, for God's sake. I can't do anything for your father, but the general can. Let's go to him.'

'But meanwhile they'll hang him,' she moaned....

I looked round. The secretary was standing not far off.

'Ivanov,' I called to him; 'run, please, over there to them, tell them to wait a little, say I've gone to petition the general.'

'Yes, sir.'

Ivanov ran off.

We were not admitted to the general's presence. In vain I begged, persuaded, swore even, at last... in vain, poor Sara tore her hair and rushed at the sentinels; they would not let us pass.

Sara looked wildly round, clutched her head in both hands, and ran at break-neck pace towards the open country, to her father. I followed her. Every one stared at us, wondering.

We ran up to the soldiers. They were standing in a ring, and picture it, gentlemen! they were laughing, laughing at poor Girshel. I flew into a rage and shouted at them. The Jew saw us and fell on his daughter's neck. Sara clung to him passionately.

The poor wretch imagined he was pardoned.... He was just beginning to thank me... I turned away.

'Your honour,' he shrieked and wrung his hands; 'I'm not pardoned?'

I did not speak.

'No?'

'No.'

'Your honour,' he began muttering; 'look, your honour, look... she, this girl, see--you know--she's my daughter.'

'I know,' I answered, and turned away again.

'Your honour,' he shrieked, 'I never went away from the tent! I wouldn't for anything...'

He stopped, and closed his eyes for an instant.... 'I wanted your money, your honour, I must own... but not for anything....'

I was silent. Girshel was loathsome to me, and she too, his accomplice....

'But now, if you save me,' the Jew articulated in a whisper, 'I'll command her... I... do you understand?... everything... I'll go to every length....'

He was trembling like a leaf, and looking about him hurriedly. Sara silently and passionately embraced him.

The adjutant came up to us.

'Cornet,' he said to me; 'his Excellency has given me orders to place you under arrest. And you...' he motioned the soldiers to the Jew... 'quickly.'

Siliavka went up to the Jew.

'Fiodor Karlitch,' I said to the adjutant (five soldiers had come with him); 'tell them, at least, to take away that poor girl....'

'Of course. Certainly.'

The unhappy girl was scarcely conscious. Girshel was muttering something to her in Yiddish....

The soldiers with difficulty freed Sara from her father's arms, and carefully carried her twenty steps away. But all at once she broke from their arms and rushed towards Girshel.... Siliavka stopped her. Sara pushed him away; her face was covered with a faint flush, her eyes flashed, she stretched out her arms.

'So may you be accursed,' she screamed in German; 'accursed, thrice accursed, you and all the hateful breed of you, with the curse of Dathan and Abiram, the curse of poverty and sterility and violent, shameful death! May the earth open under your feet, godless, pitiless, bloodthirsty dogs....'

Her head dropped back... she fell to the ground.... They lifted her up and carried her away.

The soldiers took Girshel under his arms. I saw then why it was they had been laughing at the Jew when I ran up from the camp with Sara. He was really ludicrous, in spite of all the horror of his position. The intense anguish of parting with life, his daughter, his family, showed itself in the Jew in such strange and grotesque gesticulations, shrieks, and wriggles that we all could not help smiling, though it was horrible--intensely horrible to us too. The poor wretch was half dead with terror....

'Oy! oy! oy!' he shrieked: 'oy... wait! I've something to tell you... a lot to tell you. Mr. Under-sergeant, you know me. I'm an agent, an honest agent. Don't hold me; wait a minute, a little minute, a tiny minute--wait! Let me go; I'm a poor Hebrew. Sara... where is Sara? Oh, I know, she's at his honour the quarter-lieutenant's.' (God knows why he bestowed such an unheard-of grade upon me.) 'Your honour the quarter-lieutenant, I'm not going away from the tent.' (The soldiers were taking hold of Girshel... he uttered a deafening shriek, and wriggled out of their hands.) 'Your Excellency, have pity on the unhappy father of a family. I'll give you ten golden pieces, fifteen I'll give, your Excellency!...' (They dragged him to the birch-tree.) 'Spare me! have mercy! your honour the quarter-lieutenant! your Excellency, the general and commander-in-chief!'

They put the noose on the Jew.... I shut my eyes and rushed away.

I remained for a fortnight under arrest. I was told that the widow of the luck-less Girshel came to fetch away the clothes of the deceased. The general ordered a hundred roubles to be given to her. Sara I never saw again. I was wounded; I was taken to the hospital, and by the time I was well again, Dantzig had surrendered, and I joined my regiment on the banks of the Rhine.

AN UNHAPPY GIRL

Yes, yes, began Piotr Gavrilovitch; those were painful days... and I would rather not recall them.... But I have made you a promise; I shall have to tell you the whole story. Listen.

I

I was living at that time (the winter of 1835) in Moscow, in the house of my aunt, the sister of my dead mother. I was eighteen; I had only just passed from the second into the third course in the faculty 'of Language' (that was what it was called in those days) in the Moscow University. My aunt was a gentle, quiet woman--a widow. She lived in a big, wooden house in Ostozhonka, one of those warm, cosy houses such as, I fancy, one can find nowhere else but in Moscow. She saw hardly any one, sat from morning till night in the drawing-room with two companions, drank the choicest tea, played patience, and was continually requesting that the room should be fumigated. Thereupon her companions ran into the hall; a few minutes later an old servant in livery would bring in a copper pan with a bunch of mint on a hot brick, and stepping hurriedly upon the narrow strips of carpet, he would sprinkle the mint with vinegar. White fumes always puffed up about his wrinkled face, and he frowned and turned away, while the canaries in the dining-room chirped their hardest, exasperated by the hissing of the smouldering mint.

I was fatherless and motherless, and my aunt spoiled me. She placed the whole of the ground floor at my complete disposal. My rooms were furnished very elegantly, not at all like a student's rooms in fact: there were pink curtains in the bedroom, and a muslin canopy, adorned with blue rosettes, towered over my bed.

Those rosettes were, I'll own, rather an annoyance to me; to my thinking, such 'effeminacies' were calculated to lower me in the eyes of my companions. As it was, they nicknamed me 'the boarding-school miss.' I could never succeed in forcing myself to smoke. I studied--why conceal my shortcomings?--very lazily, especially at the beginning of the course. I went out a great deal. My aunt had bestowed on me a wide sledge, fit for a general, with a pair of sleek horses. At the houses of 'the gentry' my visits were rare, but at the theatre I was quite at home, and I consumed masses of tarts at the restaurants. For all that, I permitted myself no breach of decorum, and behaved very discreetly, ***en jeune homme de bonne maison***. I would not for anything in the world have pained my kind aunt; and besides I was naturally of a rather cool temperament.

II

From my earliest years I had been fond of chess; I had no idea of the science of the game, but I didn't play badly. One day in a cafe, I was the spectator of a prolonged contest at chess, between two players, of whom one, a fair-haired young man of about five-and-twenty, struck me as playing well. The game ended in his favour; I offered to play a match with him. He agreed,... and in the course of an hour, beat me easily, three times running.

'You have a natural gift for the game,' he pronounced in a courteous tone, noticing probably that my vanity was suffering; 'but you don't know the openings. You ought to study a chess-book--Allgacir or Petrov.'

'Do you think so? But where can I get such a book?'

'Come to me; I will give you one.'

He gave me his name, and told me where he was living. Next day I went to see him, and a week later we were almost inseparable.

III

My new acquaintance was called Alexander Davidovitch Fustov. He lived with his mother, a rather wealthy woman, the widow of a privy councillor, but he occupied a little lodge apart and lived quite independently, just as I did at my aunt's. He had a post in the department of Court affairs. I became genuinely attached to him. I had never in my life met a young man more 'sympathetic.' Everything about him was charming and attractive: his graceful figure, his bearing, his voice, and especially his small, delicate face with the golden-blue eyes, the elegant, as it were coquettishly moulded little nose, the unchanging amiable smile on the crimson lips, the light curls of soft hair over the rather narrow, snow-white brow. Fustov's character was remarkable for exceptional serenity, and a sort of amiable, restrained affability; he was never pre-occupied, and was always satisfied with everything; but on the other hand he was never ecstatic over anything. Every excess, even in a good feeling, jarred upon him; 'that's savage, savage,' he would say with a faint shrug, half closing his golden eyes. Marvellous were those eyes of Fustov's! They invariably expressed sympathy, good-will, even devotion. It was only at a later period that I noticed that the expression of his eyes resulted solely from their setting, that it never changed, even when he was sipping his soup or smoking a cigar. His preciseness became a byword between us. His grandmother, indeed, had been a German. Nature had endowed him with all sorts of talents. He danced capitally, was a dashing horseman, and a first-rate swimmer; did carpentering, carving and joinery, bound books and cut out silhouettes, painted in watercolours nosegays of flowers or Napoleon in profile in a blue uniform; played the zither with feeling; knew a number of tricks, with cards and without; and had a fair knowledge of mechanics, physics, and chemistry; but everything only up to a certain point. Only for languages he had no great facility: even French he spoke rather badly. He spoke in general little, and his share in our students' discussions was mostly limited to the bright sympathy of his glance and smile. To the fair sex Fustov was attractive, undoubtedly, but on this subject, of such importance among young people, he did not care to enlarge, and fully deserved the nickname given him by his comrades, 'the discreet Don Juan.' I was not dazzled by Fustov; there was nothing in him to dazzle, but I prized his affection, though in reality it was only manifested by his never refusing to see me when I called. To my mind Fustov was the happiest man in the world. His life ran so very smoothly. His mother, brothers, sisters, aunts, and uncles all adored him, he was on exceptionally good terms with all of them, and enjoyed the reputation of a paragon in his family.

IV

One day I went round to him rather early and did not find him in his study. He called to me from the next room; sounds of panting and splashing reached me from there. Every morning Fustov took a cold shower-bath and afterwards for a quarter of an hour practised gymnastic exercises, in which he had attained remarkable proficiency. Excessive anxiety about one's physical health he did not approve of, but he did not neglect necessary care. ('Don't neglect yourself, don't over-excite yourself, work in moderation,' was his precept.) Fustov had not yet made his appearance, when the outer door of the room where I was waiting flew wide open, and there walked in a man about fifty, wearing a bluish uniform. He was a stout, squarely-built man with milky-whitish eyes in a dark-red face and a perfect cap of thick, grey, curly hair. This person stopped short, looked at me, opened his mouth wide, and with a metallic chuckle, he gave himself a smart slap on his haunch, kicking his leg up in front as he did so.

'Ivan Demianitch?' my friend inquired through the door.

'The same, at your service,' the new comer responded. 'What are you up to? At your toilette? That's right! that's right!' (The voice of the man addressed as Ivan Demianitch had the same harsh, metallic note as his laugh.) 'I've trudged all this way to give your little brother his lesson; and he's got a cold, you know, and does nothing but sneeze. He can't do his work. So I've looked in on you for a bit to warm myself.'

Ivan Demianitch laughed again the same strange guffaw, again dealt himself a sounding smack on the leg, and pulling a check handkerchief out of his pocket, blew his nose noisily, ferociously rolling his eyes, spat into the handkerchief, and ejaculated with the whole force of his lungs: 'Tfoo-o-o!'

Fustov came into the room, and shaking hands with both of us, asked us if we were acquainted.

'Not a bit of it!' Ivan Demianitch boomed at once: 'the veteran of the year twelve has not that honour!'

Fustov mentioned my name first, then, indicating the 'veteran of the year twelve,' he pronounced: 'Ivan Demianitch Ratsch, professor of... various subjects.'

'Precisely so, various they are, precisely,' Mr. Ratsch chimed in. 'Come to think of it, what is there I haven't taught, and that I'm not teaching now, for that matter! Mathematics and geography and statistics and Italian book-keeping, ha-ha ha-ha! and music! You doubt it, my dear sir?'--he pounced suddenly upon me--'ask Alexander Daviditch if I'm not first-rate on the bassoon. I should be a poor sort of Bohemian--Czech, I should say--if I weren't! Yes, sir, I'm a Czech, and my native place is ancient Prague! By the way, Alexander Daviditch, why haven't we seen you for so long! We ought to have a little duet... ha-ha! Really!'

'I was at your place the day before yesterday, Ivan Demianitch,' replied Fustov.

'But I call that a long while, ha-ha!'

When Mr. Ratsch laughed, his white eyes shifted from side to side in a strange, restless way.

'You're surprised, young man, I see, at my behaviour,' he addressed me again. 'But that's because you don't understand my temperament. You must just ask our good friend here, Alexander Daviditch, to tell you about me. What'll he tell you? He'll tell you old Ratsch is a simple, good-hearted chap, a regular Russian, in heart, if not in origin, ha-ha! At his christening named Johann Dietrich, but always called Ivan Demianitch! What's in my mind pops out on my tongue; I wear my heart, as they say, on my sleeve. Ceremony of all sorts I know naught about and don't want to neither! Can't bear it! You drop in on me one day of an evening, and you'll see for yourself. My good woman--my wife, that is--has no nonsense about her either; she'll cook and bake you... something wonderful! Alexander Daviditch, isn't it the truth I'm telling?'

Fustov only smiled, and I remained silent.

'Don't look down on the old fellow, but come round,' pursued Mr. Ratsch. 'But now...' (he pulled a fat silver watch out of his pocket and put it up to one of his goggle eyes)'I'd better be toddling on, I suppose. I've another chick expecting me.... Devil knows what I'm teaching him,... mythology, by God! And he lives a long way off, the rascal, at the Red Gate! No matter; I'll toddle off on foot. Thanks to your brother's cutting his lesson, I shall be the fifteen kopecks for sledge hire to the good! Ha-ha! A very good day to you, gentlemen, till we meet again!... Eh?... We must have a little duet!' Mr. Ratsch bawled from the passage putting on his goloshes noisily, and for the last time we heard his metallic laugh.

V

'What a strange man!' I said, turning to Fustov, who had already set to work at his turning-lathe. 'Can he be a foreigner? He speaks Russian so fluently.'

'He is a foreigner; only he's been thirty years in Russia. As long ago as 1802, some prince or other brought him from abroad... in the capacity of secretary... more likely, valet, one would suppose. He does speak Russian fluently, certainly.'

'With such go, such far-fetched turns and phrases,' I put in.

'Well, yes. Only very unnaturally too. They're all like that, these Russianised Germans.'

'But he's a Czech, isn't he?'

'I don't know; may be. He talks German with his wife.'

'And why does he call himself a veteran of the year twelve? Was he in the militia, or what?'

'In the militia! indeed! At the time of the fire he remained in Moscow and lost all his property.... That was all he did.'

'But what did he stay in Moscow for?'

Fustov still went on with his turning.

'The Lord knows. I have heard that he was a spy on our side; but that must be nonsense. But it's a fact that he received compensation from the treasury for his losses.'

'He wears some sort of uniform.... I suppose he's in government service then?'

'Yes. Professor in the cadet's corps. He has the rank of a petty councillor.'

'What's his wife like?'

'A German settled here, daughter of a sausagemaker... or butcher....'

'And do you often go to see him?'

'Yes.'

'What, is it pleasant there?'

'Rather pleasant.'

'Has he any children?'

'Yes. Three by the German, and a son and daughter by his first wife.'

'And how old is the eldest daughter?'

'About five-and-twenty,'

I fancied Fustov bent lower over his lathe, and the wheel turned more rapidly, and hummed under the even strokes of his feet.

'Is she good-looking?'

'That's a matter of taste. She has a remarkable face, and she's altogether... a remarkable person.'

'Aha!' thought I. Fustov continued his work with special earnestness, and to my next question he only responded by a grunt.

'I must make her acquaintance,' I decided.

VI

A few days later, Fustov and I set off to Mr. Ratsch's to spend the evening. He lived in a wooden house with a big yard and garden, in Krivoy Place near the Pretchistensky boulevard. He came out into the passage, and meeting us with his characteristic jarring guffaw and noise, led us at once into the drawing-room, where he presented me to a stout lady in a skimpy canvas gown, Eleonora Karpovna, his wife. Eleonora Karpovna had most likely in her first youth been possessed of what the French for some unknown reason call **beaute du diable**, that is to say, freshness; but when I made her acquaintance, she suggested involuntarily to the mind a good-sized piece of meat, freshly laid by the butcher on a clean marble table. Designedly I used the word 'clean'; not only our hostess herself seemed a model of cleanliness, but everything about her, everything in the house positively shone, and glittered; everything had been scoured, and polished, and washed: the samovar on the round table flashed like fire; the curtains before the windows, the table-napkins were crisp with starch, as were also the little frocks and shirts of Mr. Ratsch's four children sitting there, stout, chubby little creatures, exceedingly like their mother, with coarsely moulded, sturdy faces, curls on their foreheads, and red, shapeless fingers. All the four of them had rather flat noses, large, swollen-looking lips, and tiny, light-grey eyes.

'Here's my squadron!' cried Mr. Ratsch, laying his heavy hand on the children's heads one after another. 'Kolia, Olga, Sashka and Mashka! This one's eight, this one's seven, that one's four, and this one's only two! Ha! ha! ha! As you can see, my wife and I haven't wasted our time! Eh, Eleonora Karpovna?'

'You always say things like that,' observed Eleonora Karpovna and she turned away.

'And she's bestowed such Russian names on her squallers!' Mr. Ratsch pursued. 'The next thing, she'll have them all baptized into the Orthodox Church! Yes, by Jove! She's so Slavonic in her sympathies, 'pon my soul, she is, though she is of German blood! Eleonora Karpovna, are you Slavonic?'

Eleonora Karpovna lost her temper.

'I'm a petty councillor's wife, that's what I am! And so I'm a Russian lady and all you may say....'

'There, the way she loves Russia, it's simply awful!' broke in Ivan Demianitch. 'A perfect volcano, ho, ho!'

'Well, and what of it?' pursued Eleonora Karpovna. 'To be sure I love Russia, for where else could I obtain noble rank? And my children too are nobly born, you know. Kolia, sitze ruhig mit den Fussen!'

Ratsch waved his hand to her.

'There, there, princess, don't excite yourself! But where's the nobly born Viktor? To be sure, he's always gadding about! He'll come across the inspector one of these fine days! He'll give him a talking-to! Das ist ein Bummler, Fiktor!'

'Dem Fiktov kann ich nicht kommandiren, Ivan Demianitch. Sie wissen wohl!' grumbled Eleonora Karpovna.

I looked at Fustov, as though wishing finally to arrive at what induced him to visit such people... but at that instant there came into the room a tall girl in a black dress, the elder daughter of Mr. Ratsch, to whom Fustov had referred.... I perceived the explanation of my friend's frequent visits.

VII

There is somewhere, I remember, in Shakespeare, something about 'a white dove in a flock of black crows'; that was just the impression made on me by the girl, who entered the room. Between the world surrounding her and herself there seemed to be too little in common; she herself seemed secretly bewildered and wondering how she had come there. All the members of Mr. Ratsch's family looked self-satisfied, simple-hearted, healthy creatures; her beautiful, but already care-worn, face bore the traces of depression, pride and morbidity. The others, unmistakable plebeians, were unconstrained in their manners, coarse perhaps, but simple; but a painful uneasiness was manifest in all her indubitably aristocratic nature. In her very exterior there was no trace of the type characteristic of the German race; she recalled rather the children of the south. The excessively thick, lustreless black hair, the hollow, black, lifeless but beautiful eyes, the low, prominent brow, the aquiline nose, the livid pallor of the smooth skin, a certain tragic line near the delicate lips, and in the slightly sunken cheeks, something abrupt, and at the same time helpless in the movements, elegance without gracefulness... in Italy all this would not have struck me as exceptional, but in Moscow, near the Pretchistensky boulevard, it simply astonished me! I got up from my seat on her entrance; she flung me a swift, uneasy glance, and dropping her black eyelashes, sat down near the window 'like Tatiana.' (Pushkin's **Oniegin** was then fresh in every one's mind.) I glanced at Fustov, but my friend was standing with his back to me, taking a cup of tea from the plump hands of Eleonora Karpovna. I noticed further that the girl as she came in seemed to bring with her a breath of slight physical chillness.... 'What a statue!' was my thought.

VIII

'Piotr Gavrilitch,' thundered Mr. Ratsch, turning to me, 'let me introduce you to my... to my... my number one, ha, ha, ha! to Susanna Ivanovna!'

I bowed in silence, and thought at once: 'Why, the name too is not the same sort as the others,' while Susanna rose slightly, without smiling or loosening her tightly clasped hands.

'And how about the duet?' Ivan Demianitch pursued: 'Alexander Daviditch? eh? benefactor! Your zither was left with us, and I've got the bassoon out of its case already. Let us make sweet music for the honourable company!' (Mr. Ratsch liked to display his Russian; he was continually bursting out with expressions, such as those which are strewn broadcast about the ultra-national poems of Prince Viazemsky.) 'What do you say? Carried?' cried Ivan Demianitch, seeing Fustov made no objection. 'Kolka, march into the study, and look sharp with the music-stand! Olga, this way with the zither! And oblige us with candles for the stands, better-half!' (Mr. Ratsch turned round and round in the room like a top.) 'Piotr Gavrilitch, you like music, hey? If you don't care for it, you must amuse yourself with conversation, only mind, not above a whisper! Ha, ha ha! But what ever's become of that silly chap, Viktor? He ought to be here to listen too! You spoil him completely, Eleonora Karpovna.'

Eleonora Karpovna fired up angrily.

'Aber was kann ich denn, Ivan Demianitch...'

'All right, all right, don't squabble! Bleibe ruhig, hast verstanden? Alexander Daviditch! at your service, sir!'

The children had promptly done as their father had told them. The music-stands were set up, the music began. I have already mentioned that Fustov played the zither extremely well, but that instrument has always produced the most distressing impression upon me. I have always fancied, and I fancy still, that there is imprisoned in the zither the soul of a decrepit Jew money-lender, and that it emits nasal whines and complaints against the merciless musician who forces it to utter sounds. Mr. Ratsch's performance, too, was not calculated to give me much pleasure; moreover, his face became suddenly purple, and assumed a malignant expression, while his whitish eyes rolled viciously, as though he were just about to murder some one with his bassoon, and were swearing and threatening by way of preliminary, puffing out chokingly husky, coarse notes one after another. I placed myself near Susanna, and waiting for a momentary pause, I asked her if she were as fond of music as her papa.

She turned away, as though I had given her a shove, and pronounced abruptly, 'Who?'

'Your father,' I repeated,'Mr. Ratsch.'

'Mr. Ratsch is not my father.'

'Not your father! I beg your pardon... I must have misunderstood... But I remember, Alexander Daviditch...'

Susanna looked at me intently and shyly.

'You misunderstood Mr. Fustov. Mr. Ratsch is my stepfather.'

I was silent for a while.

'And you don't care for music?' I began again.

Susanna glanced at me again. Undoubtedly there was something suggesting a wild creature in her eyes. She obviously had not expected nor desired the continuation of our conversation.

'I did not say that,' she brought out slowly. 'Troo-too-too-too-too-oo-oo...' the bassoon growled with startling fury, executing the final flourishes. I turned round, caught sight of the red neck of Mr. Ratsch, swollen like a boa-constrictor's, beneath his projecting ears, and very disgusting I thought him.

'But that... instrument you surely do not care for,' I said in an undertone.

'No... I don't care for it,' she responded, as though catching my secret hint.

'Oho!' thought I, and felt, as it were, delighted at something.

'Susanna Ivanovna,' Eleonora Karpovna announced suddenly in her German Russian, 'music greatly loves, and herself very beautifully plays the piano, only she likes not to play the piano when she is greatly pressed to play.'

Susanna made Eleonora Karpovna no reply--she did not even look at her--only there was a faint movement of her eyes, under their dropped lids, in her direction. From this movement alone--this movement of her pupils--I could perceive what was the nature of the feeling Susanna cherished for the second wife of her stepfather.... And again I was delighted at something.

Meanwhile the duet was over. Fustov got up and with hesitating footsteps approached the window, near which Susanna and I were sitting, and asked her if she had received from Lengold's the music that he had promised to order her from Petersburg.

'Selections from **Robert le Diable,**' he added, turning to me, 'from that new opera that every one's making such a fuss about.'

'No, I haven't got it yet,' answered Susanna, and turning round with her face to the window she whispered hurriedly. 'Please, Alexander Daviditch, I entreat you, don't make me play to-day. I don't feel in the mood a bit.'

'What's that? Robert le Diable of Meyer-beer?' bellowed Ivan Demianitch, coming up to us: 'I don't mind betting it's a first-class article! He's a Jew, and all Jews, like all Czechs, are born musicians. Especially Jews. That's right, isn't it, Susanna Ivanovna? Hey? Ha, ha, ha, ha!'

In Mr. Ratsch's last words, and this time even in his guffaw, there could be heard something more than his usual bantering tone--the desire to wound was evident. So, at least, I fancied, and so Susanna understood him. She started instinctively, flushed red, and bit her lower lip. A spot of light, like the gleam of a tear, flashed on her eyelash, and rising quickly, she went out of the room.

'Where are you off to, Susanna Ivanovna?' Mr. Ratsch bawled after her.

'Let her be, Ivan Demianitch, 'put in Eleonora Karpovna. 'Wenn sie einmal so et was im Kopfe hat...'

'A nervous temperament,'Ratsch pronounced, rotating on his heels, and slapping himself on the haunch, 'suffers with the **plexus solaris.** Oh! you needn't look at me like that, Piotr Gavrilitch! I've had a go at anatomy too, ha, ha! I'm even a bit of a doctor! You ask Eleonora Karpovna... I cure all her little ailments! Oh, I'm a famous hand at that!'

'You must for ever be joking, Ivan Demianitch,' the latter responded with displeasure, while Fustov, laughing and gracefully swaying to and fro, looked at the husband and wife.

'And why not be joking, mein Mutterchen?' retorted Ivan Demianitch. 'Life's given us for use, and still more for beauty, as some celebrated poet has observed. Kolka, wipe your nose, little savage!'

IX

'I was put in a very awkward position this evening through your doing,' I said the same evening to Fustov, on the way home with him. 'You told me that that girl--what's her name?--Susanna, was the daughter of Mr. Ratsch, but she's his step-daughter.'

'Really! Did I tell you she was his daughter? But... isn't it all the same?'

'That Ratsch,' I went on.... 'O Alexander, how I detest him! Did you notice the peculiar sneer with which he spoke of Jews before her? Is she... a Jewess?'

Fustov walked ahead, swinging his arms; it was cold, the snow was crisp, like salt, under our feet.

'Yes, I recollect, I did hear something of the sort,' he observed at last.... 'Her mother, I fancy, was of Jewish extraction.'

'Then Mr. Ratsch must have married a widow the first time?'

'Probably.'

'H'm!... And that Viktor, who didn't come in this evening, is his stepson too?'

'No... he's his real son. But, as you know, I don't enter into other people's affairs, and I don't like asking questions. I'm not inquisitive.'

I bit my tongue. Fustov still pushed on ahead. As we got near home, I overtook him and peeped into his face.

'Oh!' I queried, 'is Susanna really so musical?'

Fustov frowned.

'She plays the piano well,' he said between his teeth. 'Only she's very shy, I warn you!' he added with a slight grimace. He seemed to be regretting having made me acquainted with her.

I said nothing and we parted.

X

Next morning I set off again to Fustov's. To spend my mornings at his rooms had become a necessity for me. He received me cordially, as usual, but of our visit of the previous evening--not a word! As though he had taken water into his mouth, as they say. I began turning over the pages of the last number of the *Telescope.*

A person, unknown to me, came into the room. It turned out to be Mr. Ratsch's son, the Viktor whose absence had been censured by his father the evening before.

He was a young man, about eighteen, but already looked dissipated and unhealthy, with a mawkishly insolent grin on his unclean face, and an expression of fatigue in his swollen eyes. He was like his father, only his features were smaller and not without a certain prettiness. But in this very prettiness there was something offensive. He was dressed in a very slovenly way; there were buttons off his undergraduate's coat, one of his boots had a hole in it, and he fairly reeked of tobacco.

'How d'ye do,' he said in a sleepy voice, with those peculiar twitchings of the head and shoulders which I have always noticed in spoilt and conceited young men. 'I meant to go to the University, but here I am. Sort of oppression on my chest. Give us a cigar.' He walked right across the room, listlessly dragging his feet, and keeping his hands in his trouser-pockets, and sank heavily upon the sofa.

'Have you caught cold?' asked Fustov, and he introduced us to each other. We were both students, but were in different faculties.

'No!... Likely! Yesterday, I must own...' (here Ratsch junior smiled, again not without a certain prettiness, though he showed a set of bad teeth) 'I was drunk, awfully drunk. Yes'--he lighted a cigar and cleared his throat--'Obihodov's farewell supper.'

'Where's he going?'

'To the Caucasus, and taking his young lady with him. You know the black-eyed girl, with the freckles. Silly fool!'

'Your father was asking after you yesterday,' observed Fustov.

Viktor spat aside. 'Yes, I heard about it. You were at our den yesterday. Well, music, eh?'

'As usual.'

'And *she*... with a new visitor' (here he pointed with his head in my direction) 'she gave herself airs, I'll be bound. Wouldn't play, eh?'

'Of whom are you speaking?' Fustov asked.

'Why, of the most honoured Susanna Ivanovna, of course!'

Viktor lolled still more comfortably, put his arm up round his head, gazed at his own hand, and cleared his throat hoarsely.

I glanced at Fustov. He merely shrugged his shoulders, as though giving me to understand that it was no use talking to such a dolt.

XI

Viktor, staring at the ceiling, fell to talking, deliberately and through his nose, of the theatre, of two actors he knew, of a certain Serafrina Serafrinovna, who had 'made a fool' of him, of the new professor, R., whom he called a brute. 'Because, only fancy, what a monstrous notion! Every lecture he begins with calling over the students' names, and he's reckoned a liberal too! I'd have all your liberals locked up in custody!' and turning at last his full face and whole body towards Fustov, he brought out in a half-plaintive, half-ironical voice: 'I wanted to ask you something, Alexander Daviditch.... Couldn't you talk my governor round somehow?... You play duets with him, you know.... Here he gives me five miserable blue notes a month.... What's the use of that! Not enough for tobacco. And then he goes on about my not making debts! I should like to put him in my place, and then we should see! I don't come in for pensions, not like *some people*.' (Viktor pronounced these last words with peculiar emphasis.) 'But he's got a lot of tin, I know! It's no use his whining about hard times, there's no taking me in. No fear! He's made a snug little pile!'

Fustov looked dubiously at Victor.

'If you like,' he began, 'I'll speak to your father. Or, if you like... meanwhile... a trifling sum....'

'Oh, no! Better get round the governor... Though,' added Viktor, scratching his nose with all his fingers at once, 'you might hand over five-and-twenty roubles, if it's the same to you.... What's the blessed total I owe you?'

'You've borrowed eighty-five roubles of me.'

'Yes.... Well, that's all right, then... make it a hundred and ten. I'll pay it all in a lump.'

Fustov went into the next room, brought back a twenty-five-rouble note and handed it in silence to Viktor. The latter took it, yawned with his mouth wide open, grumbled thanks, and, shrugging and stretching, got up from the sofa.

'Foo! though... I'm bored,' he muttered, 'might as well turn in to the "Italie."'

He moved towards the door.

Fustov looked after him. He seemed to be struggling with himself.

'What pension were you alluding to just now, Viktor Ivanitch?' he asked at last.

Viktor stopped in the doorway and put on his cap.

'Oh, don't you know? Susanna Ivanovna's pension.... She gets one. An awfully curious story, I can tell you! I'll tell it you one of these days. Quite an affair, 'pon my soul, a queer affair. But, I say, the governor, you won't forget about the governor, please! His hide is thick, of course--German, and it's had a Russian tanning too, still you can get through it. Only, mind my step-mother Elenorka's nowhere about! Dad's afraid of her, and she wants to keep everything for her brats! But there, you know your way about! Good-bye!'

'Ugh, what a low beast that boy is!' cried Fustov, as soon as the door had slammed-to.

His face was burning, as though from the fire, and he turned away from me. I did not question him, and soon retired.

XII

All that day I spent in speculating about Fustov, about Susanna, and about her relations. I had a vague feeling of something like a family drama. As far as I could judge, my friend was not indifferent to Susanna. But she? Did she care for him? Why did she seem so unhappy? And altogether, what sort of creature was she? These questions were continually recurring to my mind. An obscure but strong conviction told me that it would be no use to apply to Fustov for the solution of them. It ended in my setting off the next day alone to Mr. Ratsch's house.

I felt all at once very uncomfortable and confused directly I found myself in the dark little passage. 'She won't appear even, very likely,' flashed into my mind. 'I shall have to stop with the repulsive veteran and his cook of a wife.... And indeed, even if she does show herself, what of it? She won't even take part in the conversation.... She was anything but warm in her manner to me the other day. Why ever did I come?' While I was making these reflections, the little page ran to announce my presence, and in the adjoining room, after two or three wondering 'Who is it? Who, do you say?' I heard the heavy shuffling of slippers, the folding-door was slightly opened, and in the crack between its two halves was thrust the face of Ivan Demianitch, an unkempt and grim-looking face. It stared at me and its expression did not immediately change.... Evidently, Mr. Ratsch did not at once recognise me; but suddenly his cheeks grew rounder, his eyes narrower, and from his opening mouth, there burst, together with a guffaw, the exclamation: 'Ah! my dear sir! Is it you? Pray walk in!'

I followed him all the more unwillingly, because it seemed to me that this affable, good-humoured Mr. Ratsch was inwardly wishing me at the devil. There was nothing to be done, however. He led me into the drawing-room, and in the drawing-room who should be sitting but Susanna, bending over an account-book? She glanced at me with her melancholy eyes, and very slightly bit the finger-nails of her left hand.... It was a habit of hers, I noticed, a habit peculiar to nervous people. There was no one else in the room.

'You see, sir,' began Mr. Ratsch, dealing himself a smack on the haunch, 'what you've found Susanna Ivanovna and me busy upon: we're at our accounts. My spouse has no great head for arithmetic, and I, I must own, try to spare my eyes. I can't read without spectacles, what am I to do? Let the young people exert themselves, ha-ha! That's the proper thing. But there's no need of haste.... More haste, worse speed in catching fleas, he-he!'

Susanna closed the book, and was about to leave the room.

'Wait a bit, wait a bit,' began Mr. Ratsch. 'It's no great matter if you're not in your best dress....' (Susanna was wearing a very old, almost childish, frock with short sleeves.) 'Our dear guest is not a stickler for ceremony, and I should like just to clear up last week.... You don't mind?'--he addressed me. 'We needn't stand on ceremony with you, eh?'

'Please don't put yourself out on my account!' I cried.

'To be sure, my good friend. As you're aware, the late Tsar Alexey Nikolavitch Romanoff used to say, "Time is for business, but a minute for recreation!" We'll devote one minute only to that same business... ha-ha! What about that thirteen roubles and thirty kopecks?' he added in a low voice, turning his back on me.

'Viktor took it from Eleonora Karpovna; he said that it was with your leave,' Susanna replied, also in a low voice.

'He said... he said... my leave...' growled Ivan Demianitch. 'I'm on the spot myself, I fancy. Might be asked. And who's had that seventeen roubles?'

'The upholsterer.'

'Oh... the upholsterer. What's that for?' 'His bill.'

'His bill. Show me!' He pulled the book away from Susanna, and planting a pair of round spectacles with silver rims on his nose, he began passing his finger along the lines. 'The upholsterer,.. the upholsterer... You'd chuck all the money out of doors! Nothing pleases you better!... Wie die Croaten! A bill indeed! But, after all,' he added aloud, and he turned round facing me again, and pulled the spectacles off his nose, 'why do this now? I can go into these wretched details later. Susanna Ivanovna, be so good as to put away that account-book, and come back to us and enchant our kind guest's ears with your musical accomplishments, to wit, playing on the pianoforte... Eh?'

Susanna turned away her head.

'I should be very happy,' I hastily observed; 'it would be a great pleasure for me to hear Susanna Ivanovna play. But I would not for anything in the world be a trouble...'

'Trouble, indeed, what nonsense! Now then, Susanna Ivanovna, eins, zwei, drei!'

Susanna made no response, and went out.

XIII

I had not expected her to come back; but she quickly reappeared. She had not even changed her dress, and sitting down in a corner, she looked twice intently at me. Whether it was that she was conscious in my manner to her of the involuntary respect, inexplicable to myself, which, more than curiosity, more even than sympathy, she aroused in me, or whether she was in a softened frame of mind that day, any way, she suddenly went to the piano, and laying her hand irresolutely on the keys, and turning her head a little over her shoulder towards me, she asked what I would like her to play. Before I had time to answer she had seated herself, taken up some music, hurriedly opened it, and begun to play. I loved music from childhood, but at that time I had but little comprehension of it, and very slight knowledge of the works of the great masters, and if Mr. Ratsch had not grumbled with some dissatisfaction, 'Aha! wieder dieser Beethoven!' I should not have guessed what Susanna had chosen. It was, as I found out afterwards, the celebrated sonata in F minor, opus 57. Susanna's playing impressed me more than I can say; I had not expected such force, such fire, such bold execution. At the very first bars of the intensely passionate allegro, the beginning of the sonata, I felt that numbness, that chill and sweet terror of ecstasy, which instantaneously enwrap the soul when beauty bursts with sudden flight upon it. I did not stir a limb till the very end. I kept, wanting--and not daring--to sigh. I was sitting behind Susanna; I could not see her face; I saw only from time to time her long dark hair tossed up and down on her shoulders, her figure swaying impulsively, and her delicate arms and bare elbows swiftly, and rather angularly, moving. The last notes died away. I sighed at last. Susanna still sat before the piano.

'Ja, ja,' observed Mr. Ratsch, who had also, however, listened with attention; 'romantische Musik! That's all the fashion nowadays. Only, why not play correctly? Eh? Put your finger on two notes at once--what's that for? Eh? To be sure, all we care for is to go quickly, quickly! Turns it out hotter, eh? Hot pancakes!' he bawled like a street seller.

Susanna turned slightly towards Mr. Ratsch. I caught sight of her face in profile. The delicate eyebrow rose high above the downcast eyelid, an unsteady flush overspread the cheek, the little ear was red under the lock pushed behind it.

'I have heard all the best performers with my own ears,' pursued Mr. Ratsch, suddenly frowning, 'and compared with the late Field they were all--tfoo! nil! zero!! Das war ein Kerl! Und ein so reines Spiel! And his own compositions the finest things! But all those now "tloo-too-too," and "tra-ta-ta," are written, I suppose, more for beginners. Da braucht man keine Delicatesse! Bang the keys anyhow... no matter! It'll turn out some how! Janitscharen Musik! Pugh!' (Ivan Demianitch wiped his forehead with his handkerchief.) 'But I don't say that for you, Susanna Ivanovna; you played well, and oughtn't to be hurt by my remarks.'

'Every one has his own taste,' Susanna said in a low voice, and her lips were trembling; 'but your remarks, Ivan Demianitch, you know, cannot hurt me.'

'Oh! of course not! Only don't you imagine'--Mr. Ratsch turned to me--'don't you imagine, my young friend, that that comes from our excessive good-nature and meekness of spirit; it's simply that we fancy ourselves so highly exalted that--oo-oo!--we can't keep our cap on our head, as the Russian proverb says, and, of course, no criticism can touch us. The conceit, my dear sir, the conceit!'

I listened in surprise to Mr. Ratsch. Spite, the bitterest spite, seemed as it were boiling over in every word he uttered.... And long it must have been rankling! It choked him. He tried to conclude his tirade with his usual laugh, and fell into a husky, broken cough instead. Susanna did not let drop a syllable in reply to him, only she shook her head, raised her face, and clasping her elbows with her hands, stared straight at him. In the depths of her fixed, wide-open eyes the hatred of long years lay smouldering with dim, unquenchable fire. I felt ill at ease.

'You belong to two different musical generations,' I began, with an effort at lightness, wishing by this lightness to suggest that I noticed nothing, 'and so it is not surprising that you do not agree in your opinions.... But, Ivan Demianitch, you must allow me to take rather... the side of the younger generation. I'm an outsider, of course; but I must confess nothing in music has ever made such an impression on me as the... as what Susanna Ivanovna has just played us.'

Ratsch pounced at once upon me.

'And what makes you suppose,' he roared, still purple from the fit of coughing, 'that we want to enlist you on our side? We don't want that at all! Freedom for the free, salvation for the saved! But as to the two generations, that's right enough; we old folks find it hard to get on with you young people, very hard! Our ideas don't agree in anything: neither in art, nor in life, nor even in morals; do they, Susanna Ivanovna?'

Susanna smiled a contemptuous smile.

'Especially in regard to morals, as you say, our ideas do not agree, and cannot agree,' she responded, and something menacing seemed to flit over her brows, while her lips were faintly trembling as before.

'Of course! of course!' Ratsch broke in, 'I'm not a philosopher! I'm not capable of... rising so superior! I'm a plain man, swayed by prejudices--oh yes!'

Susanna smiled again.

'I think, Ivan Demianitch, you too have sometimes been able to place yourself above what are called prejudices.'

'Wie so? How so, I mean? I don't know what you mean.'

'You don't know what I mean? Your memory's so bad!'

Mr. Ratsch seemed utterly taken aback.

'I... I...' he repeated, 'I...'

'Yes, you, Mr. Ratsch.'

There followed a brief silence.

'Really, upon my word...' Mr. Ratsch was beginning; 'how dare you... such insolence...'

Susanna all at once drew herself up to her full height, and still holding her elbows, squeezing them tight, drumming on them with her fingers, she stood still facing Ratsch. She seemed to challenge him to conflict, to stand up to meet him. Her face was changed; it became suddenly, in one instant, extraordinarily beautiful, and terrible too; a sort of bright, cold brilliance--the brilliance of steel--gleamed in her lustreless eyes; the lips that had been quivering were compressed in one straight, mercilessly stern line. Susanna challenged Ratsch, but he gazed blankly, and suddenly subsiding into silence, all of a heap, so to say, drew his head in, even stepped back a pace. The veteran of the year twelve was afraid; there could be no mistake about that.

Susanna slowly turned her eyes from him to me, as though calling upon me to witness her victory, and the humiliation of her foe, and, smiling once more, she walked out of the room.

The veteran remained a little while motionless in his arm-chair; at last, as though recollecting a forgotten part, he roused himself, got up, and, slapping me on the shoulder, laughed his noisy guffaw.

'There, 'pon my soul! fancy now, it's over ten years I've been living with that young lady, and yet she never can see when I'm joking, and when I'm in earnest! And you too, my young friend, are a little puzzled, I do believe.... Ha-ha-ha! That's because you don't know old Ratsch!'

'No.... I do know you now,' I thought, not without a feeling of some alarm and disgust.

'You don't know the old fellow, you don't know him,' he repeated, stroking himself on the stomach, as he accompanied me into the passage. 'I may be a tiresome person, knocked about by life, ha-ha! But I'm a good-hearted fellow, 'pon my soul, I am!'

I rushed headlong from the stairs into the street. I longed with all speed to get away from that good-hearted fellow.

XIV

'They hate one another, that's clear,' I thought, as I returned homewards; 'there's no doubt either that he's a wretch of a man, and she's a good girl. But what has there been between them? What is the reason of this continual exasperation? What was the meaning of those hints? And how suddenly it broke out! On such a trivial pretext!'

Next day Fustov and I had arranged to go to the theatre, to see Shtchepkin in 'Woe from Wit.' Griboyedov's comedy had only just been licensed for performance after being first disfigured by the censors' mutilations. We warmly applauded Famusov and Skalozub. I don't remember what actor took the part of Tchatsky, but I well remember that he was indescribably bad. He made his first appearance in a Hungarian jacket, and boots with tassels, and came on later in a frockcoat of the colour 'flamme du punch,' then in fashion, and the frockcoat looked about as suitable as it would have done on our old butler. I recollect too that we were all in ecstasies over the ball in the third act. Though, probably, no one ever executed such steps in reality, it was accepted as correct and I believe it is acted in just the same way to-day. One of the guests hopped excessively high, while his wig flew from side to side, and the public roared with laughter. As we were coming out of the theatre, we jostled against Viktor in a corridor.

'You were in the theatre!' he cried, flinging his arms about. 'How was it I didn't see you? I'm awfully glad I met you. You must come and have supper with me. Come on; I'll stand the supper!'

Young Ratsch seemed in an excited, almost ecstatic, frame of mind. His little eyes darted to and fro; he was grinning, and there were spots of red on his face.

'Why this gleefulness?' asked Fustov.

'Why? Wouldn't you like to know, eh?' Viktor drew us a little aside, and pulling out of his trouser-pocket a whole bundle of the red and blue notes then in use waved them in the air.

Fustov was surprised.

'Has your governor been so liberal?'

Viktor chuckled.

'He liberal! You just try it on!... This morning, relying on your intercession, I asked him for cash. What do you suppose the old skinflint answered? "I'll pay your debts," says he, "if you like. Up to twenty-five roubles inclusive!" Do you hear, inclusive! No, sir, this was a gift from God in my destitution. A lucky chance.'

'Been robbing someone?' Fustov hazarded carelessly.

Viktor frowned.

'Robbing, no indeed! I won it, won it from an officer, a guardsman. He only arrived from Petersburg yesterday. Such a chain of circumstances! It's worth telling... only this isn't the place. Come along to Yar's; not a couple of steps. I'll stand the show, as I said!'

We ought, perhaps, to have refused; but we followed without making any objection.

XV

At Yar's we were shown into a private room; supper was served, champagne was brought. Viktor related to us, omitting no detail, how he had in a certain 'gay' house met this officer of the guards, a very nice chap and of good family, only without a hap'orth of brains; how they had made friends, how he, the officer that is, had suggested as a joke a game of 'fools' with Viktor with some old cards, for next to nothing, and with the condition that the officer's winnings should go to the benefit of Wilhelmina, but Viktor's to his own benefit; how afterwards they had got on to betting on the games.

'And I, and I,' cried Viktor, and he jumped up and clapped his hands, 'I hadn't more than six roubles in my pocket all the while. Fancy! And at first I was completely cleaned out.... A nice position! Only then--in answer to whose prayers I can't say--fortune smiled. The other fellow began to get hot and kept showing all his cards.... In no time he'd lost seven hundred and fifty roubles! He began begging me to go on playing, but I'm not quite a fool, I fancy; no, one mustn't abuse such luck; I popped on my hat and cut away. So now I've no need to eat humble pie with the governor, and can treat my friends.... Hi waiter! Another bottle! Gentlemen, let's clink glasses!'

We did clink glasses with Viktor, and continued drinking and laughing with him, though his story was by no means to our liking, nor was his society a source of any great satisfaction to us either. He began being very affable, playing the buffoon, unbending, in fact, and was more loathsome than ever. Viktor noticed at last the impression he was making on us, and began to get sulky; his remarks became more disconnected and his looks gloomier. He began yawning, announced that he was sleepy, and after swearing with his characteristic coarseness at the waiter for a badly cleaned pipe, he suddenly accosted Fustov, with a challenging expression on his distorted face.

'I say, Alexander Daviditch,' said he, 'you tell me, if you please, what do you look down on me for?'

'How so?' My friend was momentarily at a loss for a reply.

'I'll tell you how.... I'm very well aware that you look down on me, and that person does too' (he pointed at me with his finger), 'so there! As though you were yourself remarkable for such high and exalted principles, and weren't just as much a sinner as the rest of us. Worse even. Still waters... you know the proverb?'

Fustov turned rather red.

'What do you mean by that?' he asked.

'Why, I mean that I'm not blind yet, and I see very clearly everything that's going on under my nose.... And I have nothing against it: first it's not my principle to interfere, and secondly, my sister Susanna Ivanovna hasn't always been so exemplary herself.... Only, why look down on me?'

'You don't understand what you're babbling there yourself! You're drunk,' said Fustov, taking his overcoat from the wall. 'He's swindled some fool of his money, and now he's telling all sorts of lies!'

Viktor continued reclining on the sofa, and merely swung his legs, which were hanging over its arm.

'Swindled! Why did you drink the wine, then? It was paid for with the money I won, you know. As for lies, I've no need for lying. It's not my fault that in her past Susanna Ivanovna...'

'Hold your tongue!' Fustov shouted at him, 'hold your tongue... or...'

'Or what?'

'You'll find out what. Come along, Piotr.'

'Aha!' pursued Viktor; 'our noble-hearted knight takes refuge in flight. He doesn't care to hear the truth, that's evident! It stings--the truth does, it seems!'

'Come along, Piotr,' Fustov repeated, completely losing his habitual coolness and self-possession.

'Let's leave this wretch of a boy!'

'The boy's not afraid of you, do you hear,' Viktor shouted after us, 'he despises you, the boy does! Do you hear!'

Fustov walked so quickly along the street that I had difficulty in keeping up with him. All at once he stopped short and turned sharply back.

'Where are you going?' I asked.

'Oh, I must find out what the idiot.... He's drunk, no doubt, God knows what.... Only don't you follow me... we shall see each other to-morrow. Good-bye!'

And hurriedly pressing my hand, Fustov set off towards Yar's hotel.

Next day I missed seeing Fustov; and on the day after that, on going to his rooms, I learned that he had gone into the country to his uncle's, near Moscow. I inquired if he had left no note for me, but no note was forth-coming. Then I asked the servant whether he knew how long Alexander Daviditch would be away in the country. 'A fortnight, or a little more, probably,' replied the man. I took at any rate Fustov's exact address, and sauntered home, meditating deeply. This unexpected absence from Moscow, in the winter, completed my utter perplexity. My good aunt observed to me at dinner that I seemed continually expecting something, and gazed at the cabbage pie as though I were beholding it for the first time in my life. 'Pierre, vous n'etes pas amoureux?' she cried at last, having previously got rid of her companions. But I reassured her: no, I was not in love.

XVI

Three days passed. I had a secret prompting to go to the Ratschs'. I fancied that in their house I should be sure to find a solution of all that absorbed my mind, that I could not make out.... But I should have had to meet the veteran.... That thought pulled me up. One tempestuous evening--the February wind was howling angrily outside, the frozen snow tapped at the window from time to time like coarse sand flung by a mighty hand--I was sitting in my room, trying to read. My servant came, and, with a mysterious air, announced that a lady wished to see me. I was surprised... ladies did not visit me, especially at such a late hour; however, I told him to show her in. The door opened and with swift step there walked in a woman, muffled up in a light summer cloak and a yellow shawl. Abruptly she cast off the cloak and the shawl, which were covered with snow, and I saw standing before me Susanna. I was so astonished that I did not utter a word, while she went up to the window, and leaning her shoulder against the wall, remained motionless; only her bosom heaved convulsively and her eyes moved restlessly, and the breath came with a faint moan from her white lips. I realised that it was no slight trouble that had brought her to me; I realised, for all my youth and shallowness, that at that instant before my eyes the fate of a whole life was being decided--a bitter and terrible fate.

'Susanna Ivanovna,' I began, 'how...'

She suddenly clutched my hand in her icy fingers, but her voice failed her. She gave a broken sigh and looked down. Her heavy coils of black hair fell about her face.... The snow had not melted from off it.

'Please, calm yourself, sit down,' I began again, 'see here, on the sofa. What has happened? Sit down, I entreat you.'

'No,' she articulated, scarcely audibly, and she sank on to the window-seat. 'I am all right here.... Let me be.... You could not expect... but if you knew... if I could... if...'

She tried to control herself, but the tears flowed from her eyes with a violence that shook her, and sobs, hurried, devouring sobs, filled the room. I felt a tightness at my heart.... I was utterly stupefied. I had seen Susanna only twice; I had conjectured that she had a hard life, but I had regarded her as a proud girl, of strong character, and all at once these violent, despairing tears.... Mercy! Why, one only weeps like that in the presence of death!

I stood like one condemned to death myself.

'Excuse me,' she said at last, several times, almost angrily, wiping first one eye, then the other. 'It'll soon be over. I've come to you....' She was still sobbing, but without tears. 'I've come.... You know that Alexander Daviditch has gone away?'

In this single question Susanna revealed everything, and she glanced at me, as though she would say: 'You understand, of course, you will have pity, won't you?' Unhappy girl! There was no other course left her then!

I did not know what answer to make....

'He has gone away, he has gone away... he believed him!' Susanna was saying meanwhile. 'He did not care even to question me; he thought I should not tell him all the truth, he could think that of me! As though I had ever deceived him!'

She bit her lower lip, and bending a little, began to scratch with her nail the patterns of ice that covered the window-pane. I went hastily into the next room, and sending my servant away, came back at once and lighted another candle. I had no clear idea why I was doing all this.... I was greatly overcome. Susanna was sitting as before on the window-seat, and it was at this moment that I noticed how lightly she was dressed: a grey gown with white buttons and a broad leather belt, that was all. I went up to her, but she did not take any notice of me.

'He believed it,... he believed it,' she whispered, swaying softly from side to side. 'He did not hesitate, he dealt me this last... last blow!' She turned suddenly to me. 'You know his address?'

'Yes, Susanna Ivanovna.. I learnt it from his servants... at his house. He told me nothing of his intention; I had not seen him for two days--went to inquire and he had already left Moscow.'

'You know his address?' she repeated. 'Well, write to him then that he has killed me. You are a good man, I know. He did not talk to you of me, I dare say, but he talked to me about you. Write... ah, write to him to come back quickly, if he wants to find me alive!... No! He will not find me!...'

Susanna's voice grew quieter at each word, and she was quieter altogether. But this calm seemed to me more awful than the previous sobs.

'He believed him,...' she said again, and rested her chin on her clasped hands.

A sudden squall of wind beat upon the window with a sharp whistle and a thud of snow. A cold draught passed over the room.... The candles flickered.... Susanna shivered. Again I begged her to sit on the sofa.

'No, no, let me be,' she answered, 'I am all right here. Please.' She huddled up to the frozen pane, as though she had found herself a refuge in the recesses of the window. 'Please.'

'But you're shivering, you're frozen,' I cried, 'Look, your shoes are soaked.'

'Let me be... please...' she whispered,. and closed her eyes.

A panic seized me.

'Susanna Ivanovna!' I almost screamed: 'do rouse yourself, I entreat you! What is the matter with you? Why such despair? You will see, every thing will be cleared up, some misunderstanding... some unlooked-for chance.... You will see, he will soon be back. I will let him know.... I will write to him to-day.... But I will not repeat your words.... Is it possible!'

'He will not find me,' Susanna murmured, still in the same subdued voice. 'Do you suppose I would have come here, to you, to a stranger, if I had not known I should not long be living? Ah, all my past has been swept away beyond return! You see, I could not bear to die so, in solitude, in silence, without saying to some one, "I've lost every thing... and I'm dying.... Look!"'

She drew back into her cold little corner.... Never shall I forget that head, those fixed eyes with their deep, burnt-out look, those dark, disordered tresses against the pale window-pane, even the grey, narrow gown, under every fold of which throbbed such young, passionate life!

Unconsciously I flung up my hands.

'You... you die, Susanna Ivanovna! You have only to live.... You must live!'

She looked at me.... My words seemed to surprise her.

'Ah, you don't know,' she began, and she softly dropped both her hands. 'I cannot live, Too much, too much I have had to suffer, too much! I lived through it.... I hoped... but now... when even this is shattered... when...'

She raised her eyes to the ceiling and seemed to sink into thought. The tragic line, which I had once noticed about her lips, came out now still more clearly; it seemed to spread across her whole face. It seemed as though some relentless hand had drawn it immutably, had set a mark for ever on this lost soul.

She was still silent.

'Susanna Ivanovna,' I said, to break that awful silence with anything; 'he will come back, I assure you!'

Susanna looked at me again.

'What do you say?' she enunciated with visible effort.

'He will come back, Susanna Ivanovna, Alexander will come back!'

'He will come back?' she repeated. 'But even if he did come back, I cannot forgive him this humiliation, this lack of faith....'

She clutched at her head.

'My God! my God! what am I saying, and why am I here? What is it all? What... what did I come to ask... and whom? Ah, I am going mad!...'

Her eyes came to a rest.

'You wanted to ask me to write to Alexander,' I made haste to remind her.

She started.

'Yes, write, write to him... what you like.... And here...' She hurriedly fumbled in her pocket and brought out a little manuscript book. 'This I was writing for him... before he ran away.... But he believed... he believed him!'

I understood that her words referred to Viktor; Susanna would not mention him, would not utter his detested name.

'But, Susanna Ivanovna, excuse me,' I began, 'what makes you suppose that

Alexander Daviditch had any conversation... with that person?'

'What? Why, he himself came to me and told me all about it, and bragged of it... and laughed just as his father laughs! Here, here, take it,' she went on, thrusting the manuscript into my hand, 'read it, send it to him, burn it, throw it away, do what you like, as you please.... But I can't die like this with no one knowing.... Now it is time.... I must go.'

She got up from the window-seat.... I stopped her.

'Where are you going, Susanna Ivanovna, mercy on us! Listen, what a storm is raging! You are so lightly dressed.... And your home is not near here. Let me at least go for a carriage, for a sledge....'

'No, no, I want nothing,' she said resolutely, repelling me and taking up her cloak and shawl. 'Don't keep me, for God's sake! or... I can't answer for anything! I feel an abyss, a dark abyss under my feet.... Don't come near me, don't touch me!' With feverish haste she put on her cloak, arranged her shawl.... 'Good-bye... good-bye.... Oh, my unhappy people, for ever strangers, a curse lies upon us! No one has ever cared for me, was it likely he...' She suddenly ceased. 'No; one man loved me,' she began again, wringing her hands, 'but death is all about me, death and no escape! Now it is my turn.... Don't come after me,' she cried shrilly. 'Don't come! don't come!'

I was petrified, while she rushed out; and an instant later, I heard the slam downstairs of the heavy street door, and the window panes shook again under the violent onslaught of the blast.

I could not quickly recover myself. I was only beginning life in those days: I had had no experience of passion nor of suffering, and had rarely witnessed any manifestation of strong feeling in others.... But the sincerity of this suffering, of this passion, impressed me. If it had not been for the manuscript in my hands, I might have thought that I had dreamed it all--it was all so unlikely, and swooped by like a passing storm. I was till midnight reading the manuscript. It consisted of several sheets of letter-paper, closely covered with a large, irregular writing, almost without an erasure. Not a single line was quite straight, and one seemed in every one of them to feel the excited trembling of the hand that held the pen. Here follows what was in the manuscript. I have kept it to this day.

XVII
MY STORY

I am this year twenty-eight years old. Here are my earliest recollections; I was living in the Tambov province, in the country house of a rich landowner, Ivan Matveitch Koltovsky, in a small room on the second storey. With me lived my mother, a Jewess, daughter of a dead painter, who had come from abroad, a woman always ailing, with an extraordinarily beautiful face, pale as wax, and such mournful eyes, that sometimes when she gazed long at me, even without looking at her, I was aware of her sorrowful, sorrowful eyes, and I would burst into tears and rush to embrace her. I had tutors come to me; I had music lessons, and was called 'miss.' I dined at the master's table together with my mother. Mr. Koltovsky was a tall, handsome old man with a stately manner; he always smelt of *ambre*. I stood in mortal terror of him, though he called me Suzon and gave me his dry, sinewy hand to kiss under its lace-ruffles. With my mother he was elaborately courteous, but he talked little even with her. He would say two or three affable words, to which she promptly made a hurried answer; and he would be silent and sit looking about him with dignity, and slowly picking up a pinch of Spanish snuff from his round, golden snuff-box with the arms of the Empress Catherine on it.

My ninth year has always remained vivid in my memory.... I learnt then, from the maids in the servants' room, that Ivan Matveitch Koltovsky was my father, and almost on the same day, my mother, by his command, was married to Mr. Ratsch, who was something like a steward to him. I was utterly unable to comprehend the possibility of such a thing, I was bewildered, I was almost ill, my brain suffered under the strain, my mind was overclouded. 'Is it true, is it true, mamma,' I asked her, 'that scented bogey' (that was my name for Ivan Matveitch) 'is my father?' My mother was terribly scared, she shut my mouth.... 'Never speak to any one of that, do you hear, Susanna, do you hear, not a word!'... she repeated in a shaking voice, pressing my head to her bosom.... And I never did speak to any one of it.... That prohibition of my mother's I understood.... I understood that I must be silent, that my mother begged my forgiveness!

My unhappiness began from that day. Mr. Ratsch did not love my mother, and she did not love him. He married her for money, and she was obliged to submit. Mr. Koltovsky probably considered that in this way everything had been arranged for the best, *la position etait regularisee*. I remember the day before the marriage my mother and I--both locked in each other's arms--wept almost the whole morning--bitterly, bitterly--and silently. It is not strange that she was silent.... What could she say to me? But that I did not question her shows that unhappy children learn wisdom sooner than happy ones... to their cost.

Mr. Koltovsky continued to interest himself in my education, and even by degrees put me on a more intimate footing. He did not talk to me... but morning and evening, after flicking the snuff from his jabot with two fingers, he would with the same two fingers--always icy cold--pat me on the cheek and give me some sort of dark-coloured sweetmeats, also smelling of *ambre*, which I never ate. At twelve years old I became his reader---*sa petite lectrice*. I read him French books of the last century, the memoirs of Saint Simon, of Mably, Renal, Helvetius, Voltaire's correspondence, the encyclopedists, of course without understanding a word, even when, with a smile and a grimace, he ordered me, 'relire ce dernier paragraphe, qui est bien remarquable!' Ivan Matveitch was completely a Frenchman. He had lived in Paris till the Revolution, remembered Marie Antoinette, and had received an invitation to Trianon to see her. He had also seen Mirabeau, who, according to his account, wore very large buttons--*exagere en tout*, and was altogether a man of *mauvais ton, en depit de sa naissance!* Ivan Matveitch, however, rarely talked of that time; but two or three times a year, addressing himself to the crooked old emigrant whom he had taken into his house, and called for some unknown reason 'M. le Commandeur,' he recited in his deliberate, nasal voice, the impromptu he had once delivered at a soiree of the Duchesse de Polignac. I remember only the first two lines.... It had reference to a comparison between the Russians and the French:

'L'aigle se plait aux regions austeres
Ou le ramier ne saurait habiter...'

'Digne de M. de Saint Aulaire!' M. le Commandeur would every time exclaim.

Ivan Matveitch looked youngish up to the time of his death: his cheeks were rosy, his teeth white, his eyebrows thick and immobile, his eyes agreeable and expressive, clear, black eyes, perfect agate. He was not at all unreasonable, and was very courteous with every one, even with the servants.... But, my God! how wretched I was with him, with what joy I always left him, what evil thoughts confounded me in his presence! Ah, I was not to blame for them!... I was not to blame for what they had made of me....

Mr. Ratsch was, after his marriage, assigned a lodge not far from the big house. I lived there with my mother. It was a cheerless life I led there. She soon gave birth to a son, Viktor, this same Viktor whom I have every right to think and to call my enemy. From the time of his birth my mother never regained her health, which had always been weak. Mr. Ratsch did not think fit in those days to keep up such a show of good spirits as he maintains now: he always wore a morose air and tried to pass for a busy, hard-working person. To me he was cruel and rude. I felt relief when I retired from Ivan Matveitch's presence; but my own home too I was glad to leave.... Unhappy was my youth! For ever tossed from one shore to the other, with no desire to anchor at either! I would run across the courtyard in winter, through the deep snow, in a thin frock--run to the big house to read to Ivan Matveitch, and as it were be glad to go.... But when I was there, when I saw those great cheerless rooms, the bright-coloured, upholstered furniture, that courteous and heartless old man in the open silk wadded jacket, in the white jabot and white cravat, with lace ruffles falling over his fingers, with a **soupcon** of powder (so his valet expressed it) on his combed-back hair, I felt choked by the stifling scent of **ambre**, and my heart sank. Ivan Matveitch usually sat in a large low chair; on the wall behind his head hung a picture, representing a young woman, with a bright and bold expression of face, dressed in a sumptuous Hebrew costume, and simply covered with precious stones, with diamonds.... I often stole a glance at this picture, but only later on I learned that it was the portrait of my mother, painted by her father at Ivan Matveitch's request. She had changed indeed since those days! Well had he succeeded in subduing and crushing her! 'And she loved him! Loved that old man!' was my thought.... 'How could it be! Love him!' And yet, when I recalled some of my mother's glances, some half-uttered phrases and unconscious gestures.... 'Yes, yes, she did love him!' I repeated with horror. Ah, God, spare others from knowing aught of such feelings!

Every day I read to Ivan Matveitch, sometimes for three or four hours together.... So much reading in such a loud voice was harmful to me. Our doctor was anxious about my lungs and even once communicated his fears to Ivan Matveitch.

But the old man only smiled--no; he never smiled, but somehow sharpened and moved forward his lips--and told him: 'Vous ne savez pas ce qu'il y a de ressources dans cette jeunesse.' 'In former years, however, M. le Commandeur,'... the doctor ventured to observe. Ivan Matveitch smiled as before. 'Vous revez, mon cher,' he interposed: 'le commandeur n'a plus de dents, et il crache a chaque mot. J'aime les voix jeunes.'

And I still went on reading, though my cough was very troublesome in the mornings and at night.... Sometimes Ivan Matveitch made me play the piano. But music always had a soporific influence on his nerves. His eyes closed at once, his head nodded in time, and only rarely I heard, 'C'est du Steibelt, n'est-ce pas? Jouez-moi du Steibelt!' Ivan Matveitch looked upon Steibelt as a great genius, who had succeeded in overcoming in himself 'la grossiere lourdeur des Allemands,' and only found fault with him for one thing: 'trop de fougue! trop d'imagination!'... When Ivan Matveitch noticed that I was tired from playing he would offer me 'du cachou de Bologne.' So day after day slipped by....

And then one night--a night never to be forgotten!--a terrible calamity fell upon me. My mother died almost suddenly. I was only just fifteen. Oh, what a sorrow that was, with what cruel violence it swooped down upon me! How terrified I was at that first meeting with death! My poor mother! Strange were our relations; we passionately loved each other... passionately and hopelessly; we both as it were treasured up and hid from each other our common secret, kept obstinately silent about it, though we knew all that was passing at the bottom of our hearts! Even of the past, of her own early past, my mother never spoke to me, and she never complained in words, though her whole being was nothing but one dumb complaint. We avoided all conversation of any seriousness. Alas! I kept hoping that the hour would come, and she would open her heart at last, and I too should speak out, and both of us would be more at ease.... But the daily little cares, her irresolute, shrinking temper, illnesses, the presence of Mr. Ratsch, and most of all the eternal question,--what is the use? and the relentless, unbroken flowing away of time, of life.... All was ended as though by a clap of thunder, and the words which would have loosed us from the burden of our secret--even the last dying words of leave-taking--I was not destined to hear from my mother! All that is left in my memory is Mr. Ratsch's calling, 'Susanna Ivanovna, go, please, your mother wishes to give you her blessing!' and then the pale hand stretched out from the heavy counterpane, the agonised breathing, the dying eyes.... Oh, enough! enough!

With what horror, with what indignation and piteous curiosity I looked next day, and on the day of the funeral, into the face of my father... yes, my father! In my dead mother's writing-case were found his letters. I fancied he looked a little pale and drawn... but no! Nothing was stirring in that heart of stone. Exactly as before, he summoned me to his room, a week later; exactly in the same voice he asked me to read: 'Si vous le voulez bien, les observations sur l'histoire de France de Mably, a la page 74... la ou nous avons ete interrompus.' And he had not even had my mother's portrait moved! On dismissing me, he did indeed call me to him, and giving me his hand to kiss a second time, he observed: 'Suzanne, la mort de votre mere vous a privee de votre appui naturel; mais vous pourrez toujours compter sur ma protection,' but with the other hand he gave me at once a slight push on the shoulder, and, with the sharpening of the corners of the mouth habitual with him, he added, 'Allez, mon enfant.' I longed to shriek at him: 'Why, but you know you're my father!' but I said nothing and left the room.

Next morning, early, I went to the graveyard. May had come in all its glory of flowers and leaves, and a long while I sat on the new grave. I did not weep, nor grieve; one thought was filling my brain: 'Do you hear, mother? He means to extend his protection to me, too!' And it seemed to me that my mother ought not to be wounded by the smile which it instinctively called up on my lips.

At times I wonder what made me so persistently desire to wring--not a confession... no, indeed! but, at least, one warm word of kinship from Ivan Matveitch? Didn't I know what he was, and how little he was like all that I pictured in my dreams as a *father*!... But I was so lonely, so alone on earth! And then, that thought, ever recurring, gave me no rest: 'Did not she love him? She must have loved him for something?'

Three years more slipped by. Nothing changed in the monotonous round of life, marked out and arranged for us. Viktor was growing into a boy. I was eight years older and would gladly have looked after him, but Mr. Ratsch opposed my doing so. He gave him a nurse, who had orders to keep strict watch that the child was not 'spoilt,' that is, not to allow me to go near him. And Viktor himself fought shy of me. One day Mr. Ratsch came into my room, perturbed, excited, and angry.

On the previous evening unpleasant rumours had reached me about my stepfather; the servants were talking of his having been caught embezzling a considerable sum of money, and taking bribes from a merchant.

'You can assist me,' he began, tapping impatiently on the table with his fingers. 'Go and speak for me to Ivan Matveitch.'

'Speak for you? On what ground? What about?'

'Intercede for me.... I'm not like a stranger any way... I'm accused... well, the fact is, I may be left without bread to eat, and you, too.'

'But how can I go to him? How can I disturb him?'

'What next! You have a right to disturb him!'

'What right, Ivan Demianitch?'

'Come, no humbug.... He cannot refuse you, for many reasons. Do you mean to tell me you don't understand that?'

He looked insolently into my eyes, and I felt my cheeks simply burning. Hatred, contempt, rose up within me, surged in a rush upon me, drowning me.

'Yes, I understand you, Ivan Demianitch,' I answered at last--my own voice seemed strange to me--'and I am not going to Ivan Matveitch, and I will not ask him for anything. Bread, or no bread!'

Mr. Ratsch shivered, ground his teeth, and clenched his fists.

'All right, wait a bit, your highness!' he muttered huskily. 'I won't forget it!' That same day, Ivan Matveitch sent for him, and, I was told, shook his cane at him, the very cane which he had once exchanged with the Due de la Rochefoucauld, and cried, 'You be a scoundrel and extortioner! I put you outside!' Ivan Matveitch could hardly speak Russian at all, and despised our 'coarse jargon,' *ce jargon vulgaire et rude*. Some one once said before him, 'That same's self-understood.' Ivan Matveitch was quite indignant, and often afterwards quoted the phrase as an example of the senselessness and absurdity of the Russian tongue. 'What does it mean, that same's self-understood?' he would ask in Russian, with emphasis on each syllable. 'Why not simply that's understood, and why same and self?'

Ivan Matveitch did not, however, dismiss Mr. Ratsch, he did not even deprive him of his position. But my stepfather kept his word: he never forgot it.

I began to notice a change in Ivan Matveitch. He was low-spirited, depressed, his health broke down a little. His fresh, rosy face grew yellow and wrinkled; he lost a front tooth. He quite ceased going out, and gave up the reception-days he had established for the peasants, without the assistance of the priest, **sans le concours du clerge**. On such days Ivan Matveitch had been in the habit of going in to the peasants in the hall or on the balcony, with a rose in his buttonhole, and putting his lips to a silver goblet of vodka, he would make them a speech something like this: 'You are content with my actions, even as I am content with your zeal, whereat I rejoice truly. We are all **brothers**; at our birth we are equal; I drink your health!' He bowed to them, and the peasants bowed to him, but only from the waist, no prostrating themselves to the ground, that was strictly forbidden. The peasants were entertained with good cheer as before, but Ivan Matveitch no longer showed himself to his subjects. Sometimes he interrupted my reading with exclamations: 'La machine se detraque! Cela se gate!' Even his eyes--those bright, stony eyes--began to grow dim and, as it were, smaller; he dozed oftener than ever and breathed hard in his sleep. His manner with me was unchanged; only a shade of chivalrous deference began to be perceptible in it. He never failed to get up--though with difficulty--from his chair when I came in, conducted me to the door, supporting me with his hand under my elbow, and instead of Suzon began to call me sometimes, 'ma chere demoiselle,' sometimes, 'mon Antigone.' M. le Commandeur died two years after my mother's death; his death seemed to affect Ivan Matveitch far more deeply. A contemporary had disappeared: that was what distressed him. And yet in later years M. le Commandeur's sole service had consisted in crying, 'Bien joue, mal reussi!' every time Ivan Matveitch missed a stroke, playing billiards with Mr. Ratsch; though, indeed, too, when Ivan Matveitch addressed him at table with some such question as: 'N'est-ce pas, M. le Commandeur, c'est Montesquieu qui a dit cela dans ses **Lettres Persanes**?' he had still, sometimes dropping a spoonful of soup on his ruffle, responded profoundly: 'Ah, Monsieur de Montesquieu? Un grand ecrivain, monsieur, un grand ecrivain!' Only once, when Ivan Matveitch told him that 'les theophilanthropes ont eu pourtant du bon!' the old man cried in an excited voice, 'Monsieur de Kolontouskoi' (he hadn't succeeded in the course of twenty years in learning to pronounce his patron's name correctly), 'Monsieur de Kolontouskoi! Leur fondateur, l'instigateur de cette secte, ce La Reveillere Lepeaux etait un bonnet rouge!' 'Non, non,' said Ivan Matveitch, smiling and rolling together a pinch of snuff: 'des fleurs, des jeunes vierges, le culte de la Nature... ils out eu du bon, ils out eu du bon!'...I was always surprised at the extent of Ivan Matveitch's knowledge, and at the uselessness of his knowledge to himself.

Ivan Matveitch was perceptibly failing, but he still put a good face on it. One day, three weeks before his death, he had a violent attack of giddiness just after dinner. He sank into thought, said, 'C'est la fin,' and pulling himself together with a sigh, he wrote a letter to Petersburg to his sole heir, a brother with whom he had had no intercourse for twenty years. Hearing that Ivan Matveitch was unwell, a neighbour paid him a visit--a German, a Catholic--once a distinguished physician, who was living in retirement in his little place in the country. He was very rarely at Ivan Matveitch's, but the latter always received him with special deference, and in fact had a great respect for him. He was almost the only person in the world he did respect. The old man advised Ivan Matveitch to send for a priest, but Ivan Matveitch responded that 'ces messieurs et moi, nous n'avons rien a nous dire,' and begged him to change the subject. On the neighbour's departure, he gave his valet orders to admit no one in future.

Then he sent for me. I was frightened when I saw him; there were blue patches under his eyes, his face looked drawn and stiff, his jaw hung down. 'Vous voila grande, Suzon,' he said, with difficulty articulating the consonants, but still trying to smile (I was then nineteen), 'vous allez peut-etre bientot rester seule. Soyez toujours sage et vertueuse. C'est la derniere recommandation d'un'--he coughed-- 'd'un vieillard qui vous veut du bien. Je vous ai recommande a mon frere et je ne doute pas qu'il ne respecte mes volontes....' He coughed again, and anxiously felt his chest. 'Du reste, j'esepre encore pouvoir faire quelque chose pour vous... dans mon testament.' This last phrase cut me to the heart, like a knife. Ah, it was really too... too contemptuous and insulting! Ivan Matveitch probably ascribed to some other feeling--to a feeling of grief or gratitude--what was expressed in my face, and as though wishing to comfort me, he patted me on the shoulder, at the same time, as usual, gently repelling me, and observed: 'Voyons, mon enfant, du courage! Nous sommes tous mortels! Et puis il n'y a pas encore de danger. Ce n'est qu'une precaution que j'ai cru devoir prendre.... Allez!'

Again, just as when he had summoned me after my mother's death, I longed to shriek at him, 'But I'm your daughter! your daughter!' But I thought in those words, in that cry of the heart, he would doubtless hear nothing but a desire to assert my rights, my claims on his property, on his money.... Oh, no, for nothing in the world would I say a word to this man, who had not once mentioned my mother's name to me, in whose eyes I was of so little account that he did not even trouble himself to ascertain whether I was aware of my parentage! Or, perhaps, he suspected, even knew it, and did not wish 'to raise a dust' (a favourite saying of his, almost the only Russian expression he ever used), did not care to deprive himself of a good reader with a young voice! No! no! Let him go on wronging his daughter, as he had wronged her mother! Let him carry both sins to the grave! I swore it, I swore he should not hear from my lips the word which must have something of a sweet and holy sound in every ear! I would not say to him father! I would not forgive him for my mother and myself! He felt no need of that forgiveness, of that name.... It could not be, it could not be that he felt no need of it! But he should not have forgiveness, he should not, he should not!

God knows whether I should have kept my vow, and whether my heart would not have softened, whether I should not have overcome my shyness, my shame, and my pride... but it happened with Ivan Matveitch just as with my mother. Death carried him off suddenly, and also in the night. It was again Mr. Ratsch who waked me, and ran with me to the big house, to Ivan Matveitch's bedroom.... But I found not even the last dying gestures, which had left such a vivid impression on my memory at my mother's bedside. On the embroidered, lace-edged pillows lay a sort of withered, dark-coloured doll, with sharp nose and ruffled grey eyebrows.... I shrieked with horror, with loathing, rushed away, stumbled in doorways against bearded peasants in smocks with holiday red sashes, and found myself, I don't remember how, in the fresh air....

I was told afterwards that when the valet ran into the bedroom, at a violent ring of the bell, he found Ivan Matveitch not in the bed, but a few feet from it. And that he was sitting huddled up on the floor, and that twice over he repeated, 'Well, granny, here's a pretty holiday for you!' And that these were his last words. But I cannot believe that. Was it likely he would speak Russian at such a moment, and such a homely old Russian saying too!

For a whole fortnight afterwards we were awaiting the arrival of the new master, Semyon Matveitch Koltovsky. He sent orders that nothing was to be touched, no one was to be discharged, till he had looked into everything in person. All the doors, all the furniture, drawers, tables--all were locked and sealed up. All the servants were downcast and apprehensive. I became suddenly one of the most important persons in the house, perhaps the most important. I had been spoken of as 'the young lady' before; but now this expression seemed to take a new significance, and was pronounced with a peculiar emphasis. It began to be whispered that 'the old master had died suddenly, and hadn't time to send for a priest, indeed and he hadn't been at confession for many a long day; but still, a will doesn't take long to make.'

Mr. Ratsch, too, thought well to change his mode of action. He did not affect good-nature and friendliness; he knew he would not impose upon me, but his face wore an expression of sulky resignation. 'You see, I give in,' he seemed to say. Every one showed me deference, and tried to please me... while I did not know what to do or how to behave, and could only marvel that people failed to perceive how they were hurting me. At last Semyon Matveitch arrived.

Semyon Matveitch was ten years younger than Ivan Matveitch, and his whole life had taken a completely different turn. He was a government official in Petersburg, filling an important position.... He had married and been left early a widower; he had one son. In face Semyon Matveitch was like his brother, only he was shorter and stouter, and had a round bald head, bright black eyes, like Ivan Matveitch's, only more prominent, and full red lips. Unlike his brother, whom he spoke of even after his death as a French philosopher, and sometimes bluntly as a queer fish, Semyon Matveitch almost invariably talked Russian, loudly and fluently, and he was constantly laughing, completely closing his eyes as he did so and shaking all over in an unpleasant way, as though he were shaking with rage. He looked after things very sharply, went into everything himself, exacted the strictest account from every one. The very first day of his arrival he ordered a service with holy water, and sprinkled everything with water, all the rooms in the house, even the lofts and the cellars, in order, as he put it, 'radically to expel the Voltairean and Jacobin spirit.' In the first week several of Ivan Matveitch's favourites were sent to the right-about, one was even banished to a settlement, corporal punishment was inflicted on others; the old valet--he was a Turk, knew French, and had been given to Ivan Matveitch by the late field-marshal Kamensky--received his freedom, indeed, but with it a command to be gone within twenty-four hours, 'as an example to others.' Semyon Matveitch turned out to be a harsh master; many probably regretted the late owner.

'With the old master, Ivan Matveitch,' a butler, decrepit with age, wailed in my presence, 'our only trouble was to see that the linen put out was clean, and that the rooms smelt sweet, and that the servants' voices weren't heard in the passages--God forbid! For the rest, you might do as you pleased. The old master never hurt a fly in his life! Ah, it's hard times now! It's time to die!'

Rapid, too, was the change in my position, that is to say in the position in which I had been placed for a few days against my own will.... No sort of will was found among Ivan Matveitch's papers, not a line written for my benefit. At once every one seemed in haste to avoid me.... I am not speaking of Mr. Ratsch... every one else, too, was angry with me, and tried to show their anger, as though I had deceived them.

One Sunday after matins, in which he invariably officiated at the altar, Semyon Matveitch sent for me. Till that day I had seen him by glimpses, and he seemed not to have noticed me. He received me in his study, standing at the window. He was wearing an official uniform with two stars. I stood still, near the door; my heart was beating violently from fear and from another feeling, vague as yet, but still oppressive. 'I wish to see you, young lady,' began Semyon Matveitch, glancing first at my feet, and then suddenly into my eyes. The look was like a slap in the face. 'I wished to see you to inform you of my decision, and to assure you of my unhesitating inclination to be of service to you.' He raised his voice. 'Claims, of course, you have none, but as... my brother's reader you may always reckon on my... my consideration. I am... of course convinced of your good sense and of your principles. Mr. Ratsch, your stepfather, has already received from me the necessary instructions. To which I must add that your attractive exterior seems to me a pledge of the excellence of your sentiments.' Semyon Matveitch went off into a thin chuckle, while I... I was not offended exactly... but I suddenly felt very sorry for myself... and at that moment I fully realised how utterly forsaken and alone I was. Semyon Matveitch went with short, firm steps to the table, took a roll of notes out of the drawer, and putting it in my hand, he added: 'Here is a small sum from me for pocket-money. I won't forget you in future, my pretty; but good-bye for the present, and be a good girl.' I took the roll mechanically: I should have taken anything he had offered me, and going back to my own room, a long while I wept, sitting on my bed. I did not notice that I had dropped the roll of notes on the floor. Mr. Ratsch found it and picked it up, and, asking me what I meant to do with it, kept it for himself.

An important change had taken place in his fortunes too in those days. After a few conversations with Semyon Matveitch, he became a great favourite, and soon after received the position of head steward. From that time dates his cheerfulness, that eternal laugh of his; at first it was an effort to adapt himself to his patron... in the end it became a habit. It was then, too, that he became a Russian patriot. Semyon Matveitch was an admirer of everything national, he called himself 'a true Russian bear,' and ridiculed the European dress, which he wore however. He sent away to a remote village a cook, on whose training Ivan Matveitch had spent vast sums: he sent him away because he had not known how to prepare pickled giblets.

Semyon Matveitch used to stand at the altar and join in the responses with the deacons, and when the serf-girls were brought together to dance and sing choruses, he would join in their songs too, and beat time with his feet, and pinch their cheeks.... But he soon went back to Petersburg, leaving my stepfather practically in complete control of the whole property.

Bitter days began for me.... My one consolation was music, and I gave myself up to it with my whole soul. Fortunately Mr. Ratsch was very fully occupied, but he took every opportunity to make me feel his hostility; as he had promised, he 'did not forget' my refusal. He ill-treated me, made me copy his long and lying reports to Semyon Matveitch, and correct for him the mistakes in spelling. I was forced to obey him absolutely, and I did obey him. He announced that he meant to tame me, to make me as soft as silk. 'What do you mean by those mutinous eyes?' he shouted sometimes at dinner, drinking his beer, and slapping the table with his hand. 'You think, maybe, you're as silent as a sheep, so you must be all right.... Oh, no! You'll please look at me like a sheep too!' My position became a torture, insufferable,... my heart was growing bitter. Something dangerous began more and more frequently to stir within it. I passed nights without sleep and without a light, thinking, thinking incessantly; and in the darkness without and the gloom within, a fearful determination began to shape itself. The arrival of Semyon Matveitch gave another turn to my thoughts.

No one had expected him. It turned out that he was retiring in unpleasant circumstances; he had hoped to receive the Alexander ribbon, and they had presented him with a snuff-box. Discontented with the government, which had failed to appreciate his talents, and with Petersburg society, which had shown him little sympathy, and did not share his indignation, he determined to settle in the country, and devote himself to the management of his property. He arrived alone. His son, Mihail Semyonitch, arrived later, in the holidays for the New Year. My stepfather was scarcely ever out of Semyon Matveitch's room; he still stood high in his good graces. He left me in peace; he had no time for me then... Semyon Matveitch had taken it into his head to start a paper factory. Mr. Ratsch had no knowledge whatever of manufacturing work, and Semyon Matveitch was aware of the fact; but then my stepfather was an active man (the favourite expression just then), an 'Araktcheev!' That was just what Semyon Matveitch used to call him--'my Araktcheev!' 'That's all I want,' Semyon Matveitch maintained; 'if there is zeal, I myself will direct it.' In the midst of his numerous occupations--he had to superintend the factory, the estate, the foundation of a counting-house, the drawing up of counting-house regulations, the creation of new offices and duties--Semyon Matveitch still had time to attend to me.

I was summoned one evening to the drawing-room, and set to play the piano. Semyon Matveitch cared for music even less than his brother; he praised and thanked me, however, and next day I was invited to dine at the master's table. After dinner Semyon Matveitch had rather a long conversation with me, asked me questions, laughed at some of my replies, though there was, I remember, nothing amusing in them, and stared at me so strangely... I felt uncomfortable. I did not like his eyes, I did not like their open expression, their clear glance.... It always seemed to me that this very openness concealed something evil, that under that clear brilliance it was dark within in his soul. 'You shall not be my reader,' Semyon Matveitch announced to me at last, prinking and setting himself to rights in a repulsive way. 'I am, thank God, not blind yet, and can read myself; but coffee will taste better to me from your little hands, and I shall listen to your playing with pleasure.' From that day I always went over to the big house to dinner, and sometimes remained in the drawing-room till evening. I too, like my stepfather, was in favour: it was not a source of joy for me. Semyon Matveitch, I am bound to own, showed me a certain respect, but in the man there was, I felt it, something that repelled and alarmed me. And that 'something' showed itself not in words, but in his eyes, in those wicked eyes, and in his laugh. He never spoke to me of my father, of his brother, and it seemed to me that he avoided the subject, not because he did not want to excite ambitious ideas or pretensions in me, but from another cause, to which I could not give a definite shape, but which made me blush and feel bewildered.... Towards Christmas came his son, Mihail Semyonitch.

Ah, I feel I cannot go on as I have begun; these memories are too painful. Especially now I cannot tell my story calmly.... But what is the use of concealment? I loved Michel, and he loved me.

How it came to pass--I am not going to describe that either. From the very evening when he came into the drawing-room--I was at the piano, playing a sonata of Weber's when he came in--handsome and slender, in a velvet coat lined with sheepskin and high gaiters, just as he was, straight from the frost outside, and shaking his snow-sprinkled, sable cap, before he had greeted his father, glanced swiftly at me, and wondered--I knew that from that evening I could never forget him--I could never forget that good, young face. He began to speak... and his voice went straight to my heart.... A manly and soft voice, and in every sound such a true, honest nature!

Semyon Matveitch was delighted at his son's arrival, embraced him, but at once asked, 'For a fortnight, eh? On leave, eh?' and sent me away.

I sat a long while at my window, and gazed at the lights flitting to and fro in the rooms of the big house. I watched them, I listened to the new, unfamiliar voices; I was attracted by the cheerful commotion, and something new, unfamiliar, bright, flitted into my soul too.... The next day before dinner I had my first conversation with him. He had come across to see my stepfather with some message from Semyon Matveitch, and he found me in our little sitting-room. I was getting up to go; he detained me. He was very lively and unconstrained in all his movements and words, but of superciliousness or arrogance, of the tone of Petersburg superiority, there was not a trace in him, and nothing of the officer, of the guardsman.... On the contrary, in the very freedom of his manner there was something appealing, almost shamefaced, as though he were begging you to overlook something. Some people's eyes are never laughing, even at the moment of laughter; with *him* it was the lips that almost never changed their beautiful line, while his eyes were almost always smiling. So we chatted for about an hour... what about I don't remember; I remember only that I looked him straight in the face all the while, and oh, how delightfully at ease I felt with him!

In the evening I played on the piano. He was very fond of music, and he sat down in a low chair, and laying his curly head on his arm, he listened intently. He did not once praise me, but I felt that he liked my playing, and I played with ardour. Semyon Matveitch, who was sitting near his son, looking through some plans, suddenly frowned. 'Come, madam,' he said, smoothing himself down and buttoning himself up, as his manner was, 'that's enough; why are you trilling away like a canary? It's enough to make one's head ache. For us old folks you wouldn't exert yourself so, no fear...' he added in an undertone, and again he sent me away. Michel followed me to the door with his eyes, and got up from his seat. 'Where are you off to? Where are you off to?' cried Semyon Matveitch, and he suddenly laughed, and then said something more... I could not catch his words; but Mr. Ratsch, who was present, sitting in a corner of the drawing-room (he was always 'present,' and that time he had brought in the plans), laughed, and his laugh reached my ears.... The same thing, or almost the same thing, was repeated the following evening... Semyon Matveitch grew suddenly cooler to me.

Four days later I met Michel in the corridor that divided the big house in two. He took me by the hand, and led me to a room near the dining-room, which was called the portrait gallery. I followed him, not without emotion, but with perfect confidence. Even then, I believe, I would have followed him to the end of the world, though I had as yet no suspicion of all that he was to me. Alas, I loved him with all the passion, all the despair of a young creature who not only has no one to love, but feels herself an uninvited and unnecessary guest among strangers, among enemies!... Michel said to me--and it was strange! I looked boldly, directly in his face, while he did not look at me, and flushed slightly--he said to me that he understood my position, and sympathised with me, and begged me to forgive his father.... 'As far as I'm concerned,' he added, 'I beseech you always to trust me, and believe me, to me you 're a sister--yes, a sister.' Here he pressed my hand warmly. I was confused, it was my turn to look down; I had somehow expected something else, some other word. I began to thank him. 'No, please,'--he cut me short--'don't talk like that.... But remember, it's a brother's duty to defend his sister, and if you ever need protection, against any one whatever, rely upon me. I have not been here long, but I have seen a good deal already... and among other things, I see through your stepfather.' He squeezed my hand again, and left me.

I found out later that Michel had felt an aversion for Mr. Ratsch from his very first meeting with him. Mr. Ratsch tried to ingratiate himself with him too, but becoming convinced of the uselessness of his efforts, promptly took up himself an attitude of hostility to him, and not only did not disguise it from Semyon Matveitch, but, on the contrary, lost no opportunity of showing it, expressing, at the same time, his regret that he had been so unlucky as to displease the young heir. Mr. Ratsch had carefully studied Semyon Matveitch's character; his calculations did not lead him astray. 'This man's devotion to me admits of no doubt, for the very reason that after I am gone he will be ruined; my heir cannot endure him.'... This idea grew and strengthened in the old man's head. They say all persons in power, as they grow old, are readily caught by that bait, the bait of exclusive personal devotion....

Semyon Matveitch had good reason to call Mr. Ratsch his Araktcheev.... He might well have called him another name too. 'You're not one to make difficulties,' he used to say to him. He had begun in this condescendingly familiar tone with him from the very first, and my stepfather would gaze fondly at Semyon Matveitch, let his head droop deprecatingly on one side, and laugh with good-humoured simplicity, as though to say, 'Here I am, entirely in your hands.'

Ah, I feel my hands shaking, and my heart's thumping against the table on which I write at this moment. It's terrible for me to recall those days, and my blood boils.... But I will tell everything to the end... to the end!

A new element had come into Mr. Ratsch's treatment of me during my brief period of favour. He began to be deferential to me, to be respectfully familiar with me, as though I had grown sensible, and become more on a level with him. 'You've done with your airs and graces,' he said to me one day, as we were going back from the big house to the lodge. 'Quite right too! All those fine principles and delicate sentiments--moral precepts in fact--are not for us, young lady, they're not for poor folks.'

When I had fallen out of favour, and Michel did not think it necessary to disguise his contempt for Mr. Ratsch and his sympathy with me, the latter suddenly redoubled his severity with me; he was continually following me about, as though I were capable of any crime, and must be sharply looked after. 'You mind what I say,' he shouted, bursting without knocking into my room, in muddy boots and with his cap on his head; 'I won't put up with such goings on! I won't stand your stuck-up airs! You're not going to impose on me. I'll break your proud spirit.'

And accordingly, one morning he informed me that the decree had gone forth from Semyon Matveitch that I was not to appear at the dinner-table for the future without special invitation.... I don't know how all this would have ended if it had not been for an event which was the final turning-point of my destiny....

Michel was passionately fond of horses. He took it into his head to break in a young horse, which went well for a while, then began kicking and flung him out of the sledge.... He was brought home unconscious, with a broken arm and bruises on his chest. His father was panic-stricken; he sent for the best doctors from the town. They did a great deal for Michel; but he had to lie down for a month. He did not play cards, the doctor forbade him to talk, and it was awkward for him to read, holding the book up in one hand all the while. It ended by Semyon Matveitch sending me in to his son, in my old capacity of reader.

Then followed hours I can never forget! I used to go in to Michel directly after dinner, and sit at a little round table in the half-darkened window. He used to be lying down in a little room out of the drawing-room, at the further end, on a broad leather sofa in the Empire style, with a gold bas-relief on its high, straight back. The bas-relief represented a marriage procession among the ancients. Michel's head, thrown a little back on the pillow, always moved at once, and his pale face turned towards me: he smiled, his whole face brightened, he flung back his soft, damp curls, and said to me softly, 'Good-morning, my kind sweet girl.' I took up the book--Walter Scott's novels were at the height of their fame in those days--the reading of Ivanhoe has left a particularly vivid recollection in my mind.... I could not help my voice thrilling and quivering as I gave utterance to Rebecca's speeches. I, too, had Jewish blood, and was not my lot like hers? Was I not, like Rebecca, waiting on a sick man, dear to me? Every time I removed my eyes from the page and lifted them to him, I met his eyes with the same soft, bright smile over all his face. We talked very little; the door into the drawing-room was invariably open and some one was always sitting there; but whenever it was quiet there, I used, I don't know why, to cease reading and look intently at Michel, and he looked at me, and we both felt happy then and, as it were, glad and shamefaced, and everything, everything we told each other then without a gesture or a word! Alas! our hearts came together, ran to meet each other, as underground streams flow together, unseen, unheard... and irresistibly.

'Can you play chess or draughts?' he asked me one day.

'I can play chess a little,' I answered.

'That's good. Tell them to bring a chess-board and push up the table.'

I sat down beside the sofa, my heart was throbbing, I did not dare glance at Michel,... Yet from the window, across the room, how freely I had gazed at him!

I began to set the chessmen... My fingers shook.

'I suggested it... not for the game,'... Michel said in an undertone, also setting the pieces, 'but to have you nearer me.'

I made no answer, but, without asking which should begin, moved a pawn... Michel did not move in reply... I looked at him. His head was stretched a little forward; pale all over, with imploring eyes he signed towards my hand...

Whether I understood him... I don't remember, but something instantaneously whirled into my head.... Hesitating, scarcely breathing, I took up the knight and moved it right across the board. Michel bent down swiftly, and catching my fingers with his lips, and pressing them against the board, he began noiselessly and passionately kissing them.... I had no power, I had no wish to draw them back; with my other hand I hid my face, and tears, as I remember now, cold but blissful... oh, what blissful tears!... dropped one by one on the table. Ah, I knew, with my whole heart I felt at that moment, all that he was who held my hand in his power! I knew that he was not a boy, carried away by a momentary impulse, not a Don Juan, not a military Lovelace, but one of the noblest, the best of men... and he loved me!

'Oh, my Susanna!' I heard Michel whisper, 'I will never make you shed other tears than these.'

He was wrong... he did.

But what use is there in dwelling on such memories... especially, especially now?

Michel and I swore to belong to each other. He knew that Semyon Matveitch would never let him marry me, and he did not conceal it from me. I had no doubt about it myself and I rejoiced, not that he did not deceive me--he **could not** deceive--but that he did not try to delude himself. For myself I asked for nothing, and would have followed where and how he chose. 'You shall be my wife,' he repeated to me. 'I am not Ivanhoe; I know that happiness is not with Lady Rowena.'

Michel soon regained his health. I could not continue going to see him, but everything was decided between us. I was already entirely absorbed in the future; I saw nothing of what was passing around me, as though I were floating on a glorious, calm, but rushing river, hidden in mist. But we were watched, we were being spied upon. Once or twice I noticed my stepfather's malignant eyes, and heard his loathsome laugh.... But that laugh, those eyes as it were emerged for an instant from the mist... I shuddered, but forgot it directly, and surrendered myself again to the glorious, swift river...

On the day before the departure of Michel--we had planned together that he was to turn back secretly on the way and fetch me--I received from him through his trusted valet a note, in which he asked me to meet him at half-past nine in the summer billiard-room, a large, low-pitched room, built on to the big house in the garden. He wrote to me that he absolutely must speak with me and arrange things. I had twice already met Michel in the billiard-room... I had the key of the outer door. As soon as it struck half-past nine I threw a warm wrap over my shoulders, stepped quietly out of the lodge, and made my way successfully over the crackling snow to the billiard-room. The moon, wrapped in vapour, stood a dim blur just over the ridge of the roof, and the wind whistled shrilly round the corner of the wall. A shiver passed over me, but I put the key into the lock, went into the room, closed the door behind me, turned round... A dark figure became visible against one of the walls, took a couple of steps forward, stopped...

'Michel,' I whispered.

'Michel is locked up by my orders, and this is I!' answered a voice, which seemed to rend my heart...

Before me stood Semyon Matveitch!

I was rushing to escape, but he clutched at my arm.

'Where are you off to, vile hussy?' he hissed. 'You 're quite equal to stolen interviews with young fools, so you'll have to be equal to the consequences.'

I was numb with horror, but still struggled towards the door... In vain! Like iron hooks the ringers of Semyon Matveitch held me tight.

'Let me go, let me go,' I implored at last.

'I tell you you shan't stir!'

Semyon Matveitch forced me to sit down. In the half-darkness I could not distinguish his face. I had turned away from him too, but I heard him breathing hard and grinding his teeth. I felt neither fear nor despair, but a sort of senseless amazement... A captured bird, I suppose, is numb like that in the claws of the kite... and Semyon Matveitch's hand, which still held me as fast, crushed me like some wild, ferocious claw....

'Aha!' he repeated; 'aha! So this is how it is... so it's come to this... Ah, wait a bit!'

I tried to get up, but he shook me with such violence that I almost shrieked with pain, and a stream of abuse, insult, and menace burst upon me...

'Michel, Michel, where are you? save me,' I moaned.

Semyon Matveitch shook me again... That time I could not control myself... I screamed.

That seemed to have some effect on him. He became a little quieter, let go my arm, but remained where he was, two steps from me, between me and the door.

A few minutes passed... I did not stir; he breathed heavily as before.

'Sit still,' he began at last, 'and answer me. Let me see that your morals are not yet utterly corrupt, and that you are still capable of listening to the voice of reason. Impulsive folly I can overlook, but stubborn obstinacy--never! My son...' there was a catch in his breath... 'Mihail Semyonitch has promised to marry you? Hasn't he? Answer me! Has he promised, eh?'

I answered, of course, nothing. Semyon Matveitch was almost flying into fury again.

'I take your silence as a sign of assent,' he went on, after a brief pause. 'And so you were plotting to be my daughter-in-law? A pretty notion! But you're not a child of four years old, and you must be fully aware that young boobies are never sparing of the wildest promises, if only they can gain their ends... but to say nothing of that, could you suppose that I--a noble gentleman of ancient family, Semyon Matveitch Koltovsky--would ever give my consent to such a marriage? Or did you mean to dispense with the parental blessing?... Did you mean to run away, get married in secret, and then come back, go through a nice little farce, throw yourself at my feet, in the hope that the old man will be touched.... Answer me, damn you!'

I only bent my head. He could kill me, but to force me to speak--that was not in his power.

He walked up and down a little.

'Come, listen to me,' he began in a calmer voice. 'You mustn't think... don't imagine... I see one must talk to you in a different manner. Listen; I understand your position. You are frightened, upset.... Pull yourself together. At this moment I must seem to you a monster... a despot. But put yourself in my position too; how could I help being indignant, saying too much? And for all that I have shown you that I am not a monster, that I too have a heart. Remember how I treated you on my arrival here and afterwards till... till lately... till the illness of Mihail Semyonitch. I don't wish to boast of my beneficence, but I should have thought simple gratitude ought to have held you back from the slippery path on which you were determined to enter!'

Semyon Matveitch walked to and fro again, and standing still patted me lightly on the arm, on the very arm which still ached from his violence, and was for long after marked with blue bruises.

'To be sure,' he began again, 'we're headstrong... just a little headstrong! We don't care to take the trouble to think, we don't care to consider what our advantage consists in and where we ought to seek it. You ask me: where that advantage lies? You've no need to look far.... It's, maybe, close at hand.... Here am I now. As a father, as head of the family I am bound to be particular.... It's my duty. But I'm a man at the same time, and you know that very well. Undoubtedly I'm a practical person and of course cannot tolerate any sentimental nonsense; expectations that are quite inconsistent with everything, you must of course dismiss from your mind for really what sense is there in them?--not to speak of the immorality of such a proceeding.... You will assuredly realise all this yourself, when you have thought it over a little. And I say, simply and straightforwardly, I wouldn't confine myself to what I have done for you. I have always been prepared--and I am still prepared--to put your welfare on a sound footing, to guarantee you a secure position, because I know your value, I do justice to your talents, and your intelligence, and in fact... (here Semyon Matveitch stooped down to me a little)... you have such eyes that, I confess... though I am not a young man, yet to see them quite unmoved... I understand... is not an easy matter, not at all an easy matter.'

These words sent a chill through me. I could scarcely believe my ears. For the first minute I fancied that Semyon Matveitch meant to bribe me to break with Michel, to pay me 'compensation.'... But what was he saying? My eyes had begun to get used to the darkness and I could make out Semyon Matveitch's face. It was smiling, that old face, and he was walking to and fro with little steps, fidgeting restlessly before me....

'Well, what do you say,' he asked at last, 'does my offer please you?'

'Offer?'... I repeated unconsciously,... I simply did not understand a word.

Semyon Matveitch laughed... actually laughed his revolting thin laugh.

'To be sure,' he cried, 'you're all alike you young women'--he corrected himself--'young ladies... young ladies... you all dream of nothing else... you must have young men! You can't live without love! Of course not. Well, well! Youth's all very well! But do you suppose that it's only young men that can love?... There are some older men, whose hearts are warmer... and when once an old man does take a fancy to any one, well--he's simply like a rock! It's for ever! Not like these beardless, feather-brained young fools! Yes, yes; you mustn't look down on old men! They can do so much! You've only to take them the right way! Yes... yes! And as for kissing, old men know all about that too, he-he-he...' Semyon Matveitch laughed again. 'Come, please... your little hand... just as a proof... that's all....'

I jumped up from the chair, and with all my force I gave him a blow in the chest. He tottered, he uttered a sort of decrepit, scared sound, he almost fell down. There are no words in human language to express how loathsome and infinitely vile he seemed to me. Every vestige of fear had left me.

'Get away, despicable old man,' broke from my lips; 'get away, Mr. Koltovsky, you noble gentleman of ancient family! I, too, am of your blood, the blood of the Koltovskys, and I curse the day and the hour when I was born of that ancient family!'

'What!... What are you saying!... What!' stammered Semyon Matveitch, gasping for breath. 'You dare... at the very minute when I've caught you... when you came to meet Misha... eh? eh? eh?'

But I could not stop myself.... Something relentless, desperate was roused up within me.

'And you, you, the brother... of your brother, you had the insolence, you dared... What did you take me for? Can you be so blind as not to have seen long ago the loathing you arouse in me?... You dare use the word offer!... Let me out at once, this instant!'

I moved towards the door.

'Oh, indeed! oh, oh! so this is what she says!' Semyon Matveitch piped shrilly, in a fit of violent fury, but obviously not able to make up his mind to come near me.... 'Wait a bit, Mr. Ratsch, Ivan Demianitch, come here!'

The door of the billiard-room opposite the one I was near flew wide open, and my stepfather appeared, with a lighted candelabrum in each hand. His round, red face, lighted up on both sides, was beaming with the triumph of satisfied revenge, and slavish delight at having rendered valuable service.... Oh, those loathsome white eyes! when shall I cease to behold them?

'Be so good as to take this girl at once,' cried Semyon Matveitch, turning to my stepfather and imperiously pointing to me with a shaking hand. 'Be so good as to take her home and put her under lock and key... so that she... can't stir a finger, so that not a fly can get in to her! Till further orders from me! Board up the windows if need be! You'll answer for her with your head!'

Mr. Ratsch set the candelabra on the billiard-table, made Semyon Matveitch a low bow, and with a slight swagger and a malignant smile, moved towards me. A cat, I imagine, approaches a mouse who has no chance of escape in that way. All my daring left me in an instant. I knew the man was capable of... beating me. I began to tremble; yes; oh, shame! oh ignominy! I shivered.

'Now, then, madam,' said Mr. Ratsch, 'kindly come along.'

He took me, without haste, by the arm above the elbow.... He saw that I should not resist. Of my own accord I pushed forward towards the door; at that instant I had but one thought in my mind, to escape as quickly as possible from the presence of Semyon Matveitch.

But the loathsome old man darted up to us from behind, and Ratsch stopped me and turned me round face to face with his patron.

'Ah!' the latter shouted, shaking his fist; 'ah! So I'm the brother... of my brother, am I? Ties of blood! eh? But a cousin, a first cousin you could marry? You could? eh? Take her, you!' he turned to my stepfather. 'And remember, keep a sharp look-out! The slightest communication with her--and no punishment will be too severe.... Take her!'

Mr. Ratsch conducted me to my room. Crossing the courtyard, he said nothing, but kept laughing noiselessly to himself. He closed the shutters and the doors, and then, as he was finally returning, he bowed low to me as he had to Semyon Matveitch, and went off into a ponderous, triumphant guffaw!

'Good-night to your highness,' he gasped out, choking: 'she didn't catch her fairy prince! What a pity! It wasn't a bad idea in its way! It's a lesson for the future: not to keep up correspondence! Ho-ho-ho! How capitally it has all turned out though!' He went out, and all of a sudden poked his head in at the door. 'Well? I didn't forget you, did I? Hey? I kept my promise, didn't I? Ho-ho!' The key creaked in the lock. I breathed freely. I had been afraid he would tie my hands... but they were my own, they were free! I instantly wrenched the silken cord off my dressing-gown, made a noose, and was putting it on my neck, but I flung the cord aside again at once. 'I won't please you!' I said aloud. 'What madness, really! Can I dispose of my life without Michel's leave, my life, which I have surrendered into his keeping? No, cruel wretches! No! You have not won your game yet! He will save me, he will tear me out of this hell, he... my Michel!'

But then I remembered that he was shut up just as I was, and I flung myself, face downwards, on my bed, and sobbed... and sobbed.... And only the thought that my tormentor was perhaps at the door, listening and triumphing, only that thought forced me to swallow my tears....

I am worn out. I have been writing since morning, and now it is evening; if once I tear myself from this sheet of paper, I shall not be capable of taking up the pen again.... I must hasten, hasten to the finish! And besides, to dwell on the hideous things that followed that dreadful day is beyond my strength!

Twenty-four hours later I was taken in a closed cart to an isolated hut, surrounded by peasants, who were to watch me, and kept shut up for six whole weeks! I was not for one instant alone.... Later on I learnt that my stepfather had set spies to watch both Michel and me ever since his arrival, that he had bribed the servant, who had given me Michel's note. I ascertained too that an awful, heart-rending scene had taken place the next morning between the son and the father.... The father had cursed him. Michel for his part had sworn he would never set foot in his father's house again, and had set off to Petersburg. But the blow aimed at me by my stepfather rebounded upon himself. Semyon Matveitch announced that he could not have him remaining there, and managing the estate any longer. Awkward service, it seems, is an unpardonable offence, and some one must be fixed upon to bear the brunt of the **scandal**. Semyon Matveitch recompensed Mr. Ratsch liberally, however: he gave him the necessary means to move to Moscow and to establish himself there. Before the departure for Moscow, I was brought back to the lodge, but kept as before under the strictest guard. The loss of the 'snug little berth,' of which he was being deprived 'thanks to me,' increased my stepfather's vindictive rage against me more than ever.

'Why did you make such a fuss?' he would say, almost snorting with indignation; 'upon my word! The old chap, of course, got a little too hot, was a little too much in a hurry, and so he made a mess of it; now, of course, his vanity's hurt, there's no setting the mischief right again now! If you'd only waited a day or two, it'd all have been right as a trivet; you wouldn't have been kept on dry bread, and I should have stayed what I was! Ah, well, women's hair is long... but their wit is short! Never mind; I'll be even with you yet, and that pretty young gentleman shall smart for it too!'

I had, of course, to bear all these insults in silence. Semyon Matveitch I did not once see again. The separation from his son had been a shock to him too. Whether he felt remorse or--which is far more likely--wished to bind me for ever to my home, to my family--my family!--anyway, he assigned me a pension, which was to be paid into my stepfather's hands, and to be given to me till I married.... This humiliating alms, this pension I still receive... that is to say, Mr. Ratsch receives it for me....

We settled in Moscow. I swear by the memory of my poor mother, I would not have remained two days, not two hours, with my stepfather, after once reaching the town... I would have gone away, not knowing where... to the police; I would have flung myself at the feet of the governor-general, of the senators; I don't know what I would have done, if it had not happened, at the very moment of our starting from the country, that the girl who had been our maid managed to give me a letter from Michel! Oh, that letter! How many times I read over each line, how many times I covered it with kisses! Michel besought me not to lose heart, to go on hoping, to believe in his unchanging love; he swore that he would never belong to any one but me; he called me his wife, he promised to overcome all hindrances, he drew a picture of our future, he asked of me only one thing, to be patient, to wait a little....

And I resolved to wait and be patient. Alas! what would I not have agreed to, what would I not have borne, simply to do his will! That letter became my holy thing, my guiding star, my anchor. Sometimes when my stepfather would begin abusing and insulting me, I would softly lay my hand on my bosom (I wore Michel's letter sewed into an amulet) and only smile. And the more violent and abusive was Mr. Ratsch, the easier, lighter, and sweeter was the heart within me.... I used to see, at last, by his eyes, that he began to wonder whether I was going out of my mind.... Following on this first letter came a second, still more full of hope.... It spoke of our meeting soon.

Alas! instead of that meeting there came a morning... I can see Mr. Ratsch coming in--and triumph again, malignant triumph, in his face--and in his hands a page of the *Invalid*, and there the announcement of the death of the Captain of the Guards--Mihail Koltovsky.

What can I add? I remained alive, and went on living in Mr. Ratsch's house. He hated me as before--more than before--he had unmasked his black soul too much before me, he could not pardon me that. But that was of no consequence to me. I became, as it were, without feeling; my own fate no longer interested me. To think of him, to think of him! I had no interest, no joy, but that. My poor Michel died with my name on his lips.... I was told so by a servant, devoted to him, who had been with him when he came into the country. The same year my stepfather married Eleonora Karpovna. Semyon Matveitch died shortly after. In his will he secured to me and increased the pension he had allowed me.... In the event of my death, it was to pass to Mr. Ratsch....

Two--three--years passed... six years, seven years.... Life has been passing, ebbing away... while I merely watched how it was ebbing. As in childhood, on some river's edge one makes a little pond and dams it up, and tries in all sorts of ways to keep the water from soaking through, from breaking in. But at last the water breaks in, and then you abandon all your vain efforts, and you are glad instead to watch all that you had guarded ebbing away to the last drop....

So I lived, so I existed, till at last a new, unhoped-for ray of warmth and light....'

The manuscript broke off at this word; the following leaves had been torn off, and several lines completing the sentence had been crossed through and blotted out.

XVIII

The reading of this manuscript so upset me, the impression made by Susanna's visit was so great, that I could not sleep all night, and early in the morning I sent an express messenger to Fustov with a letter, in which I besought him to come to Moscow as soon as possible, as his absence might have the most terrible results. I mentioned also my interview with Susanna, and the manuscript she had left in my hands. After having sent off the letter, I did not go out of the house all day, and pondered all the time on what might be happening at the Ratsches'. I could not make up my mind to go there myself. I could not help noticing though that my aunt was in a continual fidget; she ordered pastilles to be burnt every minute, and dealt the game of patience, known as 'the traveller,' which is noted as a game in which one can never succeed. The visit of an unknown lady, and at such a late hour, had not been kept secret from her: her imagination at once pictured a yawning abyss on the edge of which I was standing, and she was continually sighing and moaning and murmuring French sentences, quoted from a little manuscript book entitled **Extraits de Lecture**. In the evening I found on the little table at my bedside the treatise of De Girando, laid open at the chapter: On the evil influence of the passions. This book had been put in my room, at my aunt's instigation of course, by the elder of her companions, who was called in the household Amishka, from her resemblance to a little poodle of that name, and was a very sentimental, not to say romantic, though elderly, maiden lady. All the following day was spent in anxious expectation of Fustov's coming, of a letter from him, of news from the Ratsches' house... though on what ground could they have sent to me? Susanna would be more likely to expect me to visit her.... But I positively could not pluck up courage to see her without first talking to Fustov. I recalled every expression in my letter to him.... I thought it was strong enough; at last, late in the evening, he appeared.

XIX

He came into my room with his habitual, rapid, but deliberate step. His face struck me as pale, and though it showed traces of the fatigue of the journey, there was an expression of astonishment, curiosity, and dissatisfaction--emotions of which he had little experience as a rule. I rushed up to him, embraced him, warmly thanked him for obeying me, and after briefly describing my conversation with Susanna, handed him the manuscript. He went off to the window, to the very window in which Susanna had sat two days before, and without a word to me, he fell to reading it. I at once retired to the opposite corner of the room, and for appearance' sake took up a book; but I must own I was stealthily looking over the edge of the cover all the while at Fustov. At first he read rather calmly, and kept pulling with his left hand at the down on his lip; then he let his hand drop, bent forward and did not stir again. His eyes seemed to fly along the lines and his mouth slightly opened. At last he finished the manuscript, turned it over, looked round, thought a little, and began reading it all through a second time from beginning to end. Then he got up, put the manuscript in his pocket and moved towards the door; but he turned round and stopped in the middle of the room.

'Well, what do you think?' I began, not waiting for him to speak.

'I have acted wrongly towards her,' Fustov declared thickly. 'I have behaved... rashly, unpardonably, cruelly. I believed that... Viktor--'

'What!' I cried; 'that Viktor whom you despise so! But what could he say to you?'

Fustov crossed his arms and stood obliquely to me. He was ashamed, I saw that.

'Do you remember,' he said with some effort, 'that... Viktor alluded to... a pension. That unfortunate word stuck in my head. It's the cause of everything. I began questioning him.... Well, and he--'

'What did he say?'

'He told me that the old man... what's his name?... Koltovsky, had allowed Susanna that pension because... on account of... well, in fact, by way of damages.'

I flung up my hands.

'And you believed him?'

Fustov nodded.

'Yes! I believed him.... He said, too, that with the young one... In fact, my behaviour is unjustifiable.'

'And you went away so as to break everything off?'

'Yes; that's the best way... in such cases. I acted savagely, savagely,' he repeated.

We were both silent. Each of us felt that the other was ashamed; but it was easier for me; I was not ashamed of myself.

XX

'I would break every bone in that Viktor's body now,' pursued Fustov, clenching his teeth, 'if I didn't recognise that I'm in fault. I see now what the whole trick was contrived for, with Susanna's marriage they would lose the pension.... Wretches!'

I took his hand.

'Alexander,' I asked him, 'have you been to her?'

'No; I came straight to you on arriving. I'll go to-morrow... early to-morrow. Things can't be left so. On no account!'

'But you... love her, Alexander?'

Fustov seemed offended.

'Of course I love her. I am very much attached to her.'

'She's a splendid, true-hearted girl!' I cried.

Fustov stamped impatiently.

'Well, what notion have you got in your head? I was prepared to marry her--she's been baptized--I'm ready to marry her even now, I'd been thinking of it, though she's older than I am.'

At that instant I suddenly fancied that a pale woman's figure was seated in the window, leaning on her arms. The lights had burnt down; it was dark in the room. I shivered, looked more intently, and saw nothing, of course, in the window seat; but a strange feeling, a mixture of horror, anguish and pity, came over me.

'Alexander!' I began with sudden intensity, 'I beg you, I implore you, go at once to the Ratsches', don't put it off till to-morrow! An inner voice tells me that you really ought to see Susanna to-day!'

Fustov shrugged his shoulders.

'What are you talking about, really! It's eleven o'clock now, most likely they're all in bed.'

'No matter.... Do go, for goodness' sake! I have a presentiment.... Please do as I say! Go at once, take a sledge....'

'Come, what nonsense!' Fustov responded coolly; 'how could I go now? To-morrow morning I will be there, and everything will be cleared up.'

'But, Alexander, remember, she said that she was dying, that you would not find her... And if you had seen her face! Only think, imagine, to make up her mind to come to me... what it must have cost her....'

'She's a little high-flown,' observed Fustov, who had apparently regained his self-possession completely. 'All girls are like that... at first. I repeat, everything will be all right to-morrow. Meanwhile, good-bye. I'm tired, and you're sleepy too.'

He took his cap, and went out of the room.

'But you promise to come here at once, and tell me all about it?' I called after him.

'I promise.... Good-bye!'

I went to bed, but in my heart I was uneasy, and I felt vexed with my friend. I fell asleep late and dreamed that I was wandering with Susanna along underground, damp passages of some sort, and crawling along narrow, steep staircases, and continually going deeper and deeper down, though we were trying to get higher up out into the air. Some one was all the while incessantly calling us in monotonous, plaintive tones.

XXI

Some one's hand lay on my shoulder and pushed it several times.... I opened my eyes and in the faint light of the solitary candle, I saw Fustov standing before me. He frightened me. He was staggering; his face was yellow, almost the same colour as his hair; his lips seemed hanging down, his muddy eyes were staring senselessly away. What had become of his invariably amiable, sympathetic expression? I had a cousin who from epilepsy was sinking into idiocy.... Fustov looked like him at that moment.

I sat up hurriedly.

'What is it? What is the matter? Heavens!'

He made no answer.

'Why, what has happened? Fustov! Do speak! Susanna?...'

Fustov gave a slight start.

'She...' he began in a hoarse voice, and broke off.

'What of her? Have you seen her?'

He stared at me.

'She's no more.'

'No more?'

'No. She is dead.'

I jumped out of bed.

'Dead? Susanna? Dead?'

Fustov turned his eyes away again.

'Yes; she is dead; she died at midnight.'

'He's raving!' crossed my mind.

'At midnight! And what's the time now?'

'It's eight o'clock in the morning now.

They sent to tell me. She is to be buried to-morrow.'

I seized him by the hand.

'Alexander, you're not delirious? Are you in your senses?'

'I am in my senses,' he answered. 'Directly I heard it, I came straight to you.'

My heart turned sick and numb, as always happens on realising an irrevocable misfortune.

'My God! my God! Dead!' I repeated. 'How is it possible? So suddenly! Or perhaps she took her own life?'

'I don't know,' said Fustov, 'I know nothing. They told me she died at midnight. And to-morrow she will be buried.'

'At midnight!' I thought.... 'Then she was still alive yesterday when I fancied I saw her in the window, when I entreated him to hasten to her....'

'She was still alive yesterday, when you wanted to send me to Ivan Demianitch's,' said Fustov, as though guessing my thought.

'How little he knew her!' I thought again. 'How little we both knew her! "Highflown," said he, "all girls are like that.".... And at that very minute, perhaps, she was putting to her lips... Can one love any one and be so grossly mistaken in them?'

Fustov stood stockstill before my bed, his hands hanging, like a guilty man.

XXII

I dressed hurriedly.

'What do you mean to do now, Alexander?' I asked.

He gazed at me in bewilderment, as though marvelling at the absurdity of my question. And indeed what was there to do?

'You simply must go to them, though,' I began. 'You're bound to ascertain how it happened; there is, possibly, a crime concealed. One may expect anything of those people.... It is all to be thoroughly investigated. Remember the statement in her manuscript, the pension was to cease on her marriage, but in event of her death it was to pass to Ratsch. In any case, one must render her the last duty, pay homage to her remains!'

I talked to Fustov like a preceptor, like an elder brother. In the midst of all that horror, grief, bewilderment, a sort of unconscious feeling of superiority over Fustov had suddenly come to the surface in me.... Whether from seeing him crushed by the consciousness of his fault, distracted, shattered, whether that a misfortune befalling a man almost always humiliates him, lowers him in the opinion of others, 'you can't be much,' is felt, 'if you hadn't the wit to come off better than that!' God knows! Any way, Fustov seemed to me almost like a child, and I felt pity for him, and saw the necessity of severity. I held out a helping hand to him, stooping down to him from above. Only a woman's sympathy is free from condescension.

But Fustov continued to gaze with wild and stupid eyes at me--my authoritative tone obviously had no effect on him, and to my second question, 'You're going to them, I suppose?' he replied--

'No, I'm not going.'

'What do you mean, really? Don't you want to ascertain for yourself, to investigate, how, and what? Perhaps, she has left a letter... a document of some sort....'

Fustov shook his head.

'I can't go there,' he said. 'That's what I came to you for, to ask you to go... for me... I can't... I can't....'

Fustov suddenly sat down to the table, hid his face in both hands, and sobbed bitterly.

'Alas, alas!' he kept repeating through his tears; 'alas, poor girl... poor girl... I loved... I loved her... alas!'

I stood near him, and I am bound to confess, not the slightest sympathy was excited in me by those incontestably sincere sobs. I simply marvelled that Fustov could cry *like that*, and it seemed to me that *now* I knew what a small person he was, and that I should, in his place, have acted quite differently. What's one to make of it? If Fustov had remained quite unmoved, I should perhaps have hated him, have conceived an aversion for him, but he would not have sunk in my esteem.... He would have kept his prestige. Don Juan would have remained Don Juan! Very late in life, and only after many experiences, does a man learn, at the sight of a fellow-creature's real failing or weakness, to sympathise with him, and help him without a secret self-congratulation at his own virtue and strength, but on the contrary, with every humility and comprehension of the naturalness, almost the inevitableness, of sin.

XXIII

I was very bold and resolute in sending Fustov to the Ratsches'; but when I set out there myself at twelve o'clock (nothing would induce Fustov to go with me, he only begged me to give him an exact account of everything), when round the corner of the street their house glared at me in the distance with a yellowish blur from the coffin candles at one of the windows, an indescribable panic made me hold my breath, and I would gladly have turned back.... I mastered myself, however, and went into the passage. It smelt of incense and wax; the pink cover of the coffin, edged with silver lace, stood in a corner, leaning against the wall. In one of the adjoining rooms, the dining-room, the monotonous muttering of the deacon droned like the buzzing of a bee. From the drawing-room peeped out the sleepy face of a servant girl, who murmured in a subdued voice, 'Come to do homage to the dead?' She indicated the door of the dining-room. I went in. The coffin stood with the head towards the door; the black hair of Susanna under the white wreath, above the raised lace of the pillow, first caught my eyes. I went up sidewards, crossed myself, bowed down to the ground, glanced... Merciful God! what a face of agony! Unhappy girl! even death had no pity on her, had denied her--beauty, that would be little-- even that peace, that tender and impressive peace which is often seen on the faces of the newly dead. The little, dark, almost brown, face of Susanna recalled the vis- ages on old, old holy pictures. And the expression on that face! It looked as though she were on the point of shrieking--a shriek of despair--and had died so, uttering no sound... even the line between the brows was not smoothed out, and the fingers on the hands were bent back and clenched. I turned away my eyes involuntarily; but, after a brief interval, I forced myself to look, to look long and attentively at her. Pity filled my soul, and not pity alone. 'That girl died by violence,' I decided inwardly; 'that's beyond doubt.' While I was standing looking at the dead girl, the deacon, who on my entrance had raised his voice and uttered a few disconnected sounds, relapsed into droning again, and yawned twice. I bowed to the ground a second time, and went out into the passage.

In the doorway of the drawing-room Mr. Ratsch was already on the look-out for me, dressed in a gay-coloured dressing-gown. Beckoning to me with his hand, he led me to his own room--I had almost said, to his lair. The room, dark and close, soaked through and through with the sour smell of stale tobacco, suggested a com- parison with the lair of a wolf or a fox.

XXIV

'Rupture! rupture of the external... of the external covering.... You under- stand.., the envelopes of the heart!' said Mr. Ratsch, directly the door closed. 'Such a misfortune! Only yesterday evening there was nothing to notice, and all of a sud- den, all in a minute, all was over! It's a true saying, "heute roth, morgen todt!" It's true; it's what was to be expected. I always expected it. At Tambov the regimental doctor, Galimbovsky, Vikenty Kasimirovitch.... you've probably heard of him... a first-rate medical man, a specialist--'

'It's the first time I've heard the name,' I observed.

'Well, no matter; any way he was always,' pursued Mr. Ratsch, at first in a low voice, and then louder and louder, and, to my surprise, with a perceptible German accent, 'he was always warning me: "Ay, Ivan Demianitch! ay! my dear boy, you must be careful! Your stepdaughter has an organic defect in the heart--hypertrophia cordialis! The least thing and there'll be trouble! She must avoid all exciting emotions above all.... You must appeal to her reason."... But, upon my word, with a young lady... can one appeal to reason? Ha... ha... ha...'

Mr. Ratsch was, through long habit, on the point of laughing, but he recollected himself in time, and changed the incipient guffaw into a cough.

And this was what Mr. Ratsch said! After all that I had found out about him!... I thought it my duty, however, to ask him whether a doctor was called in.

Mr. Ratsch positively bounced into the air.

'To be sure there was.... Two were summoned, but it was already over--abgemacht! And only fancy, both, as though they were agreeing' (Mr. Ratsch probably meant, as though they had agreed), 'rupture! rupture of the heart! That's what, with one voice, they cried out. They proposed a post-mortem; but I... you understand, did not consent to that.'

'And the funeral's to-morrow?' I queried.

'Yes, yes, to-morrow, to-morrow we bury our dear one! The procession will leave the house precisely at eleven o'clock in the morning.... From here to the church of St. Nicholas on Hen's Legs... what strange names your Russian churches do have, you know! Then to the last resting-place in mother earth. You will come! We have not been long acquainted, but I make bold to say, the amiability of your character and the elevation of your sentiments!...'

I made haste to nod my head.

'Yes, yes, yes,' sighed Mr. Ratsch. 'It... it really has been, as they say, a thunderbolt from a clear sky! Ein Blitz aus heiterem Himmel!'

'And Susanna Ivanovna said nothing before her death, left nothing?'

'Nothing, positively! Not a scrap of anything! Not a bit of paper! Only fancy, when they called me to her, when they waked me up--she was stiff already! Very distressing it was for me; she has grieved us all terribly! Alexander Daviditch will be sorry too, I dare say, when he knows.... They say he is not in Moscow.'

'He did leave town for a few days...' I began.

'Viktor Ivanovitch is complaining they're so long getting his sledge harnessed,' interrupted a servant girl coming in--the same girl I had seen in the passage. Her face, still looking half-awake, struck me this time by the expression of coarse insolence to be seen in servants when they know that their masters are in their power, and that they do not dare to find fault or be exacting with them.

'Directly, directly,' Ivan Demianitch responded nervously. 'Eleonora Karpovna! Leonora! Lenchen! come here!'

There was a sound of something ponderous moving the other side of the door, and at the same instant I heard Viktor's imperious call: 'Why on earth don't they put the horses in? You don't catch me trudging off to the police on foot!'

'Directly, directly,' Ivan Demianitch faltered again. 'Eleonora Karpovna, come here!'

'But, Ivan Demianitch,' I heard her voice, 'ich habe keine Toilette gemacht!'

'Macht nichts. Komm herein!'

Eleonora Karpovna came in, holding a kerchief over her neck with two fingers. She had on a morning wrapper, not buttoned up, and had not yet done her hair. Ivan Demianitch flew up to her.

'You hear, Viktor's calling for the horses,' he said, hurriedly pointing his finger first to the door, then to the window. 'Please, do see to it, as quick as possible! Der Kerl schreit so!'

'Der Viktor schreit immer, Ivan Demianitch, Sie wissen wohl,' responded Eleonora Karpovna, 'and I have spoken to the coachman myself, but he's taken it into his head to give the horses oats. Fancy, what a calamity to happen so suddenly,' she added, turning to me; 'who could have expected such a thing of Susanna Ivanovna?'

'I was always expecting it, always!' cried Ratsch, and threw up his arms, his dressing-gown flying up in front as he did so, and displaying most repulsive unmentionables of chamois leather, with buckles on the belt. 'Rupture of the heart! rupture of the external membrane! Hypertrophy!'

'To be sure,' Eleonora Karpovna repeated after him, 'hyper... Well, so it is.

Only it's a terrible, terrible grief to me, I say again...' And her coarse-featured face worked a little, her eyebrows rose into the shape of triangles, and a tiny tear rolled over her round cheek, that looked varnished like a doll's.... 'I'm very sorry that such a young person who ought to have lived and enjoyed everything... everything... And to fall into despair so suddenly!'

'Na! gut, gut... geh, alte!' Mr. Ratsch cut her short.

'Geh' schon, geh' schon,' muttered Eleonora Karpovna, and she went away, still holding the kerchief with her fingers, and shedding tears.

And I followed her. In the passage stood Viktor in a student's coat with a beaver collar and a cap stuck jauntily on one side. He barely glanced at me over his shoulder, shook his collar up, and did not nod to me, for which I mentally thanked him.

I went back to Fustov.

XXV

I found my friend sitting in a corner of his room with downcast head and arms folded across his breast. He had sunk into a state of numbness, and he gazed around him with the slow, bewildered look of a man who has slept very heavily and has only just been waked. I told him all about my visit to Ratsch's, repeated the veteran's remarks and those of his wife, described the impression they had made on me and informed him of my conviction that the unhappy girl had taken her own life.... Fustov listened to me with no change of expression, and looked about him with the same bewildered air.

'Did you see her?' he asked me at last.

'Yes.'

'In the coffin?'

Fustov seemed to doubt whether Susanna were really dead.

'In the coffin.'

Fustov's face twitched and he dropped his eyes and softly rubbed his hands.

'Are you cold?' I asked him.

'Yes, old man, I'm cold,' he answered hesitatingly, and he shook his head stupidly.

I began to explain my reasons for thinking that Susanna had poisoned herself or perhaps had been poisoned, and that the matter could not be left so....

Fustov stared at me.

'Why, what is there to be done?' he said, slowly opening his eyes wide and slowly closing them. 'Why, it'll be worse... if it's known about. They won't bury her. We must let things... alone.'

This idea, simple as it was, had never entered my head. My friend's practical sense had not deserted him.

'When is... her funeral?' he went on.

'To-morrow.'

'Are you going?'

'Yes.'

'To the house or straight to the church?'

'To the house and to the church too; and from there to the cemetery.'

'But I shan't go... I can't, I can't!' whispered Fustov and began crying. It was at these same words that he had broken into sobs in the morning. I have noticed that it is often so with weeping; as though to certain words, for the most of no great meaning,--but just to these words and to no others--it is given to open the fount of tears in a man, to break him down, and to excite in him the feeling of pity for others and himself... I remember a peasant woman was once describing before me the sudden death of her daughter, and she fairly dissolved and could not go on with her tale as soon as she uttered the phrase, 'I said to her, Fekla. And she says, "Mother, where have you put the salt... the salt... sa-alt?"' The word 'salt' overpowered her.

But again, as in the morning, I was but little moved by Fustov's tears. I could not conceive how it was he did not ask me if Susanna had not left something for him. Altogether their love for one another was a riddle to me; and a riddle it remained to me.

After weeping for ten minutes Fustov got up, lay down on the sofa, turned his face to the wall, and remained motionless. I waited a little, but seeing that he did not stir, and made no answer to my questions, I made up my mind to leave him. I am perhaps doing him injustice, but I almost believe he was asleep. Though indeed that would be no proof that he did not feel sorrow... only his nature was so constituted as to be unable to support painful emotions for long... His nature was too awfully well-balanced!

XXVI

The next day exactly at eleven o'clock I was at the place. Fine hail was falling from the low-hanging sky, there was a slight frost, a thaw was close at hand, but there were cutting, disagreeable gusts of wind flitting across in the air.... It was the most thoroughly Lenten, cold-catching weather. I found Mr. Ratsch on the steps of his house. In a black frock-coat adorned with crape, with no hat on his head, he fussed about, waved his arms, smote himself on the thighs, shouted up to the house, and then down into the street, in the direction of the funeral car with a white catafalque, already standing there with two hired carriages. Near it four garrison soldiers, with mourning capes over their old coats, and mourning hats pulled over their screwed-up eyes, were pensively scratching in the crumbling snow with the long stems of their unlighted torches. The grey shock of hair positively stood up straight above the red face of Mr. Ratsch, and his voice, that brazen voice, was cracking from the strain he was putting on it. 'Where are the pine branches? pine branches! this way! the branches of pine!' he yelled. 'They'll be bearing out the coffin directly! The pine! Hand over those pine branches! Look alive!' he cried once more, and dashed into the house. It appeared that in spite of my punctuality, I was late: Mr. Ratsch had thought fit to hurry things forward. The service in the house was already over; the priests--of whom one wore a calotte, and the other, rather younger, had most carefully combed and oiled his hair--appeared with all their retinue on the steps. The coffin too appeared soon after, carried by a coachman, two door-keepers, and a water-carrier. Mr. Ratsch walked behind, with the tips of his fingers on the coffin lid, continually repeating, 'Easy, easy!' Behind him waddled Eleonora Karpovna in a black dress, also adorned with crape, surrounded by her whole family; after all of them, Viktor stepped out in a new uniform with a sword with crape round the handle. The coffin-bearers, grumbling and altercating among themselves, laid the coffin on the hearse; the garrison soldiers lighted their torches, which at once began crackling and smoking; a stray old woman, who had joined herself on to the party, raised a wail; the deacons began to chant, the fine snow suddenly fell faster and whirled round like 'white flies.' Mr. Ratsch bawled, 'In God's name! start!' and the procession started. Besides Mr. Ratsch's family, there were in all five men accompanying the hearse: a retired and extremely shabby officer of roads and highways, with a faded Stanislas ribbon--not improbably hired--on his neck; the police superintendent's assistant, a diminutive man with a meek face and greedy eyes; a little old man in a fustian smock; an extremely fat fishmonger in a tradesman's bluejacket, smelling strongly of his calling, and I. The absence of the female sex (for one could hardly count as such two aunts of Eleonora Karpovna, sisters of the sausagemaker, and a hunchback old maiden lady with blue spectacles on her blue nose), the absence of girl friends and acquaintances struck me at first; but on thinking it over I realised that Susanna, with her character, her education, her memories, could not have made friends in the circle in which she was living. In the church there were a good many people assembled, more outsiders than acquaintances, as one could see by the expression of their faces. The service did not last long. What surprised me was that Mr. Ratsch crossed himself with great fervour, quite as though he were of the orthodox faith, and even chimed in with the deacons in the responses, though only with the notes not with the words. When at last it came to taking leave of the dead, I bowed low, but did not give the last kiss. Mr. Ratsch, on the contrary, went through this terrible ordeal with the utmost composure, and with a deferential inclination of his person invited the officer of the Stanislas ribbon to the coffin, as though offering him entertainment, and picking his children up under the arms swung them up in turn and held them up to the body. Eleonora Karpovna, on taking farewell of Susanna, suddenly broke into a roar that filled the church; but she was soon soothed and continually asked in an exasperated whisper, 'But where's my reticule?' Viktor held himself aloof, and seemed to be trying by his whole demeanour to convey that he was out of sympathy with all such customs and was only performing a social duty. The person who showed the most sympathy was the little old man in the smock, who had been, fifteen years before, a land surveyor in the Tambov province, and had not seen Ratsch since then. He did not know Susanna at all, but had drunk a couple of glasses of spirits at the sideboard before starting. My aunt had also come to the church. She had somehow or other found out that the deceased woman was the very lady who had paid me a visit, and had been thrown into a state of indescribable agitation! She could not bring herself to suspect me of any sort of misconduct, but neither could she explain such a strange chain of circumstances.... Not improbably she imagined that Susanna had been led by love for me to commit suicide, and attired in her darkest garments, with an aching heart and tears, she prayed on her knees for the peace of the soul of the departed, and put a rouble candle before the picture of the Consolation of Sorrow.... 'Amishka' had come with her too, and she too prayed, but was for the most part gazing at me, horror-stricken.... That elderly spinster, alas! did not regard me with indifference. On leaving the church, my aunt distributed all her money, more than ten roubles, among the poor.

At last the farewell was over. They began closing the coffin. During the whole service I had not courage to look straight at the poor girl's distorted face; but every time that my eyes passed by it--'he did not come, he did not come,' it seemed to me that it wanted to say. They were just going to lower the lid upon the coffin. I could not restrain myself: I turned a rapid glance on to the dead woman. 'Why did you do it?' I was unconsciously asking.... 'He did not come!' I fancied for the last time.... The hammer was knocking in the nails, and all was over.

XXVII

We followed the hearse towards the cemetery. We were forty in number, of all sorts and conditions, nothing else really than an idle crowd. The wearisome journey lasted more than an hour. The weather became worse and worse. Halfway there Viktor got into a carriage, but Mr. Ratsch stepped gallantly on through the sloppy snow; just so must he have stepped through the snow when, after the fateful interview with Semyon Matveitch, he led home with him in triumph the girl whose life he had ruined for ever. The 'veteran's' hair and eyebrows were edged with snow; he kept blowing and uttering exclamations, or manfully drawing deep breaths and puffing out his round, dark-red cheeks.... One really might have thought he was laughing. 'On my death the pension was to pass to Ivan Demianitch'; these words from Susanna's manuscript recurred again to my mind. We reached the cemetery at last; we moved up to a freshly dug grave. The last ceremony was quickly performed;

all were chilled through, all were in haste. The coffin slid on cords into the yawning hole; they began to throw earth on it. Mr. Ratsch here too showed the energy of his spirit, so rapidly, with such force and vigour, did he fling clods of earth on to the coffin lid, throwing himself into an heroic pose, with one leg planted firmly before him... he could not have shown more energy if he had been stoning his bitterest foe. Viktor, as before, held himself aloof; he kept muffling himself up in his coat, and rubbing his chin in the fur of his collar. Mr. Ratsch's other children eagerly imitated their father. Flinging sand and earth was a source of great enjoyment to them, for which, of course, they were in no way to blame. A mound began to rise up where the hole had been; we were on the point of separating, when Mr. Ratsch, wheeling round to the left in soldierly fashion, and slapping himself on the thigh, announced to all of us 'gentlemen present,' that he invited us, and also the 'reverend clergy,' to a 'funeral banquet,' which had been arranged at no great distance from the cemetery, in the chief saloon of an extremely superior restaurant, 'thanks to the kind offices of our honoured friend Sigismund Sigismundovitch.'... At these words he indicated the assistant of the police superintendent, and added that for all his grief and his Lutheran faith, he, Ivan Demianitch Ratsch, as a genuine Russian, put the old Russian usages before everything. 'My spouse,' he cried, 'with the ladies that have accompanied her, may go home, while we gentlemen commemorate in a modest repast the shade of Thy departed servant!' Mr. Ratsch's proposal was received with genuine sympathy; 'the reverend clergy' exchanged expressive glances with one another, while the officer of roads and highways slapped Ivan Demianitch on the shoulder, and called him a patriot and the soul of the company.

We set off all together to the restaurant. In the restaurant, in the middle of a long, wide, and quite empty room on the first storey, stood two tables laid for dinner, covered with bottles and eatables, and surrounded by chairs. The smell of white-wash, mingled with the odours of spirits and salad oil, was stifling and oppressive. The police superintendent's assistant, as the organiser of the banquet, placed the clergy in the seats of honour, near which the Lenten dishes were crowded together conspicuously; after the priests the other guests took their seats; the banquet began. I would not have used such a festive word as banquet by choice, but no other word would have corresponded with the real character of the thing. At first the proceedings were fairly quiet, even slightly mournful; jaws munched busily, and glasses were emptied, but sighs too were audible--possibly sighs of digestion, but possibly also of feeling. There were references to death, allusions to the brevity of human life, and the fleeting nature of earthly hopes. The officer of roads and highways related a military but still edifying anecdote. The priest in the calotte expressed his approval, and himself contributed an interesting fact from the life of the saint, Ivan the Warrior. The priest with the superbly arranged hair, though his attention was chiefly engrossed by the edibles, gave utterance to something improving on the subject of chastity. But little by little all this changed. Faces grew redder, and voices grew louder, and laughter reasserted itself; one began to hear disconnected exclamations, caressing appellations, after the manner of 'dear old boy,' 'dear heart alive,' 'old cock,' and even 'a pig like that'--everything, in fact, of which the Russian nature is so lavish, when, as they say, 'it comes unbuttoned.' By the time that the corks of home-made champagne were popping, the party had become noisy; some one even crowed like a cock, while another guest was offering to bite up and swallow the glass out of which he had just been drinking. Mr. Ratsch, no longer red but purple, suddenly rose from his seat; he had been guffawing and making a great noise before, but now he asked leave to make a speech. 'Speak! Out with it!' every one roared; the old man in the smock even bawled 'bravo!' and clapped his hands... but he was already sitting on the floor. Mr. Ratsch lifted his glass high above his head, and announced that he proposed in brief but 'impressionable' phrases to refer to the qualities of the noble soul which,'leaving here, so to say, its earthly husk (die irdische Hulle) has soared to heaven, and plunged...' Mr. Ratsch corrected himself: 'and plashed....' He again corrected himself: 'and plunged...'

'Father deacon! Reverend sir! My good soul!' we heard a subdued but insistent whisper, 'they say you've a devilish good voice; honour us with a song, strike up: "We live among the fields!"'

'Sh! sh!... Shut up there!' passed over the lips of the guests.

...'Plunged all her devoted family,' pursued Mr. Ratsch, turning a severe glance in the direction of the lover of music, 'plunged all her family into the most irreplaceable grief! Yes!' cried Ivan Demianitch, 'well may the Russian proverb say, "Fate spares not the rod."...'

'Stop! Gentlemen!' shouted a hoarse voice at the end of the table, 'my purse has just been stolen!...'

'Ah, the swindler!' piped another voice, and slap! went a box on the ear.

Heavens! What followed then! It was as though the wild beast, till then only growling and faintly stirring within us, had suddenly broken from its chains and reared up, ruffled and fierce in all its hideousness. It seemed as though every one had been secretly expecting 'a scandal,' as the natural outcome and sequel of a banquet, and all, as it were, rushed to welcome it, to support it.... Plates, glasses clattered and rolled about, chairs were upset, a deafening din arose, hands were waving in the air, coat-tails were flying, and a fight began in earnest.

'Give it him! give it him!' roared like mad my neighbour, the fishmonger, who had till that instant seemed to be the most peaceable person in the world; it is true he had been silently drinking some dozen glasses of spirits. 'Thrash him!...'

Who was to be thrashed, and what he was to be thrashed for, he had no idea, but he bellowed furiously.

The police superintendent's assistant, the officer of roads and highways, and Mr. Ratsch, who had probably not expected such a speedy termination to his eloquence, tried to restore order... but their efforts were unavailing. My neighbour, the fishmonger, even fell foul of Mr. Ratsch himself.

'He's murdered the young woman, the blasted German,' he yelled at him, shaking his fists; 'he's bought over the police, and here he's crowing over it!!'

At this point the waiters ran in.... What happened further I don't know; I snatched up my cap in all haste, and made off as fast as my legs would carry me! All I remember is a fearful crash; I recall, too, the remains of a herring in the hair of the old man in the smock, a priest's hat flying right across the room, the pale face of Viktor huddled up in a corner, and a red beard in the grasp of a muscular hand.... Such were the last impressions I carried away of the 'memorial banquet,' arranged by the excellent Sigismund Sigismundovitch in honour of poor Susanna.

After resting a little, I set off to see Fustov, and told him all of which I had been a witness during that day. He listened to me, sitting still, and not raising his head, and putting both hands under his legs, he murmured again, 'Ah! my poor girl, my poor girl!' and again lay down on the sofa and turned his back on me.

A week later he seemed to have quite got over it, and took up his life as before. I asked him for Susanna's manuscript as a keepsake: he gave it me without raising any objection.

XXVIII

Several years passed by. My aunt was dead; I had left Moscow and settled in Petersburg. Fustov too had moved to Petersburg. He had entered the department of the Ministry of Finance, but we rarely met and I saw nothing much in him then. An official like every one else, and nothing more! If he is still living and not married, he is, most likely, unchanged to this day; he carves and carpenters and uses dumb-bells, and is as much a lady-killer as ever, and sketches Napoleon in a blue uniform in the albums of his lady friends. It happened that I had to go to Moscow on business. In Moscow I learned, with considerable surprise, that the fortunes of my former acquaintance, Mr. Ratsch, had taken an adverse turn. His wife had, indeed, presented him with twins, two boys, whom as a true Russian he had christened Briacheslav and Viacheslav, but his house had been burnt down, he had been forced to retire from his position, and worst of all, his eldest son, Viktor, had become practically a permanent inmate of the debtors' prison. During my stay in Moscow, among a company at a friendly gathering, I chanced to hear an allusion made to Susanna, and a most slighting, most insulting allusion! I did all I could to defend the memory of the unhappy girl, to whom fate had denied even the charity of oblivion, but my arguments did not make much impression on my audience. One of them, a young student poet, was, however, a little moved by my words. He sent me next day a poem, which I have forgotten, but which ended in the following four lines:

'Her tomb lies cold, forlorn, but even death
Her gentle spirit's memory cannot save
From the sly voice of slander whispering on,
Withering the flowers on her forsaken tomb....'

I read these lines and unconsciously sank into musing. Susanna's image rose before me; once more I seemed to see the frozen window in my room; I recalled that evening and the blustering snowstorm, and those words, those sobs.... I began to ponder how it was possible to explain Susanna's love for Fustov, and why she had so quickly, so impulsively given way to despair, as soon as she saw herself forsaken. How was it she had had no desire to wait a little, to hear the bitter truth from the lips of the man she loved, to write to him, even? How could she fling herself at once headlong into the abyss? Because she was passionately in love with Fustov, I shall be told; because she could not bear the slightest doubt of his devotion, of his respect for her. Perhaps; or perhaps because she was not at all so passionately in love with Fustov; that she did not deceive herself about him, but simply rested her last hopes on him, and could not get over the thought that even this man had at once, at the first breath of slander, turned away from her with contempt! Who can say what killed her; wounded pride, or the wretchedness of her helpless position, or the very memory of that first, noble, true-hearted nature to whom she had so joyfully pledged herself in the morning of her early days, who had so deeply trusted her, and so honoured her? Who knows; perhaps at the very instant when I fancied that her dead lips were murmuring, 'he did not come!' her soul was rejoicing that she had gone herself to him, to her Michel? The secrets of human life are great, and love itself, the most impenetrable of those secrets.... Anyway, to this day, whenever the image of Susanna rises before me, I cannot overcome a feeling of pity for her, and of angry reproach against fate, and my lips whisper instinctively, 'Unhappy girl! unhappy girl!'

1868.

THE DUELLIST

I

A regiment of cuirassiers was quartered in 1829 in the village of Kirilovo, in the K--- province. That village, with its huts and hay-stacks, its green hemp-patches, and gaunt willows, looked from a distance like an island in a boundless sea of ploughed, black-earth fields. In the middle of the village was a small pond, invariably covered with goose feathers, with muddy, indented banks; a hundred paces from the pond, on the other side of the road, rose the wooden manor-house, long, empty, and mournfully slanting on one side. Behind the house stretched the deserted garden; in the garden grew old apple-trees that bore no fruit, and tall birch-trees, full of rooks' nests. At the end of the principal garden-walk, in a little house, once the bath-house, lived a decrepit old steward. Every morning, gasping and groaning, he would, from years of habit, drag himself across the garden to the seignorial apartments, though there was nothing to take care of in them except a dozen white arm-chairs, upholstered in faded stuff, two podgy chests on carved legs with copper handles, four pictures with holes in them, and one black alabaster Arab with a broken nose. The owner of the house, a careless young man, lived partly at Petersburg, partly abroad, and had completely forgotten his estate. It had come to him eight years before, from a very old uncle, once noted all over the countryside for his excellent liqueurs. The empty, dark-green bottles are to this day lying about in the storeroom, in company with rubbish of all sorts, old manuscript books in parti-coloured covers, scantily filled with writing, old-fashioned glass lustres, a nobleman's uniform of the Catherine period, a rusty sabre with a steel handle and so forth. In one of the lodges of the great house the colonel himself took up his abode. He was a married man, tall, sparing of his words, grim and sleepy. In another lodge lived the regimental adjutant, an emotional person of fine sentiments and many perfumes, fond of flowers and female society. The social life of the officers of this regiment did not differ from any other kind of society. Among their number were good people and bad, clever and silly.... One of them, a certain Avdey Ivanovitch Lutchkov, staff captain, had a reputation as a duellist. Lutchkov was a short and not thick-set man; he had a small, yellowish, dry face, lank, black hair, unnoticeable features, and dark, little eyes. He had early been left an orphan, and had grown up among privations and hardships. For weeks together he would be quiet enough,... and then all at once--as though he were possessed by some devil--he would let no one alone, annoying everybody, staring every one insolently in the face; trying, in fact, to pick a quarrel. Avdey Ivanovitch did not, however, hold aloof from intercourse with his comrades, but he was not on intimate terms with any one but the perfumed adjutant. He did not play cards, and did not drink spirits.

In the May of 1829, not long before the beginning of the manoeuvres, there joined the regiment a young cornet, Fyodor Fedorovitch Kister, a Russian nobleman of German extraction, very fair-haired and very modest, cultivated and well read. He had lived up to his twentieth year in the home of his fathers, under the wings of his mother, his grandmother, and his two aunts. He was going into the army in deference solely to the wishes of his grandmother, who even in her old age could not see a white plumed helmet without emotion.... He served with no special enthusiasm but with energy, as it were conscientiously doing his duty. He was not a dandy, but was always cleanly dressed and in good taste. On the day of his arrival Fyodor Fedoritch paid his respects to his superior officers, and then proceeded to arrange his quarters. He had brought with him some cheap furniture, rugs, shelves, and so forth. He papered all the walls and the doors, put up some screens, had the yard cleaned, fixed up a stable, and a kitchen, even arranged a place for a bath.... For a whole week he was busily at work; but it was a pleasure afterwards to go into his room. Before the window stood a neat table, covered with various little things; in one corner was a set of shelves for books, with busts of Schiller and Goethe; on the walls hung maps, four Grevedon heads, and guns; near the table was an elegant row of pipes with clean mouthpieces; there was a rug in the outer room; all the doors shut and locked; the windows were hung with curtains. Everything in Fyodor Fedoritch's room had a look of cleanliness and order.

It was quite a different thing in his comrades' quarters. Often one could scarcely make one's way across the muddy yard; in the outer room, behind a canvas screen, with its covering peeling off it, would lie stretched the snoring orderly; on the floor rotten straw; on the stove, boots and a broken jam-pot full of blacking; in the room itself a warped card-table, marked with chalk; on the table, glasses, half-full of cold, dark-brown tea; against the wall, a wide, rickety, greasy sofa; on the window-sills, tobacco-ash.... In a podgy, clumsy arm-chair one would find the master of the place in a grass-green dressing-gown with crimson plush facings and an embroidered smoking-cap of Asiatic extraction, and a hideously fat, unpleasant dog in a stinking brass collar would be snoring at his side.... All the doors always ajar....

Fyodor Fedoritch made a favourable impression on his new comrades. They liked him for his good-nature, modesty, warm-heartedness, and natural inclination for everything beautiful, for everything, in fact, which in another officer they might, very likely, have thought out of place. They called Kister a young lady, and were kind and gentle in their manners with him. Avdey Ivanovitch was the only one who eyed him dubiously. One day after drill Lutchkov went up to him, slightly pursing up his lips and inflating his nostrils:

'Good-morning, Mr. Knaster.'

Kister looked at him in some perplexity.

'A very good day to you, Mr. Knaster,' repeated Lutchkov.

'My name's Kister, sir.'

'You don't say so, Mr. Knaster.'

Fyodor Fedoritch turned his back on him and went homewards. Lutchkov looked after him with a grin.

Next day, directly after drill he went up to Kister again.

'Well, how are you getting on, Mr. Kinderbalsam?'

Kister was angry, and looked him straight in the face. Avdey Ivanovitch's little bilious eyes were gleaming with malignant glee.

'I'm addressing you, Mr. Kinderbalsam!'

'Sir,' Fyodor Fedoritch replied, 'I consider your joke stupid and ill-bred--do you hear?--stupid and ill-bred.'

'When shall we fight?' Lutchkov responded composedly.

'When you like,... to-morrow.'

Next morning they fought a duel. Lutchkov wounded Kister slightly, and to the extreme astonishment of the seconds went up to the wounded man, took him by the hand and begged his pardon. Kister had to keep indoors for a fortnight. Avdey Ivanovitch came several times to ask after him and on Fyodor Fedoritch's recovery made friends with him. Whether he was pleased by the young officer's pluck, or whether a feeling akin to remorse was roused in his soul--it's hard to say... but from the time of his duel with Kister, Avdey Ivanovitch scarcely left his side, and called him first Fyodor, and afterwards simply Fedya. In his presence he became quite another man and--strange to say!--the change was not in his favour. It did not suit him to be gentle and soft. Sympathy he could not call forth in any one anyhow; such was his destiny! He belonged to that class of persons to whom has somehow been granted the privilege of authority over others; but nature had denied him the gifts essential for the justification of such a privilege. Having received no education, not being distinguished by intelligence, he ought not to have revealed himself; possibly his malignancy had its origin in his consciousness of the defects of his bringing up, in the desire to conceal himself altogether under one unchanging mask. Avdey Ivanovitch had at first forced himself to despise people, then he began to notice that it was not a difficult matter to intimidate them, and he began to despise them in reality. Lutchkov enjoyed cutting short by his very approach all but the most vulgar conversation. 'I know nothing, and have learned nothing, and I have no talents,' he said to himself; 'and so you too shall know nothing and not show off your talents before me....' Kister, perhaps, had made Lutchkov abandon the part he had taken up--just because before his acquaintance with him, the bully had never met any one genuinely idealistic, that is to say, unselfishly and simple-heartedly absorbed in dreams, and so, indulgent to others, and not full of himself.

Avdey Ivanovitch would come sometimes to Kister, light a pipe and quietly sit down in an arm-chair. Lutchkov was not in Kister's company abashed by his own ignorance; he relied--and with good reason--on his German modesty.

'Well,' he would begin, 'what did you do yesterday? Been reading, I'll bet, eh?'

'Yes, I read....'

'Well, and what did you read? Come, tell away, old man, tell away.' Avdey

Ivanovitch kept up his bantering tone to the end.

'I read Kleist's *Idyll*. Ah, what a fine thing it is! If you don't mind, I'll translate you a few lines....' And Kister translated with fervour, while Lutchkov, wrinkling up his forehead and compressing his lips, listened attentively.... 'Yes, yes,' he would repeat hurriedly, with a disagreeable smile,'it's fine... very fine... I remember, I've read it... very fine.'

'Tell me, please,' he added affectedly, and as it were reluctantly, 'what's your view of Louis the Fourteenth?'

And Kister would proceed to discourse upon Louis the Fourteenth, while Lutchkov listened, totally failing to understand a great deal, misunderstanding a part... and at last venturing to make a remark.... This threw him into a cold sweat; 'now, if I'm making a fool of myself,' he thought. And as a fact he often did make a fool of himself. But Kister was never off-hand in his replies; the good-hearted youth was inwardly rejoicing that, as he thought, the desire for enlightenment was awakened in a fellow-creature. Alas! it was from no desire for enlightenment that Avdey Ivanovitch questioned Kister; God knows why he did! Possibly he wished to ascertain for himself what sort of head he, Lutchkov, had, whether it was really dull, or simply untrained. 'So I really am stupid,' he said to himself more than once with a bitter smile; and he would draw himself up instantly and look rudely and insolently about him, and smile malignantly to himself if he caught some comrade dropping his eyes before his glance. 'All right, my man, you're so learned and well educated,...' he would mutter between his teeth. 'I'll show you... that's all....'

The officers did not long discuss the sudden friendship of Kister and Lutchkov; they were used to the duellist's queer ways. 'The devil's made friends with the baby,' they said.... Kister was warm in his praises of his friend on all hands; no one disputed his opinion, because they were afraid of Lutchkov; Lutchkov himself never mentioned Kister's name before the others, but he dropped his intimacy with the perfumed adjutant.

II

The landowners of the South of Russia are very keen on giving balls, inviting officers to their houses, and marrying off their daughters.

About seven miles from the village of Kirilovo lived just such a country gentleman, a Mr. Perekatov, the owner of four hundred souls, and a fairly spacious house. He had a daughter of eighteen, Mashenka, and a wife, Nenila Makarievna. Mr. Perekatov had once been an officer in the cavalry, but from love of a country life and from indolence he had retired and had begun to live peaceably and quietly, as landowners of the middling sort do live. Nenila Makarievna owed her existence in a not perfectly legitimate manner to a distinguished gentleman of Moscow.

Her protector had educated his little Nenila very carefully, as it is called, in his own house, but got her off his hands rather hurriedly, at the first offer, as a not very marketable article. Nenila Makarievna was ugly; the distinguished gentleman was giving her no more than ten thousand as dowry; she snatched eagerly at Mr. Perekatov. To Mr. Perekatov it seemed extremely gratifying to marry a highly educated, intellectual young lady... who was, after all, so closely related to so illustrious a personage. This illustrious personage extended his patronage to the young people even after the marriage, that is to say, he accepted presents of salted quails from them and called Perekatov 'my dear boy,' and sometimes simply, 'boy.' Nenila Makarievna took complete possession of her husband, managed everything, and looked after the whole property--very sensibly, indeed; far better, any way, than Mr. Perekatov could have done. She did not hamper her partner's liberty too much; but she kept him well in hand, ordered his clothes herself, and dressed him in the English style, as is fitting and proper for a country gentleman. By her instructions, Mr. Perekatov grew a little Napoleonic beard on his chin, to cover a large wart, which looked like an over-ripe raspberry. Nenila Makarievna, for her part, used to inform visitors that her husband played the flute, and that all flute-players always let the beard grow under the lower lip; they could hold their instrument more comfortably. Mr. Perekatov always, even in the early morning, wore a high, clean stock, and was well combed and washed. He was, moreover, well content with his lot; he dined very well, did as he liked, and slept all he could. Nenila Makarievna had introduced into her household 'foreign ways,' as the neighbours used to say; she kept few servants, and had them neatly dressed. She was fretted by ambition; she wanted at least to be the wife of the marshal of the nobility of the district; but the gentry of the district, though they dined at her house to their hearts' content, did not choose her husband, but first the retired premier-major Burkolts, and then the retired second major Burundukov. Mr. Perekatov seemed to them too extreme a product of the capital.

Mr. Perekatov's daughter, Mashenka, was in face like her father. Nenila Makarievna had taken the greatest pains with her education. She spoke French well, and played the piano fairly. She was of medium height, rather plump and white; her rather full face was lighted up by a kindly and merry smile; her flaxen, not over-abundant hair, her hazel eyes, her pleasant voice--everything about her was gently pleasing, and that was all. On the other hand the absence of all affectation and conventionality, an amount of culture exceptional in a country girl, the freedom of her expressions, the quiet simplicity of her words and looks could not but be striking in her. She had developed at her own free will; Nenila Makarievna did not keep her in restraint.

One morning at twelve o'clock the whole family of the Perekatovs were in the drawing-room. The husband in a round green coat, a high check cravat, and pea-green trousers with straps, was standing at the window, very busily engaged in catching flies. The daughter was sitting at her embroidery frame; her small dimpled little hand rose and fell slowly and gracefully over the canvas. Nenila Makarievna was sitting on the sofa, gazing in silence at the floor.

'Did you send an invitation to the regiment at Kirilovo, Sergei Sergeitch?' she asked her husband.

'For this evening? To be sure I did, ma chere.' (He was under the strictest orders not to call her 'little mother.') 'To be sure!'

'There are positively no gentlemen,' pursued Nenila Makarievna. 'Nobody for the girls to dance with.'

Her husband sighed, as though crushed by the absence of partners.

'Mamma,' Masha began all at once, 'is Monsieur Lutchkov asked?'

'What Lutchkov?'

'He's an officer too. They say he's a very interesting person.'

'How's that?'

'Oh, he's not good-looking and he's not young, but every one's afraid of him. He's a dreadful duellist.' (Mamma frowned a little.) 'I should so like to see him.'

Sergei Sergeitch interrupted his daughter.

'What is there to see in him, my darling? Do you suppose he must look like Lord Byron?' (At that time we were only just beginning to talk about Lord Byron.) 'Nonsense! Why, I declare, my dear, there was a time when I had a terrible character as a fighting man.'

Masha looked wonderingly at her parent, laughed, then jumped up and kissed him on the cheek. His wife smiled a little, too... but Sergei Sergeitch had spoken the truth.

'I don't know if that gentleman is coming,' observed Nenila Makarievna. 'Possibly he may come too.'

The daughter sighed.

'Mind you don't go and fall in love with him,' remarked Sergei Sergeitch. 'I know you girls are all like that nowadays--so--what shall I say?--romantic...'

'No,' Masha responded simply.

Nenila Makarievna looked coldly at her husband. Sergei Sergeitch played with his watch-chain in some embarrassment, then took his wide-brimmed, English hat from the table, and set off to see after things on the estate.

His dog timidly and meekly followed him. As an intelligent animal, she was well aware that her master was not a person of very great authority in the house, and behaved herself accordingly with modesty and circumspection.

Nenila Makarievna went up to her daughter, gently raised her head, and looked affectionately into her eyes. 'Will you tell me when you fall in love?' she asked.

Masha kissed her mother's hand, smiling, and nodded her head several times in the affirmative.

'Mind you do,' observed Nenila Makarievna, stroking her cheek, and she went out after her husband. Masha leaned back in her chair, dropped her head on her bosom, interlaced her fingers, and looked long out of window, screwing up her eyes... A slight flush passed over her fresh cheeks; with a sigh she drew herself up, was setting to work again, but dropped her needle, leaned her face on her hand, and biting the tips of her nails, fell to dreaming... then glanced at her own shoulder, at her outstretched hand, got up, went to the window, laughed, put on her hat and went out into the garden.

That evening at eight o'clock, the guests began to arrive. Madame Perekatov with great affability received and 'entertained' the ladies, Mashenka the girls; Sergei Sergeitch talked about the crops with the gentlemen and continually glanced towards his wife. Soon there arrived the young dandies, the officers, intentionally a little late; at last the colonel himself, accompanied by his adjutants, Kister and Lutchkov. He presented them to the lady of the house. Lutchkov bowed without speaking, Kister muttered the customary 'extremely delighted'... Mr. Perekatov went up to the colonel, pressed his hand warmly and looked him in the face with great cordiality. The colonel promptly looked forbidding. The dancing began. Kister asked Mashenka for a dance. At that time the **Ecossaise** was still flourishing.

'Do tell me, please,' Masha said to him, when, after galloping twenty times to the end of the room, they stood at last, the first couple, 'why isn't your friend dancing?'

'Which friend?'

Masha pointed with the tip of her fan at Lutchkov.

'He never dances,' answered Kister.

'Why did he come then?'

Kister was a little disconcerted. 'He wished to have the pleasure...'

Mashenka interrupted him. 'You've not long been transferred into our regiment, I think?'

'Into your regiment,' observed Kister, with a smile: 'no, not long.'

'Aren't you dull here?'

'Oh no... I find such delightful society here... and the scenery!'... Kister launched into eulogies of the scenery. Masha listened to him, without raising her head. Avdey Ivanovitch was standing in a corner, looking indifferently at the dancers.

'How old is Mr. Lutchkov?' she asked suddenly.

'Oh... thirty-five, I fancy,' answered Kister.

'They say he's a dangerous man... hot-tempered,' Masha added hurriedly.

'He is a little hasty... but still, he's a very fine man.'

'They say every one's afraid of him.'

Kister laughed.

'And you?'

'I'm a friend of his.'

'Really?'

'Your turn, your turn,' was shrieked at them from all sides. They started and began galloping again right across the room.

'Well, I congratulate you,' Kister said to Lutchkov, going up to him after the dance; 'the daughter of the house does nothing but ask questions about you.'

'Really?' Lutchkov responded scornfully.

'On my honour! And you know she's extremely nice-looking; only look at her.'

'Which of them is she?'

Kister pointed out Masha.

'Ah, not bad.' And Lutchkov yawned.

'Cold-hearted person!' cried Kister, and he ran off to ask another girl to dance.

Avdey Ivanovitch was extremely delighted at the fact Kister had mentioned to him, though he did yawn, and even yawned loudly. To arouse curiosity flattered his vanity intensely: love he despised--in words--but inwardly he was himself aware that it would be a hard and difficult task for him to win love.... A hard and difficult task for him to win love, but easy and simple enough to wear a mask of indifference, of silent haughtiness. Avdey Ivanovitch was unattractive and no longer young; but on the other hand he enjoyed a terrible reputation--and consequently he had every right to pose. He was used to the bitter, unspoken enjoyment of grim loneliness. It was not the first time he had attracted the attention of women; some had even tried to get upon more friendly terms with him, but he repelled their advances with exasperated obstinacy; he knew that sentiment was not in his line (during tender interviews, avowals, he first became awkward and vulgar, and, through anger, rude to the point of grossness, of insult); he remembered that the two or three women with whom he had at different times been on a friendly footing had rapidly grown cool to him after the first moment of closer intimacy, and had of their own impulse made haste to get away from him... and so he had at last schooled himself to remain an enigma, and to scorn what destiny had denied him.... This is, I fancy, the only sort of scorn people in general do feel. No sort of frank, spontaneous, that is to say good, demonstration of passion suited Lutchkov; he was bound to keep a continual check on himself, even when he was angry. Kister was the only person who was not disgusted when Lutchkov broke into laughter; the kind-hearted German's eyes shone with the generous delight of sympathy, when he read Avdey his favourite passages from Schiller, while the bully would sit facing him with lowering looks, like a wolf.... Kister danced till he was worn out, Lutchkov never left his corner, scowled, glanced stealthily at Masha, and meeting her eyes, at once threw an expression of indifference into his own. Masha danced three times with Kister. The enthusiastic youth inspired her with confidence. She chatted with him gaily enough, but at heart she was not at ease. Lutchkov engrossed her thoughts.

A mazurka tune struck up. The officers fell to bounding up and down, tapping with their heels, and tossing the epaulettes on their shoulders; the civilians tapped with their heels too. Lutchkov still did not stir from his place, and slowly followed the couples with his eyes, as they whirled by. Some one touched his sleeve... he looked round; his neighbour pointed him out Masha. She was standing before him with downcast eyes, holding out her hand to him. Lutchkov for the first moment gazed at her in perplexity, then he carelessly took off his sword, threw his hat on the floor, picked his way awkwardly among the arm-chairs, took Masha by the hand, and went round the circle, with no capering up and down nor stamping, as it were unwillingly performing an unpleasant duty.... Masha's heart beat violently.

'Why don't you dance?' she asked him at last.

'I don't care for it,' answered Lutchkov.

'Where's your place?'

'Over there.'

Lutchkov conducted Masha to her chair, coolly bowed to her and coolly returned to his corner... but there was an agreeable stirring of the spleen within him.

Kister asked Masha for a dance.

'What a strange person your friend is!'

'He does interest you...' said Fyodor Fedoritch, with a sly twinkle of his blue and kindly eyes.

'Yes... he must be very unhappy.'

'He unhappy? What makes you suppose so?' And Fyodor Fedoritch laughed.

'You don't know... you don't know...' Masha solemnly shook her head with an important air.

'Me not know? How's that?'...

Masha shook her head again and glanced towards Lutchkov. Avdey Ivanovitch noticed the glance, shrugged his shoulders imperceptibly, and walked away into the other room.

III

Several months had passed since that evening. Lutchkov had not once been at the Perekatovs'. But Kister visited them pretty often. Nenila Makarievna had taken a fancy to him, but it was not she that attracted Fyodor Fedoritch. He liked Masha. Being an inexperienced person who had not yet talked himself out, he derived great pleasure from the interchange of ideas and feelings, and he had a simple-hearted faith in the possibility of a calm and exalted friendship between a young man and a young girl.

One day his three well-fed and skittish horses whirled him rapidly along to Mr. Perekatov's house. It was a summer day, close and sultry. Not a cloud anywhere. The blue of the sky was so thick and dark on the horizon that the eye mistook it for storm-cloud. The house Mr. Perekatov had erected for a summer residence had been, with the foresight usual in the steppes, built with every window directly facing the sun. Nenila Makarievna had every shutter closed from early morning. Kister walked into the cool, half-dark drawing-room. The light lay in long lines on the floor and in short, close streaks on the walls. The Perekatov family gave Fyodor Fedoritch a friendly reception. After dinner Nenila Makarievna went away to her own room to lie down; Mr. Perekatov settled himself on the sofa in the drawing-room; Masha sat near the window at her embroidery frame, Kister facing her. Masha, without opening her frame, leaned lightly over it, with her head in her hands. Kister began telling her something; she listened inattentively, as though waiting for something, looked from time to time towards her father, and all at once stretched out her hand.

'Listen, Fyodor Fedoritch... only speak a little more softly... papa's asleep.'

Mr. Perekatov had indeed as usual dropped asleep on the sofa, with his head hanging and his mouth a little open.

'What is it?' Kister inquired with curiosity.

'You will laugh at me.'

'Oh, no, really!...'

Masha let her head sink till only the upper part of her face remained uncovered by her hands and in a half whisper, not without hesitation, asked Kister why it was he never brought Mr. Lutchkov with him. It was not the first time Masha had mentioned him since the ball.... Kister did not speak. Masha glanced timorously over her interlaced fingers.

'May I tell you frankly what I think?' Kister asked her.

'Oh, why not? of course.'

'It seems to me that Lutchkov has made a great impression on you.'

'No!' answered Masha, and she bent over, as though wishing to examine the pattern more closely; a narrow golden streak of light lay on her hair; 'no... but...'

'Well, but?' said Kister, smiling.

'Well, don't you see,' said Masha, and she suddenly lifted her head, so that the streak of light fell straight in her eyes; 'don't you see... he...'

'He interests you....'

'Well... yes...' Masha said slowly; she flushed a little, turned her head a little away and in that position went on talking. 'There is something about him so... There, you're laughing at me,' she added suddenly, glancing swiftly at Fyodor Fedoritch.

Fyodor Fedoritch smiled the gentlest smile imaginable.

'I tell you everything, whatever comes into my head,' Masha went on: 'I know that you are a very'... (she nearly said great) 'good friend of mine.'

Kister bowed. Masha ceased speaking, and shyly held out her hand to him; Fyodor Fedoritch pressed the tips of her fingers respectfully.

'He must be a very queer person!' observed Masha, and again she propped her elbows on the frame.

'Queer?'

'Of course; he interests me just because he is queer!' Masha added slily.

'Lutchkov is a noble, a remarkable man,' Kister rejoined solemnly. 'They don't know him in our regiment, they don't appreciate him, they only see his external side. He's embittered, of course, and strange and impatient, but his heart is good.'

Masha listened greedily to Fyodor Fedoritch.

'I will bring him to see you, I'll tell him there's no need to be afraid of you, that it's absurd for him to be so shy... I'll tell him... Oh! yes, I know what to say... Only you mustn't suppose, though, that I would...' (Kister was embarrassed, Masha too was embarrassed.)... 'Besides, after all, of course you only... like him....'

'Of course, just as I like lots of people.'

Kister looked mischievously at her.

'All right, all right,' he said with a satisfied air; 'I'll bring him to you....'

'Oh, no....'

'All right, I tell you it will be all right.... I'll arrange everything.'

'You are so...' Masha began with a smile, and she shook her finger at him. Mr. Perekatov yawned and opened his eyes.

'Why, I almost think I've been asleep,' he muttered with surprise. This doubt and this surprise were repeated daily. Masha and Kister began discussing Schiller.

Fyodor Fedoritch was not however quite at ease; he felt something like a stir of envy within him... and was generously indignant with himself. Nenila Makarievna came down into the drawing-room. Tea was brought in. Mr. Perekatov made his dog jump several times over a stick, and then explained he had taught it everything himself, while the dog wagged its tail deferentially, licked itself and blinked. When at last the great heat began to lessen, and an evening breeze blew up, the whole family went out for a walk in the birch copse. Fyodor Fedoritch was continually glancing at Masha, as though giving her to understand that he would carry out her behests; Masha felt at once vexed with herself, and happy and uncomfortable. Kister suddenly, apropos of nothing, plunged into a rather high-flown discourse upon love in the abstract, and upon friendship... but catching Nenila Makarievna's bright and vigilant eye he, as abruptly, changed the subject. The sunset was brilliant and glowing. A broad, level meadow lay outstretched before the birch copse. Masha took it into her head to start a game of 'catch-catch.' Maid-servants and footmen came out; Mr. Perekatov stood with his wife, Kister with Masha. The maids ran with deferential little shrieks; Mr. Perekatov's valet had the temerity to separate Nenila Makarievna from her spouse; one of the servant-girls respectfully paired off with her master; Fyodor Fedoritch was not parted from Masha. Every time as he regained his place, he said two or three words to her; Masha, all flushed with running, listened to him with a smile, passing her hand over her hair. After supper, Kister took leave.

It was a still, starlight night. Kister took off his cap. He was excited; there was a lump in his throat. 'Yes,' he said at last, almost aloud; 'she loves him: I will bring them together; I will justify her confidence in me.' Though there was as yet nothing to prove a definite passion for Lutchkov on Masha's part, though, according to her own account, he only excited her curiosity, Kister had by this time made up a complete romance, and worked out his own duty in the matter. He resolved to sacrifice his feelings--the more readily as 'so far I have no other sentiment for her but sincere devotion,' thought he. Kister really was capable of sacrificing himself to friendship, to a recognised duty. He had read a great deal, and so fancied himself a person of experience and even of penetration; he had no doubt of the truth of his suppositions; he did not suspect that life is endlessly varied, and never repeats itself. Little by little, Fyodor Fedoritch worked himself into a state of ecstasy. He began musing with emotion on his mission. To be the mediator between a shy, loving girl and a man possibly embittered only because he had never once in his life loved and been loved; to bring them together; to reveal their own feelings to them, and then to withdraw, letting no one know the greatness of his sacrifice, what a splendid feat! In spite of the coolness of the night, the simple-hearted dreamer's face burned....

Next day he went round to Lutchkov early in the morning.

Avdey Ivanovitch was, as usual, lying on the sofa, smoking a pipe. Kister greeted him.

'I was at the Perekatovs yesterday,' he said with some solemnity.

'Ah!' Lutchkov responded indifferently, and he yawned.

'Yes. They are splendid people.'

'Really?'

'We talked about you.'

'Much obliged; with which of them was that?'

'With the old people... and the daughter too.'

'Ah! that... little fat thing?'

'She's a splendid girl, Lutchkov.'

'To be sure, they're all splendid.'

'No, Lutchkov, you don't know her. I have never met such a clever, sweet and sensitive girl.'

Lutchkov began humming through his nose:

'In the Hamburg Gazette,
You've read, I dare say,
How the year before last,
Munich gained the day....'

'But I assure you....'

'You 're in love with her, Fedya,' Lutchkov remarked sarcastically.

'Not at all. I never even thought of it.'

'Fedya, you're in love with her!'

'What nonsense! As if one couldn't...'

'You're in love with her, friend of my heart, beetle on my hearth,' Avdey Iva-novitch chanted drawling.

'Ah, Avdey, you really ought to be ashamed!' Kister said with vexation.

With any one else Lutchkov would thereupon have kept on more than before; Kister he did not tease. 'Well, well, sprechen Sie deutsch, Ivan Andreitch,' he muttered in an undertone, 'don't be angry.'

'Listen, Avdey,' Kister began warmly, and he sat down beside him. 'You know I care for you.' (Lutchkov made a wry face.) 'But there's one thing, I'll own, I don't like about you... it's just that you won't make friends with any one, that you will stick at home, and refuse all intercourse with nice people. Why, there are nice people in the world, hang it all! Suppose you have been deceived in life, have been embittered, what of it; there's no need to rush into people's arms, of course, but why turn your back on everybody? Why, you'll cast me off some day, at that rate, I suppose.'

Lutchkov went on smoking coolly.

'That's how it is no one knows you... except me; goodness knows what some people think of you... Avdey!' added Kister after a brief silence; 'do you disbelieve in virtue, Avdey?'

'Disbelieve... no, I believe in it,'... muttered Lutchkov.

Kister pressed his hand feelingly.

'I want,' he went on in a voice full of emotion, 'to reconcile you with life. You will grow happier, blossom out... yes, blossom out. How I shall rejoice then! Only you must let me dispose of you now and then, of your time. To-day it's--what? Monday... to-morrow's Tuesday... on Wednesday, yes, on Wednesday we'll go together to the Perekatovs'. They will be so glad to see you... and we shall have such a jolly time there... and now let me have a pipe.'

Avdey Ivanovitch lay without budging on the sofa, staring at the ceiling. Kister lighted a pipe, went to the window, and began drumming on the panes with his fingers.

'So they've been talking about me?' Avdey asked suddenly.

'They have,' Kister responded with meaning.

'What did they say?'

'Oh, they talked. There're very anxious to make your acquaintance.'

'Which of them's that?'

'I say, what curiosity!'

Avdey called his servant, and ordered his horse to be saddled.

'Where are you off to?'

'The riding-school.'

'Well, good-bye. So we're going to the Perekatovs', eh?'

'All right, if you like,' Lutchkov said lazily, stretching.

'Bravo, old man!' cried Kister, and he went out into the street, pondered, and sighed deeply.

IV

Masha was just approaching the drawing-room door when the arrival of Kister and Lutchkov was announced. She promptly returned to her own room, and went up to the looking-glass.... Her heart was throbbing violently. A girl came to summon her to the drawing-room. Masha drank a little water, stopped twice on the stairs, and at last went down. Mr. Perekatov was not at home. Nenila Makarievna was sitting on the sofa; Lutchkov was sitting in an easy-chair, wearing his uniform, with his hat on his knees; Kister was near him. They both got up on Masha's entrance--Kister with his usual friendly smile, Lutchkov with a solemn and constrained air. She bowed to them in confusion, and went up to her mother. The first ten minutes passed off favourably. Masha recovered herself, and gradually began to watch Lutchkov. To the questions addressed to him by the lady of the house, he answered briefly, but uneasily; he was shy, like all egoistic people. Nenila Makarievna suggested a stroll in the garden to her guests, but did not herself go beyond the balcony. She did not consider it essential never to lose sight of her daughter, and to be constantly hobbling after her with a fat reticule in her hands, after the fashion of many mothers in the steppes. The stroll lasted rather a long while. Masha talked more with Kister, but did not dare to look either at him or at Lutchkov. Avdey Ivanovitch did not address a remark to her; Kister's voice showed agitation. He laughed and chattered a little over-much.... They reached the stream. A couple of yards or so from the bank there was a water-lily, which seemed to rest on the smooth surface of the water, encircled by its broad, round leaves.

'What a beautiful flower!' observed Masha.

She had hardly uttered these words when Lutchkov pulled out his sword, clutched with one hand at the frail twigs of a willow, and, bending his whole body over the water, cut off the head of the flower. 'It's deep here, take care!' Masha cried in terror. Lutchkov with the tip of his sword brought the flower to the bank, at her very feet. She bent down, picked up the flower, and gazed with tender, delighted amazement at Avdey. 'Bravo!' cried Kister. 'And I can't swim...' Lutchkov observed abruptly. Masha did not like that remark. 'What made him say that?' she wondered.

Lutchkov and Kister remained at Mr. Perekatov's till the evening. Something new and unknown was passing in Masha's soul; a dreamy perplexity was reflected more than once in her face. She moved somehow more slowly, she did not flush on meeting her mother's eyes--on the contrary, she seemed to seek them, as though she would question her. During the whole evening, Lutchkov paid her a sort of awkward attention; but even this awkwardness gratified her innocent vanity. When they had both taken leave, with a promise to come again in a few days, she quietly went off to her own room, and for a long while, as it were, in bewilderment she looked about her. Nenila Makarievna came to her, kissed and embraced her as usual. Masha opened her lips, tried to say something--and did not utter a word. She wanted to confess---she did not know what. Her soul was gently wandering in dreams. On the little table by her bedside the flower Lutchkov had picked lay in water in a clean glass. Masha, already in bed, sat up cautiously, leaned on her elbow, and her maiden lips softly touched the fresh white petals....

'Well,' Kister questioned his friend next day, 'do you like the Perekatovs? Was I right? eh? Tell me.'

Lutchkov did not answer.

'No, do tell me, do tell me!'

'Really, I don't know.'

'Nonsense, come now!'

'That... what's her name... Mashenka's all right; not bad-looking.'

'There, you see...' said Kister--and he said no more.

Five days later Lutchkov of his own accord suggested that they should call on the Perekatovs.

Alone he would not have gone to see them; in Fyodor Fedoritch's absence he would have had to keep up a conversation, and that he could not do, and as far as possible avoided.

On the second visit of the two friends, Masha was much more at her ease. She was by now secretly glad that she had not disturbed her mamma by an uninvited avowal. Before dinner, Avdey had offered to try a young horse, not yet broken in, and, in spite of its frantic rearing, he mastered it completely. In the evening he thawed, and fell into joking and laughing--and though he soon pulled himself up, yet he had succeeded in making a momentary unpleasant impression on Masha. She could not yet be sure herself what the feeling exactly was that Lutchkov excited in her, but everything she did not like in him she set down to the influence of misfortune, of loneliness.

V

The friends began to pay frequent visits to the Perekatovs'. Kister's position became more and more painful. He did not regret his action... no, but he desired at least to cut short the time of his trial. His devotion to Masha increased daily; she too felt warmly towards him; but to be nothing more than a go-between, a confidant, a friend even--it's a dreary, thankless business! Coldly idealistic people talk a great deal about the sacredness of suffering, the bliss of suffering... but to Kister's warm and simple heart his sufferings were not a source of any bliss whatever. At last, one day, when Lutchkov, ready dressed, came to fetch him, and the carriage was waiting at the steps, Fyodor Fedoritch, to the astonishment of his friend, announced point-blank that he should stay at home. Lutchkov entreated him, was vexed and angry... Kister pleaded a headache. Lutchkov set off alone.

The bully had changed in many ways of late. He left his comrades in peace, did not annoy the novices, and though his spirit had not 'blossomed out,' as Kister had foretold, yet he certainly had toned down a little. He could not have been called 'disillusioned' before--he had seen and experienced almost nothing--and so it is not surprising that Masha engrossed his thoughts. His heart was not touched though; only his spleen was satisfied. Masha's feelings for him were of a strange kind. She almost never looked him straight in the face; she could not talk to him.... When they happened to be left alone together, Masha felt horribly awkward. She took him for an exceptional man, and felt overawed by him and agitated in his presence, fancied she did not understand him, and was unworthy of his confidence; miserably, drearily--but continually--she thought of him. Kister's society, on the contrary, soothed her and put her in a good humour, though it neither overjoyed nor excited her. With him she could chatter away for hours together, leaning on his arm, as though he were her brother, looking affectionately into his face, and laughing with his laughter--and she rarely thought of him. In Lutchkov there was something enigmatic for the young girl; she felt that his soul was 'dark as a forest,' and strained every effort to penetrate into that mysterious gloom.... So children stare a long while into a deep well, till at last they make out at the very bottom the still, black water.

On Lutchkov's coming into the drawing-room alone, Masha was at first scared... but then she felt delighted. She had more than once fancied that there existed some sort of misunderstanding between Lutchkov and her, that he had not hitherto had a chance of revealing himself. Lutchkov mentioned the cause of Kister's absence; the parents expressed their regret, but Masha looked incredulously at Avdey, and felt faint with expectation. After dinner they were left alone; Masha did not know what to say, she sat down to the piano; her fingers flitted hurriedly and tremblingly over the keys; she was continually stopping and waiting for the first word... Lutchkov did not understand nor care for music. Masha began talking to him about Rossini (Rossini was at that time just coming into fashion) and about Mozart.... Avdey Ivanovitch responded: 'Quite so,' 'by no means,' 'beautiful,' 'indeed,' and that was all. Masha played some brilliant variations on one of Rossini's airs. Lutchkov listened and listened... and when at last she turned to him, his face expressed such unfeigned boredom, that Masha jumped up at once and closed the piano. She went up to the window, and for a long while stared into the garden; Lutchkov did not stir from his seat, and still remained silent. Impatience began to take the place of timidity in Masha's soul. 'What is it?' she wondered, 'won't you... or can't you?' It was Lutchkov's turn to feel shy. He was conscious again of his miserable, over-whelming diffidence; already he was raging!... 'It was the devil's own notion to have anything to do with the wretched girl,' he muttered to himself.... And all the while how easy it was to touch Masha's heart at that instant! Whatever had been said by such an extraordinary though eccentric man, as she imagined Lutchkov, she would have understood everything, have excused anything, have believed anything.... But this burdensome, stupid silence! Tears of vexation were standing in her eyes. 'If he doesn't want to be open, if I am really not worthy of his confidence, why does he go on coming to see us? Or perhaps it is that I don't set the right way to work to make him reveal himself?'... And she turned swiftly round, and glanced so inquiringly, so searchingly at him, that he could not fail to understand her glance, and could not keep silence any longer....

'Marya Sergievna,' he pronounced falteringly; 'I... I've... I ought to tell you something....'

'Speak,' Masha responded rapidly.

Lutchkov looked round him irresolutely.

'I can't now...'

'Why not?'

'I should like to speak to you... alone....'

'Why, we are alone now.'

'Yes... but... here in the house....'

Masha was at her wits' end.... 'If I refuse,' she thought, 'it's all over.'... Curiosity was the ruin of Eve....

'I agree,' she said at last.

'When then? Where?'

Masha's breathing came quickly and unevenly.

'To-morrow... in the evening. You know the copse above the Long Meadow?'...

'Behind the mill?'

Masha nodded.

'What time?'

'Wait...'

She could not bring out another word; her voice broke... she turned pale and went quickly out of the room.

A quarter of an hour later, Mr. Perekatov, with his characteristic politeness, conducted Lutchkov to the hall, pressed his hand feelingly, and begged him 'not to forget them'; then, having let out his guest, he observed with dignity to the footman that it would be as well for him to shave, and without awaiting a reply, returned with a careworn air to his own room, with the same careworn air sat down on the sofa, and guilelessly dropped asleep on the spot.

'You're a little pale to-day,' Nenila Makarievna said to her daughter, on the evening of the same day. 'Are you quite well?'

'Yes, mamma.'

Nenila Makarievna set straight the kerchief on the girl's neck.

'You are very pale; look at me,' she went on, with that motherly solicitude in which there is none the less audible a note of parental authority: 'there, now, your eyes look heavy too. You're not well, Masha.'

'My head does ache a little,' said Masha, to find some way of escape.

'There, I knew it.' Nenila Makarievna put some scent on Masha's forehead. 'You're not feverish, though.'

Masha stooped down, and picked a thread off the floor.

Nenila Makarievna's arms lay softly round Masha's slender waist.

'It seems to me you have something you want to tell me,' she said caressingly, not loosing her hands.

Masha shuddered inwardly.

'I? Oh, no, mamma.'

Masha's momentary confusion did not escape her mother's attention.

'Oh, yes, you do.... Think a little.'

But Masha had had time to regain her self-possession, and instead of answering, she kissed her mother's hand with a laugh.

'And so you've nothing to tell me?'

'No, really, nothing.'

'I believe you,' responded Nenila Makarievna, after a short silence. 'I know you keep nothing secret from me.... That's true, isn't it?'

'Of course, mamma.'

Masha could not help blushing a little, though.

'You do quite rightly. It would be wrong of you to keep anything from me.... You know how I love you, Masha.'

'Oh yes, mamma.'

And Masha hugged her.

'There, there, that's enough.' (Nenila Makarievna walked about the room.) 'Oh tell me,' she went on in the voice of one who feels that the question asked is of no special importance; 'what were you talking about with Avdey Ivanovitch to-day?'

'With Avdey Ivanovitch?' Masha repeated serenely. 'Oh, all sorts of things....'

'Do you like him?'

'Oh yes, I like him.'

'Do you remember how anxious you were to get to know him, how excited you were?'

Masha turned away and laughed.

'What a strange person he is!' Nenila Makarievna observed good-humouredly.

Masha felt an inclination to defend Lutchkov, but she held her tongue.

'Yes, of course,' she said rather carelessly; 'he is a queer fish, but still he's a nice man!'

'Oh, yes!... Why didn't Fyodor Fedoritch come?'

'He was unwell, I suppose. Ah! by the way, Fyodor Fedoritch wanted to make me a present of a puppy.... Will you let me?'

'What? Accept his present?'

'Yes.'

'Of course.'

'Oh, thank you!' said Masha, 'thank you, thank you!'

Nenila Makarievna got as far as the door and suddenly turned back again.

'Do you remember your promise, Masha?'

'What promise?'

'You were going to tell me when you fall in love.'

'I remember.'

'Well... hasn't the time come yet?' (Masha laughed musically.) 'Look into my eyes.'

Masha looked brightly and boldly at her mother.

'It can't be!' thought Nenila Makarievna, and she felt reassured. 'As if she could deceive me!... How could I think of such a thing!... She's still a perfect baby....'

She went away....

'But this is really wicked,' thought Masha.

VI

Kister had already gone to bed when Lutchkov came into his room. The bully's face never expressed *one* feeling; so it was now: feigned indifference, coarse delight, consciousness of his own superiority... a number of different emotions were playing over his features.

'Well, how was it? how was it?' Kister made haste to question him.

'Oh! I went. They sent you greetings.'

'Well? Are they all well?'

'Of course, why not?'

'Did they ask why I didn't come?'

'Yes, I think so.'

Lutchkov stared at the ceiling and hummed out of tune. Kister looked down and mused.

'But, look here,' Lutchkov brought out in a husky, jarring voice, 'you're a clever fellow, I dare say, you're a cultured fellow, but you're a good bit out in your ideas sometimes for all that, if I may venture to say so.'

'How do you mean?'

'Why, look here. About women, for instance. How you're always cracking them up! You're never tired of singing their praises! To listen to you, they're all angels.... Nice sort of angels!'

'I like and respect women, but------'

'Oh, of course, of course,' Avdey cut him short. 'I am not going to argue with you. That's quite beyond me! I'm a plain man.'

'I was going to say that... But why just to-day... just now,... are you talking about women?'

'Oh, nothing!' Avdey smiled with great meaning. 'Nothing!'

Kister looked searchingly at his friend. He imagined (simple heart!) that Masha had been treating him badly; had been torturing him, perhaps, as only women can....

'You are feeling hurt, my poor Avdey; tell me...'

Lutchkov went off into a chuckle.

'Oh, well, I don't fancy I've much to feel hurt about,' he said, in a drawling tone, complacently stroking his moustaches. 'No, only, look here, Fedya,' he went on with the manner of a preceptor, 'I was only going to point out that you're altogether out of it about women, my lad. You believe me, Fedya, they 're all alike. One's only got to take a little trouble, hang about them a bit, and you've got things in your own hands. Look at Masha Perekatov now....'

'Oh!'

Lutchkov tapped his foot on the floor and shook his head.

'Is there anything so specially attractive about me, hey? I shouldn't have thought there was anything. There isn't anything, is there? And here, I've a clandestine appointment for to-morrow.'

Kister sat up, leaned on his elbow, and stared in amazement at Lutchkov.

'For the evening, in a wood...' Avdey Ivanovitch continued serenely. 'Only don't you go and imagine it means much. It's only a bit of fun. It's slow here, don't you know. A pretty little girl,... well, says I, why not? Marriage, of course, I'm not going in for... but there, I like to recall my young days. I don't care for hanging about petticoats--but I may as well humour the baggage. We can listen to the nightingales together. Of course, it's really more in your line; but the wench has no eyes, you see. I should have thought I wasn't worth looking at beside you.'

Lutchkov talked on a long while. But Kister did not hear him. His head was going round. He turned pale and passed his hand over his face. Lutchkov swayed up and down in his low chair, screwed up his eyes, stretched, and putting down Kister's emotion to jealousy, was almost gasping with delight. But it was not jealousy that was torturing Kister; he was wounded, not by the fact itself, but by Avdey's coarse carelessness, his indifferent and contemptuous references to Masha. He was still staring intently at the bully, and it seemed as if for the first time he was thoroughly seeing his face. So this it was he had been scheming for! This for which he had sacrificed his own inclinations! Here it was, the blessed influence of love.

'Avdey... do you mean to say you don't care for her?' he muttered at last.

'O innocence! O Arcadia!' responded Avdey, with a malignant chuckle.

Kister in the goodness of his heart did not give in even then; perhaps, thought he, Avdey is in a bad temper and is 'humbugging' from old habit... he has not yet found a new language to express new feelings. And was there not in himself some other feeling lurking under his indignation? Did not Lutchkov's avowal strike him so unpleasantly simply because it concerned Masha? How could one tell, perhaps Lutchkov really was in love with her.... Oh, no! no! a thousand times no! That man in love?... That man was loathsome with his bilious, yellow face, his nervous, cat-like movements, crowing with conceit... loathsome! No, not in such words would Kister have uttered to a devoted friend the secret of his love.... In overflowing happiness, in dumb rapture, with bright, blissful tears in his eyes would he have flung himself on his bosom....

'Well, old man,' queried Avdey, 'own up now you didn't expect it, and now you feel put out. Eh? jealous? Own up, Fedya. Eh? eh?'

Kister was about to speak out, but he turned with his face to the wall. 'Speak openly... to him? Not for anything!' he whispered to himself. 'He wouldn't understand me... so be it! He supposes none but evil feelings in me--so be it!...'

Avdey got up.

'I see you're sleepy,' he said with assumed sympathy: 'I don't want to be in your way. Pleasant dreams, my boy... pleasant dreams!'

And Lutchkov went away, very well satisfied with himself.

Kister could not get to sleep before the morning. With feverish persistence he turned over and over and thought over and over the same single idea--an occupation only too well known to unhappy lovers.

'Even if Lutchkov doesn't care for her,' he mused, 'if she has flung herself at his head, anyway he ought not even with me, with his friend, to speak so disrespectfully, so offensively of her! In what way is she to blame? How could any one have no feeling for a poor, inexperienced girl?

'But can she really have a secret appointment with him? She has--yes, she certainly has. Avdey's not a liar, he never tells a lie. But perhaps it means nothing, a mere freak....

'But she does not know him.... He is capable, I dare say, of insulting her. After to-day, I wouldn't answer for anything.... And wasn't it I myself that praised him up and exalted him? Wasn't it I who excited her curiosity?... But who could have known this? Who could have foreseen it?...

'Foreseen what? Has he so long ceased to be my friend?... But, after all, was he ever my friend? What a disenchantment! What a lesson!'

All the past turned round and round before Kister's eyes. 'Yes, I did like him,' he whispered at last. 'Why has my liking cooled so suddenly?... And do I dislike him? No, why did I ever like him? I alone?'

Kister's loving heart had attached itself to Avdey for the very reason that all the rest avoided him. But the good-hearted youth did not know himself how great his good-heartedness was.

'My duty,' he went on, 'is to warn Marya Sergievna. But how? What right have I to interfere in other people's affairs, in other people's love? How do I know the nature of that love? Perhaps even in Lutchkov.... No, no!' he said aloud, with irritation, almost with tears, smoothing out his pillow, 'that man's stone....

'It is my own fault... I have lost a friend.... A precious friend, indeed! And she's not worth much either!... What a sickening egoist I am! No, no! from the bottom of my soul I wish them happiness.... Happiness! but he is laughing at her!... And why does he dye his moustaches? I do, really, believe he does.... Ah, how ridiculous I am!' he repeated, as he fell asleep.

VII

The next morning Kister went to call on the Perekatovs. When they met, Kister noticed a great change in Masha, and Masha, too, found a change in him, but neither spoke of it. The whole morning they both, contrary to their habit, felt uncomfortable. Kister had prepared at home a number of hints and phrases of double meaning and friendly counsels... but all this previous preparation turned out to be quite thrown away. Masha was vaguely aware that Kister was watching her; she fancied that he pronounced some words with intentional significance; but she was conscious, too, of her own excitement, and did not trust her own observations. 'If only he doesn't mean to stay till evening!' was what she was thinking incessantly, and she tried to make him realise that he was not wanted. Kister, for his part, took her awkwardness and her uneasiness for obvious signs of love, and the more afraid he was for her the more impossible he found it to speak of Lutchkov; while Masha obstinately refrained from uttering his name. It was a painful experience for poor Fyodor Fedoritch. He began at last to understand his own feelings. Never had Masha seemed to him more charming. She had, to all appearances, not slept the whole night. A faint flush stood in patches on her pale face; her figure was faintly drooping; an unconscious, weary smile never left her lips; now and then a shiver ran over her white shoulders; a soft light glowed suddenly in her eyes, and quickly faded away. Nenila Makarievna came in and sat with them, and possibly with intention mentioned Avdey Ivanovitch. But in her mother's presence Masha was armed *jusqu'aux dents,* as the French say, and she did not betray herself at all. So passed the whole morning.

'You will dine with us?' Nenila Makarievna asked Kister.

Masha turned away.

'No,' Kister said hurriedly, and he glanced towards Masha. 'Excuse me... duties of the service...'

Nenila Makarievna duly expressed her regret. Mr. Perekatov, following her lead, also expressed something or other. 'I don't want to be in the way,' Kister wanted to say to Masha, as he passed her, but he bowed down and whispered instead: 'Be happy... farewell... take care of yourself...' and was gone.

Masha heaved a sigh from the bottom of her heart, and then felt panic-stricken at his departure. What was it fretting her? Love or curiosity? God knows; but, we repeat, curiosity alone was enough to ruin Eve.

VIII

Long Meadow was the name of a wide, level stretch of ground on the right of the little stream Sniezhinka, nearly a mile from the Perekatovs' property. The left bank, completely covered by thick young oak bushes, rose steeply up over the stream, which was almost overgrown with willow bushes, except for some small 'breeding-places,' the haunts of wild ducks. Half a mile from the stream, on the right side of Long Meadow, began the sloping, undulating uplands, studded here and there with old birch-trees, nut bushes, and guelder-roses.

The sun was setting. The mill rumbled and clattered in the distance, sounding louder or softer according to the wind. The seignorial drove of horses was lazily wandering about the meadows; a shepherd walked, humming a tune, after a flock of greedy and timorous sheep; the sheepdogs, from boredom, were running after the crows. Lutchkov walked up and down in the copse, with his arms folded. His horse, tied up near by, more than once whinnied in response to the sonorous neighing of the mares and fillies in the meadow. Avdey was ill-tempered and shy, as usual. Not yet convinced of Masha's love, he felt wrathful with her and annoyed with himself... but his excitement smothered his annoyance. He stopped at last before a large nut bush, and began with his riding-whip switching off the leaves at the ends of the twigs....

He heard a light rustle... he raised his head.... Ten paces from him stood Masha, all flushed from her rapid walk, in a hat, but with no gloves, in a white dress, with a hastily tied kerchief round her neck. She dropped her eyes instantly, and softly nodded....

Avdey went awkwardly up to her with a forced smile.

'How happy I am...' he was beginning, scarcely audibly.

'I am very glad... to meet you...' Masha interrupted breathlessly. 'I usually walk here in the evening... and you...'

But Lutchkov had not the sense even to spare her modesty, to keep up her innocent deception.

'I believe, Marya Sergievna,' he pronounced with dignity, 'you yourself suggested...'

'Yes... yes...' rejoined Masha hurriedly. 'You wished to see me, you wanted...' Her voice died away.

Lutchkov did not speak. Masha timidly raised her eyes.

'Excuse me,' he began, not looking at her, 'I'm a plain man, and not used to talking freely... to ladies... I... I wished to tell you... but, I fancy, you 're not in the humour to listen to me....'

'Speak.'

'Since you tell me to... well, then, I tell you frankly that for a long while now, ever since I had the honour of making your acquaintance...'

Avdey stopped. Masha waited for the conclusion of his sentence.

'I don't know, though, what I'm telling you all this for.... There's no changing one's destiny...'

'How can one know?...'

'I know!' responded Avdey gloomily. 'I am used to facing its blows!'

It struck Masha that this was not exactly the befitting moment for Lutchkov to rail against destiny.

'There are kind-hearted people in the world,' she observed with a smile; 'some even too kind....'

'I understand you, Marya Sergievna, and believe me, I appreciate your friendliness... I... I... You won't be angry?'

'No.... What do you want to say?'

'I want to say... that I think you charming... Marya Sergievna, awfully charming....'

'I am very grateful to you,' Masha interrupted him; her heart was aching with anticipation and terror. 'Ah, do look, Mr. Lutchkov,' she went on--'look, what a view!'

She pointed to the meadow, streaked with long, evening shadows, and flushed red with the sunset.

Inwardly overjoyed at the abrupt change in the conversation, Lutchkov began admiring the view. He was standing near Masha....

'You love nature?' she asked suddenly, with a rapid turn of her little head, looking at him with that friendly, inquisitive, soft glance, which is a gift only vouch-safed to young girls.

'Yes... nature... of course...' muttered Avdey. 'Of course... a stroll's pleasant in the evening, though, I confess, I'm a soldier, and fine sentiments are not in my line.'

Lutchkov often repeated that he 'was a soldier.' A brief silence followed. Masha was still looking at the meadow.

'How about getting away?' thought Avdey. 'What rot it is, though! Come, more pluck!... Marya Sergievna...' he began, in a fairly resolute voice.

Masha turned to him.

'Excuse me,' he began, as though in joke, 'but let me on my side know what you think of me, whether you feel at all... so to say,... amiably disposed towards my person?'

'Mercy on us, how uncouth he is!' Masha said to herself. 'Do you know, Mr. Lutchkov,' she answered him with a smile, 'it's not always easy to give a direct answer to a direct question.'

'Still...'

'But what is it to you?'

'Oh, really now, I want to know...'

'But... Is it true that you are a great duellist? Tell me, is it true?' said Masha, with shy curiosity. 'They do say you have killed more than one man?'

'It has happened so,' Avdey responded indifferently, and he stroked his moustaches.

Masha looked intently at him.

'This hand then...' she murmured. Meanwhile Lutchkov's blood had caught fire. For more than a quarter of an hour a young and pretty girl had been moving before his eyes.

'Marya Sergievna,' he began again, in a sharp and strange voice, 'you know my feelings now, you know what I wanted to see you for.... You've been so kind.... You tell me, too, at last what I may hope for....'

Masha twisted a wildflower in her hands.... She glanced sideways at Lutchkov, flushed, smiled, said,' What nonsense you do talk,' and gave him the flower.

Avdey seized her hand.

'And so you love me!' he cried.

Masha turned cold all over with horror. She had not had the slightest idea of making a declaration of love to Avdey: she was not even sure herself as yet whether she did care for him, and here he was forestalling her, forcing her to speak out--he must be misunderstanding her then.... This idea flashed quicker than lightning into Masha's head. She had never expected such a speedy ***denouement***.... Masha, like an inquisitive child, had been asking herself all day: 'Can it be that Lutchkov cares for me?' She had dreamed of a delightful evening walk, a respectful and tender dialogue; she had fancied how she would flirt with him, make the wild creature feel at home with her, permit him at parting to kiss her hand... and instead of that...

Instead of that, she was suddenly aware of Avdey's rough moustaches on her cheek....

'Let us be happy,' he was whispering: 'there's no other happiness on earth!'

Masha shuddered, darted horror-stricken on one side, and pale all over, stopped short, one hand leaning on a birch-tree. Avdey was terribly confused.

'Excuse me,' he muttered, approaching her, 'I didn't expect really...'

Masha gazed at him, wide-eyed and speechless... A disagreeable smile twisted his lips... patches of red came out on his face....

'What are you afraid of?' he went on; 'it's no such great matter.... Why, we understand each other... and so....'

Masha did not speak.

'Come, stop that!... that's all nonsense! it's nothing but...' Lutchkov stretched out his hand to her.

Masha recollected Kister, his 'take care of yourself,' and, sinking with terror, in a rather shrill voice screamed, 'Taniusha!'

From behind a nutbush emerged the round face of her maid.... Avdey was completely disconcerted. Reassured by the presence of her hand-maiden, Masha did not stir. But the bully was shaking all over with rage; his eyes were half closed; he clenched his fists and laughed nervously.

'Bravo! bravo! Clever trick--no denying that!' he cried out.

Masha was petrified.

'So you took every care, I see, to be on the safe side, Marya Sergievna! Prudence is never thrown away, eh? Upon my word! Nowadays young ladies see further than old men. So this is all your love amounts to!'

'I don't know, Mr. Lutchkov, who has given you any right to speak about love... what love?'

'Who? Why, you yourself!' Lutchkov cut her short: 'what next!' He felt he was ship-wrecking the whole business, but he could not restrain himself.

'I have acted thoughtlessly,' said Masha.... 'I yielded to your request, relying upon your ***delicatesse***... but you don't know French... on your courtesy, I mean....'

Avdey turned pale. Masha had stung him to the quick.

'I don't know French... may be; but I know... I know very well that you have been amusing yourself at my expense.'

'Not at all, Avdey Ivanovitch... indeed, I'm very sorry...'

'Oh, please, don't talk about being sorry for me,' Avdey cut her short peremptorily; 'spare me that, anyway!'

'Mr. Lutchkov...'

'Oh, you needn't put on those grand-duchess airs... It's trouble thrown away! you don't impress me.'

Masha stepped back a pace, turned swiftly round and walked away.

'Won't you give me a message for your friend, your shepherd lad, your tender sweet-heart, Kister,' Avdey shouted after her. He had lost his head. 'Isn't he the happy man?'...

Masha made him no reply, and hurriedly, gladly retreated. She felt light at heart, in spite of her fright and excitement. She felt as though she had waked up from a troubled sleep, had stepped out of a dark room into air and sunshine.... Avdey glared about him like a madman; in speechless frenzy he broke a young tree, jumped on to his mare, and so viciously drove the spurs into her, so mercilessly pulled and tugged at the reins that the wretched beast galloped six miles in a quarter of an hour and almost expired the same night.

Kister waited for Lutchkov in vain till midnight, and next morning he went round himself to see him. The orderly informed Fyodor Fedoritch that his master was lying down and had given orders that he would see no one. 'He won't see me even?'. 'Not even your honour.' Kister walked twice up and down the street, tortured by the keenest apprehensions, and then went home again. His servant handed him a note.

'From whom?'

'From the Perekatovs. Artiomka the postillion brought it.'

Kister's hands began to tremble.

'He had orders to give you their greetings. He had orders to wait for your answer. Am I to give Artiomka some vodka?'

Kister slowly unfolded the note, and read as follows:

'DEAR GOOD FYODOR FEDORITCH,--I want very, very much to see you. Come to-day, if you can. Don't refuse my request, I entreat you, for the sake of our old friendship. If only you knew... but you shall know everything. Good-bye for a little while,--eh?

MARIE.

'P.S.--Be sure to come to-morrow.'

'So your honour, am I to give Artiomka some vodka?'

Kister turned a long, bewildered stare at his servant's countenance, and went out without uttering a word.

'The master has told me to get you some vodka, and to have a drink with you,' said Kister's servant to Artiomka the postillion.

IX

Masha came with such a bright and grateful face to meet Kister, when he came into the drawing-room, she pressed his hand so warmly and affectionately, that his heart throbbed with delight, and a weight seemed rolled from his mind. Masha did not, however, say a single word, and she promptly left the room. Sergei Sergeitch was sitting on the sofa, playing patience. Conversation sprang up. Sergei Sergeitch had not yet succeeded with his usual skill in bringing the conversation round from all extraneous topics to his dog, when Masha reappeared, wearing a plaid silk sash, Kister's favourite sash. Nenila Makarievna came in and gave Fyodor Fedoritch a friendly greeting. At dinner they were all laughing and making jokes; even Sergei

Sergeitch plucked up spirit and described one of the merriest pranks of his youthful days, hiding his head from his wife like an ostrich, as he told the story.

'Let us go for a walk, Fyodor Fedoritch,' Masha said to Kister after dinner with that note of affectionate authority in her voice which is, as it were, conscious that you will gladly submit to it. 'I want to talk to you about something very, very important,' she added with enchanting solemnity, as she put on her suede gloves. 'Are you coming with us, **maman**?'

'No,' answered Nenila Makarievna.

'But we are not going into the garden.'

'Where then?'

'To Long Meadow, to the copse.'

'Take Taniusha with you.'

'Taniusha, Taniusha!' Masha cried musically, flitting lightly as a bird from the room.

A quarter of an hour later Masha walked with Kister into the Long Meadow. As she passed the cattle, she gave a piece of bread to her favourite cow, patted it on the head and made Kister stroke it. Masha was in great good humour and chatted merrily. Kister responded willingly, though he awaited explanations with impatience.... Taniusha walked behind at a respectful distance, only from time to time stealing a sly glance at her young lady.

'You're not angry with me, Fyodor Fedoritch?' queried Masha.

'With you, Marya Sergievna? Why, whatever for?'

'The day before yesterday... don't you remember?'

'You were out of humour... that was all.'

'What are we walking in single file for? Give me your arm. That's right.... You were out of humour too.'

'Yes, I was too.'

'But to-day I'm in good humour, eh?'

'Yes, I think so, to-day...'

'And do you know why? Because...'

Masha nodded her head gravely. 'Well, I know why.... Because I am with you,' she added, not looking at Kister.

Kister softly pressed her hand.

'But why don't you question me?...' Masha murmured in an undertone.

'What about?'

'Oh, don't pretend... about my letter.'

'I was waiting for...'

'That's just why I am happy with you,' Masha interrupted him impulsively: 'because you are a gentle, good-hearted person, because you are incapable... ***parceque vous avez de la delicatesse***. One can say that to you: you understand French.'

Kister did understand French, but he did not in the least understand Masha.

'Pick me that flower, that one... how pretty it is!' Masha admired it, and suddenly, swiftly withdrawing her hand from his arm, with an anxious smile she began carefully sticking the tender stalk in the buttonhole of Kister's coat. Her slender fingers almost touched his lips. He looked at the fingers and then at her. She nodded her head to him as though to say 'you may.'... Kister bent down and kissed the tips of her gloves.

Meanwhile they drew near the already familiar copse. Masha became suddenly more thoughtful, and at last kept silent altogether. They came to the very place where Lutchkov had waited for her. The trampled grass had not yet grown straight again; the broken sapling had not yet withered, its little leaves were only just beginning to curl up and fade. Masha stared about her, and turned quickly to Kister.

'Do you know why I have brought you here?'

'No, I don't.'

'Don't you know? Why is it you haven't told me anything about your friend Lutchkov to-day? You always praise him so...'

Kister dropped his eyes, and did not speak.

'Do you know,' Masha brought out with some effort, 'that I made... an appointment... to meet him here... yesterday?'

'I know that,' Kister rejoined hurriedly.

'You know it?... Ah! now I see why the day before yesterday... Mr. Lutchkov was in a hurry it seems to boast of his ***conquest***.'

Kister was about to answer....

'Don't speak, don't say anything in opposition.... I know he's your friend. You are capable of taking his part. You knew, Kister, you knew.... How was it you didn't prevent me from acting so stupidly? Why didn't you box my ears, as if I were a child? You knew... and didn't you care?'

'But what right had I...'

'What right!... the right of a friend. But he too is your friend.... I'm ashamed, Kister.... He your friend.... That man behaved to me yesterday, as if...'

Masha turned away. Kister's eyes flamed; he turned pale.

'Oh, never mind, don't be angry.... Listen, Fyodor Fedoritch, don't be angry. It's all for the best. I am very glad of yesterday's explanation... yes, that's just what it was,' added Masha. 'What do you suppose I am telling you about it for? To complain of Mr. Lutchkov? Nonsense! I've forgotten about him. But I have done you a wrong, my good friend.... I want to speak openly to you, to ask your forgiveness... your advice. You have accustomed me to frankness; I am at ease with you.... You are not a Mr. Lutchkov!'

'Lutchkov is clumsy and coarse,' Kister brought out with difficulty; 'but...'

'Why **but**? Aren't you ashamed to say **but**? He is coarse, **and** clumsy, **and** ill-natured, **and** conceited.... Do you hear?--**and**, not **but**.'

'You are speaking under the influence of anger, Marya Sergievna,' Kister observed mournfully.

'Anger? A strange sort of anger! Look at me; are people like this when they 're angry? Listen,' pursued Masha; 'you may think what you like of me... but if you imagine I am flirting with you to-day from pique, well... well...' (tears stood in her eyes)'I shall be angry in earnest.'

'Do be open with me, Marya Sergievna...'

'O, silly fellow! how slow you are! Why, look at me, am I not open with you, don't you see right through me?'

'Oh, very well... yes; I believe you,' Kister said with a smile, seeing with what anxious insistence she tried to catch his eyes. 'But tell me, what induced you to arrange to meet Lutchkov?'

'What induced me? I really don't know. He wanted to speak to me alone. I fancied he had never had time, never had an opportunity to speak freely. He has spoken freely now! Do you know, he may be an extraordinary man, but he's a fool, really.... He doesn't know how to put two words together. He's simply an ignoramus. Though, indeed, I don't blame him much... he might suppose I was a giddy, mad, worthless girl. I hardly ever talked to him.... He did excite my curiosity, certainly, but I imagined that a man who was worthy of being your friend...'

'Don't, please, speak of him as my friend,' Kister interposed.

'No, no, I don't want to separate you.'

'Oh, my God, for you I'm ready to sacrifice more than a friend.... Everything is over between me and Mr. Lutchkov,' Kister added hurriedly.

Masha looked intently into his face.

'Well, enough of him,' she said. 'Don't let us talk of him. It's a lesson to me for the future. It's I that am to blame. For several months past I have almost every day seen a man who is good, clever, bright, friendly who...' (Masha was confused, and stammered) 'who, I think, cared... a little... for me too... and I like a fool,' she went on quickly, 'preferred to him... no, no, I didn't prefer him, but...'

She drooped her head, and ceased speaking in confusion.

Kister was in a sort of terror. 'It can't be!' he kept repeating to himself.

'Marya Sergievna!' he began at last.

Masha lifted her head, and turned upon him eyes heavy with unshed tears.

'You don't guess of whom I am speaking?' she asked.

Scarcely daring to breathe, Kister held out his hand. Masha at once clutched it warmly.

'You are my friend as before, aren't you?... Why don't you answer?'

'I am your friend, you know that,' he murmured.

'And you are not hard on me? You forgive me?... You understand me? You're not laughing at a girl who made an appointment only yesterday with one man, and to-day is talking to another, as I am talking to you.... You're not laughing at me, are you?...' Masha's face glowed crimson, she clung with both hands to Kister's hand....

'Laugh at you,' answered Kister: 'I... I... why, I love you... I love you,' he cried.

Masha hid her face.

'Surely you've long known that I love you, Marya Sergievna?'

X

Three weeks after this interview, Kister was sitting alone in his room, writing the following letter to his mother:--

Dearest Mother!--I make haste to share my great happiness with you; I am going to get married. This news will probably only surprise you from my not having, in my previous letters, even hinted at so important a change in my life--and you know that I am used to sharing all my feelings, my joys and my sorrows, with you. My reasons for silence are not easy to explain to you. To begin with, I did not know till lately that I was loved; and on my own side too, it is only lately that I have realised myself all the strength of my own feeling. In one of my first letters from here, I wrote to you of our neighbours, the Perekatovs; I am engaged to their only daughter, Marya. I am thoroughly convinced that we shall both be happy. My feeling for her is not a fleeting passion, but a deep and genuine emotion, in which friendship is mingled with love. Her bright, gentle disposition is in perfect harmony with my tastes. She is well-educated, clever, plays the piano splendidly.... If you could only see her! I enclose her portrait sketched by me. I need hardly say she is a hundred times better-looking than her portrait. Masha loves you already, like a daughter, and is eagerly looking forward to seeing you. I mean to retire, to settle in the country, and to go in for farming. Mr. Perekatov has a property of four hundred serfs in excellent condition. You see that even from the material point of view, you cannot but approve of my plans. I will get leave and come to Moscow and to you. Expect me in a fortnight, not later. My own dearest mother, how happy I am!... Kiss me...' and so on.

Kister folded and sealed the letter, got up, went to the window, lighted a pipe, thought a little, and returned to the table. He took out a small sheet of notepaper, carefully dipped his pen into the ink, but for a long while he did not begin to write, knitted his brows, lifted his eyes to the ceiling, bit the end of his pen.... At last he made up his mind, and in the course of a quarter of an hour he had composed the following:

'Dear Avdey Ivanovitch,--Since the day of your last visit (that is, for three weeks) you have sent me no message, have not said a word to me, and have seemed to avoid meeting me. Every one is, undoubtedly, free to act as he pleases; you have chosen to break off our acquaintance, and I do not, believe me, in addressing you intend to reproach you in any way. It is not my intention or my habit to force myself upon any one whatever; it is enough for me to feel that I am not to blame in the matter. I am writing to you now from a feeling of duty. I have made an offer to Marya Sergievna Perekatov, and have been accepted by her, and also by her parents. I inform *you* of this fact--directly and immediately--to avoid any kind of misapprehension or suspicion. I frankly confess, sir, that I am unable to feel great concern about the good opinion of a man who himself shows so little concern for the opinions and feelings of other people, and I am writing to you solely because I do not care in this matter even to appear to have acted or to be acting underhandedly. I make bold to say, you know me, and will not ascribe my present action to any other lower motive. Addressing you for the last time, I cannot, for the sake of our old friendship, refrain from wishing you all good things possible on earth.--I remain, sincerely, your obedient servant, Fyodor Kister.'

Fyodor Fedoritch despatched this note to the address, changed his uniform, and ordered his carriage to be got ready. Light-hearted and happy, he walked up and down his little room humming, even gave two little skips in the air, twisted a book of songs into a roll, and was tying it up with blue ribbon.... The door opened, and Lutchkov, in a coat without epaulettes, with a cap on his head, came into the room. Kister, astounded, stood still in the middle of the room, without finishing the bow he was tying.

'So you're marrying the Perekatov girl?' queried Avdey in a calm voice.

Kister fired up.

'Sir,' he began; 'decent people take off their caps and say good-morning when they come into another man's room.'

'Beg pardon,' the bully jerked out; and he took off his cap. 'Good-morning.'

'Good-morning, Mr. Lutchkov. You ask me if I am about to marry Miss Perekatov? Haven't you read my letter, then?'

'I have read your letter. You're going to get married. I congratulate you.'

'I accept your congratulation, and thank you for it. But I must be starting.'

'I should like to have a few words of explanation with you, Fyodor Fedoritch.'

'By all means, with pleasure,' responded the good-natured fellow. 'I must own I was expecting such an explanation. Your behaviour to me has been so strange, and I think, on my side, I have not deserved... at least, I had no reason to expect... But won't you sit down? Wouldn't you like a pipe?'

Lutchkov sat down. There was a certain weariness perceptible in his movements. He stroked his moustaches and lifted his eyebrows.

'I say, Fyodor Fedoritch,' he began at last; 'why did you keep it up with me so long?...'

'How do you mean?'

'Why did you pose as such... a disinterested being, when you were just such another as all the rest of us sinners all the while?'

'I don't understand you.... Can I have wounded you in some way?...'

'You don't understand me... all right. I'll try and speak more plainly. Just tell me, for instance, openly, Have you had a liking for the Perekatov girl all along, or is it a case of sudden passion?'

'I should prefer, Avdey Ivanitch, not to discuss with you my relations with Marya Sergievna,' Kister responded coldly.

'Oh, indeed! As you please. Only you'll kindly allow me to believe that you've been humbugging me.'

Avdey spoke very deliberately and emphatically.

'You can't believe that, Avdey Ivanitch; you know me.'

'I know you?... who knows you? The heart of another is a dark forest, and the best side of goods is always turned uppermost. I know you read German poetry with great feeling and even with tears in your eyes; I know that you've hung various maps on your walls; I know you keep your person clean; that I know,... but beyond that, I know nothing...'

Kister began to lose his temper.

'Allow me to inquire,' he asked at last, 'what is the object of your visit? You have sent no message to me for three weeks, and now you come to me, apparently with the intention of jeering at me. I am not a boy, sir, and I do not allow any one...'

'Mercy on us,' Lutchkov interrupted him; 'mercy on us, Fyodor Fedoritch, who would venture to jeer at you? It's quite the other way; I've come to you with a most humble request, that is, that you'd do me the favour to explain your behaviour to me. Allow me to ask you, wasn't it you who forced me to make the acquaintance of the Perekatov family? Didn't you assure your humble servant that it would make his soul blossom into flower? And lastly, didn't you throw me with the virtuous Marya Sergievna? Why am I not to presume that it's to **you** I'm indebted for that final agreeable scene, of which you have doubtless been informed in befitting fashion? An engaged girl, of course, tells her betrothed of everything, especially of her **innocent** indiscretions. How can I help supposing that it's thanks to you I've been made such a terrific fool of? You took such a mighty interest in my "blossoming out," you know!'

Kister walked up and down the room.

'Look here, Lutchkov,' he said at last; 'if you really--joking apart--are convinced of what you say, which I confess I don't believe, then let me tell you, it's shameful and wicked of you to put such an insulting construction on my conduct and intentions. I don't want to justify myself... I appeal to your own conscience, to your memory.'

'Yes; I remember you were continually whispering with Marya Sergievna. Besides that, let me ask you another question: Weren't you at the Perekatovs' after a certain conversation with me, after that evening when I like a fool chattered to you, thinking you my greatest friend, of the meeting she'd arranged?'

'What! you suspect me...'

'I suspect other people of nothing,' Avdey cut him short with cutting iciness, 'of which I would not suspect myself; but I have the weakness to suppose that other men are no better than I am.'

'You are mistaken,' Kister retorted emphatically; 'other men are better than you.'

'I congratulate them upon it,' Lutchkov dropped carelessly; 'but...'

'But remember,' broke in Kister, now in his turn thoroughly infuriated, 'in what terms you spoke of... of that meeting... of... But these explanations are leading to nothing, I see.... Think what you choose of me, and act as you think best.'

'Come, that's better,' observed Avdey. 'At last you're beginning to speak plainly.'

'As you think best,' repeated Kister.

'I understand your position, Fyodor Fedoritch,' Avdey went on with an affectation of sympathy; 'it's disagreeable, certainly. A man has been acting, acting a part, and no one has recognised him as a humbug; and all of a sudden...'

'If I could believe,' Kister interrupted, setting his teeth, 'that it was wounded love that makes you talk like this, I should feel sorry for you; I could excuse you.... But in your abuse, in your false charges, I hear nothing but the shriek of mortified pride... and I feel no sympathy for you.... You have deserved what you've got.'

'Ugh, mercy on us, how the fellow talks!' Avdey murmured. 'Pride,' he went on; 'may be; yes, yes, my pride, as you say, has been mortified intensely and insufferably. But who isn't proud? Aren't you? Yes, I'm proud, and for instance, I permit no one to feel sorry for me....'

'You don't permit it!' Kister retorted haughtily. 'What an expression, sir! Don't forget, the tie between us you yourself have broken. I must beg you to behave with me as with a complete outsider.'

'Broken! Broken the tie between us!' repeated Avdey. 'Understand me; I have sent you no message, and have not been to see you because I was sorry for you; you must allow me to be sorry for you, since you 're sorry for me!... I didn't want to put you in a false position, to make your conscience prick.... You talk of a tie between us... as though you could remain my friend as before your marriage! Rubbish! Why, you were only friendly with me before to gloat over your fancied superiority...'

Avdey's duplicity overwhelmed, confounded Kister.

'Let us end this unpleasant conversation!' he cried at last. 'I must own I don't see why you've been pleased to come to me.'

'You don't see what I've come to you for?' Avdey asked inquiringly.

'I certainly don't see why.'

'N--o?'

'No, I tell you...'

'Astonishing!... This is astonishing! Who'd have thought it of a fellow of your intelligence!'

'Come, speak plainly...'

'I have come, Mr. Kister,' said Avdey, slowly rising to his feet, 'I have come to challenge you to a duel. Do you understand now? I want to fight you. Ah! you thought you could get rid of me like that! Why, didn't you know the sort of man you have to do with? As if I'd allow...'

'Very good,' Kister cut in coldly and abruptly. 'I accept your challenge. Kindly send me your second.'

'Yes, yes,' pursued Avdey, who, like a cat, could not bear to let his victim go so soon: 'it'll give me great pleasure I'll own to put a bullet into your fair and idealistic countenance to-morrow.'

'You are abusive after a challenge, it seems,' Kister rejoined contemptuously. 'Be so good as to go. I'm ashamed of you.'

'Oh, to be sure, **delicatesse**!... Ah, Marya Sergievna, I don't know French!' growled Avdey, as he put on his cap. 'Till we meet again, Fyodor Fedoritch!'

He bowed and walked out.

Kister paced several times up and down the room. His face burned, his breast heaved violently. He felt neither fear nor anger; but it sickened him to think what this man really was that he had once looked upon as a friend. The idea of the duel with Lutchkov was almost pleasant to him.... Once get free from the past, leap over this rock in his path, and then to float on an untroubled tide... 'Good,' he thought, 'I shall be fighting to win my happiness.' Masha's image seemed to smile to him, to promise him success. 'I'm not going to be killed! not I!' he repeated with a serene smile. On the table lay the letter to his mother.... He felt a momentary pang at his heart. He resolved any way to defer sending it off. There was in Kister that quickening of the vital energies of which a man is aware in face of danger. He calmly thought over all the possible results of the duel, mentally placed Masha and himself in all the agonies of misery and parting, and looked forward to the future with hope. He swore to himself not to kill Lutchkov... He felt irresistibly drawn to Masha. He paused a second, hurriedly arranged things, and directly after dinner set off to the Perekatovs. All the evening Kister was in good spirits, perhaps in too good spirits.

Masha played a great deal on the piano, felt no foreboding of evil, and flirted charmingly with him. At first her unconsciousness wounded him, then he took Masha's very unconsciousness as a happy omen, and was rejoiced and reassured by it. She had grown fonder and fonder of him every day; happiness was for her a much more urgent need than passion. Besides, Avdey had turned her from all exaggerated desires, and she renounced them joyfully and for ever. Nenila Makarievna loved Kister like a son. Sergei Sergeitch as usual followed his wife's lead.

'Till we meet,' Masha said to Kister, following him into the hall and gazing at him with a soft smile, as he slowly and tenderly kissed her hands.

'Till we meet,' Fyodor Fedoritch repeated confidently; 'till we meet.'

But when he had driven half a mile from the Perekatovs' house, he stood up in the carriage, and with vague uneasiness began looking for the lighted windows.... All in the house was dark as in the tomb.

XI

Next day at eleven o'clock in the morning Kister's second, an old major of tried merit, came for him. The good old man growled to himself, bit his grey moustaches, and wished Avdey Ivanovitch everything unpleasant.... The carriage was brought to the door. Kister handed the major two letters, one for his mother, the other for Masha.

'What's this for?'

'Well, one can never tell...'

'Nonsense! we'll shoot him like a partridge...'

'Any way it's better...'

The major with vexation stuffed the two letters in the side pocket of his coat.

'Let us start.'

They set off. In a small copse, a mile and a half from the village of Kirilovo, Lutchkov was awaiting them with his former friend, the perfumed adjutant. It was lovely weather, the birds were twittering peacefully; not far from the copse a peasant was tilling the ground. While the seconds were marking out the distance, fixing the barrier, examining and loading the pistols, the opponents did not even glance at one another.... Kister walked to and fro with a careless air, swinging a flower he had gathered; Avdey stood motionless, with folded arms and scowling brow. The decisive moment arrived. 'Begin, gentlemen!' Kister went rapidly towards the barrier, but he had not gone five steps before Avdey fired, Kister started, made one more step forward, staggered. His head sank... His knees bent under him... He fell like a sack on the grass. The major rushed up to him.... 'Is it possible?' whispered the dying man.

Avdey went up to the man he had killed. On his gloomy and sunken face was a look of savage, exasperated regret.... He looked at the adjutant and the major, bent his head like a guilty man, got on his horse without a word, and rode slowly straight to the colonel's quarters.

Masha... is living to this day.

THREE PORTRAITS

Neighbours' constitute one of the most serious drawbacks of life in the country. I knew a country gentleman of the Vologodsky district, who used on every suitable occasion to repeat the following words, 'Thank God, I have no neighbours,' and I confess I could not help envying that happy mortal. My own little place is situated in one of the most thickly peopled provinces of Russia. I am surrounded by a vast number of dear neighbours, from highly respectable and highly respected country gentlemen, attired in ample frock-coats and still more ample waistcoats, down to regular loafers, wearing jackets with long sleeves and a so-called shooting-bag on their back. In this crowd of gentlefolks I chanced, however, to discover one very pleasant fellow. He had served in the army, had retired and settled for good and all in the country. According to his story, he had served for two years in the B------ regiment. But I am totally unable to comprehend how that man could have performed any sort of duty, not merely for two years, but even for two days. He was born 'for a life of peace and country calm,' that is to say, for lazy, careless vegetation, which, I note parenthetically, is not without great and inexhaustible charms. He possessed a very fair property, and without giving too much thought to its management, spent about ten thousand roubles a year, had obtained an excellent cook--my friend was fond of good fare--and ordered too from Moscow all the newest French books and magazines. In Russian he read nothing but the reports of his bailiff, and that with great difficulty. He used, when he did not go out shooting, to wear a dressing-gown from morning till dinner-time and at dinner. He would look through plans of some sort, or go round to the stables or to the threshing barn, and joke with the peasant women, who, to be sure, in his presence wielded their flails in leisurely fashion. After dinner my friend would dress very carefully before the looking-glass, and drive off to see some neighbour possessed of two or three pretty daughters. He would flirt serenely and unconcernedly with one of them, play blind-man's-buff with them, return home rather late and promptly fall into a heroic sleep. He could never be bored, for he never gave himself up to complete inactivity; and in the choice of occupations he was not difficult to please, and was amused like a child with the smallest trifle. On the other hand, he cherished no particular attachment to life, and at times, when he chanced to get a glimpse of the track of a wolf or a fox, he would let his horse go at full gallop over such ravines that to this day I cannot understand how it was he did not break his neck a hundred times over. He belonged to that class of persons who inspire in one the idea that they do not know their own value, that under their appearance of indifference strong and violent passions lie concealed. But he would have laughed in one's face if he could have guessed that one cherished such an opinion of him. And indeed I must own I believe myself that even supposing my friend had had in youth some strong impulse, however vague, towards what is so sweetly called 'higher things,' that impulse had long, long ago died out. He was rather stout and enjoyed superb health. In our day one cannot help liking people who think little about themselves, because they are exceedingly rare... and my friend had almost forgotten his own personality. I fancy, though, that I have said too much about him already, and my prolixity is the more uncalled for as he is not the hero of my story. His name was Piotr Fedorovitch Lutchinov.

One autumn day there were five of us, ardent sportsmen, gathered together at Piotr Fedorovitch's. We had spent the whole morning out, had run down a couple of foxes and a number of hares, and had returned home in that supremely agreeable frame of mind which comes over every well-regulated person after a successful day's shooting. It grew dusk. The wind was frolicking over the dark fields and noisily swinging the bare tops of the birches and lime-trees round Lutchinov's house. We reached the house, got off our horses.... On the steps I stood still and looked round: long storm-clouds were creeping heavily over the grey sky; a dark-brown bush was writhing in the wind, and murmuring plaintively; the yellow grass helplessly and forlornly bowed down to the earth; flocks of thrushes were fluttering in the mountain-ashes among the bright, flame-coloured clusters of berries. Among the light brittle twigs of the birch-trees blue-tits hopped whistling. In the village there was the hoarse barking of dogs. I felt melancholy... but it was with a genuine sense of comfort that I walked into the dining-room. The shutters were closed; on a round table, covered with a tablecloth of dazzling whiteness, amid cut-glass decanters of red wine, there were eight lighted candles in silver candlesticks; a fire glowed cheerfully on the hearth, and an old and very stately-looking butler, with a huge bald head, wearing an English dress, stood before another table on which was pleasingly conspicuous a large soup-tureen, encircled by light savoury-smelling steam. In the hall we passed by another venerable man, engaged in icing champagne-- 'according to the strictest rules of the art.' The dinner was, as is usual in such cases, exceedingly pleasant. We laughed and talked of the incidents of the day's shooting, and recalled with enthusiasm two glorious 'runs.' After dining pretty heartily, we settled comfortably into ample arm-chairs round the fire; a huge silver bowl made its appearance on the table, and in a few minutes the white flame of the burning rum announced our host's agreeable intention 'to concoct a punch.' Piotr Fedoritch was a man of some taste; he was aware, for instance, that nothing has so fatal an influence on the fancy as the cold, steady, pedantic light of a lamp, and so he gave orders that only two candles should be left in the room. Strange half-shadows quivered on the walls, thrown by the fanciful play of the fire in the hearth and the flame of the punch... a soft, exceedingly agreeable sense of soothing comfort replaced in our hearts the somewhat boisterous gaiety that had reigned at dinner.

Conversations have their destinies, like books, as the Latin proverb says, like everything in the world. Our conversation that evening was particularly many-sided and lively. From details it passed to rather serious general questions, and lightly and casually came back to the daily incidents of life.... After chatting a good deal, we suddenly all sank into silence. At such times they say an angel of peace is flying over.

I cannot say why my companions were silent, but I held my tongue because my eyes had suddenly come to rest on three dusty portraits in black wooden frames. The colours were rubbed and cracked in places, but one could still make out the faces. The portrait in the centre was that of a young woman in a white gown with lace ruffles, her hair done up high, in the style of the eighties of last century. On her right, upon a perfectly black background, there stood out the full, round face of a good-natured country gentleman of five-and-twenty, with a broad, low brow, a thick nose, and a good-humoured smile. The French powdered coiffure was utterly out of keeping with the expression of his Slavonic face. The artist had portrayed him wearing a long loose coat of crimson colour with large paste buttons; in his hand he was holding some unlikely-looking flower. The third portrait, which was the work of some other more skilful hand, represented a man of thirty, in the green uniform, with red facings, of the time of Catherine, in a white shirt, with a fine cambric cravat. One hand leaned on a gold-headed cane, the other lay on his shirt front. His dark, thinnish face was full of insolent haughtiness. The fine long eyebrows almost grew together over the pitch-black eyes, about the thin, scarcely discernible lips played an evil smile.

'Why do you keep staring at those faces?' Piotr Fedoritch asked me.

'Oh, I don't know!' I answered, looking at him.

'Would you care to hear a whole story about those three persons?'

'Oh, please tell it,' we all responded with one voice.

Piotr Fedoritch got up, took a candle, carried it to the portraits, and in the tone of a showman at a wild beast show, 'Gentlemen!' he boomed, 'this lady was the adopted child of my great-grandfather, Olga Ivanovna N.N., called Lutchinov, who died forty years ago unmarried. This gentleman,' he pointed to the portrait of a man in uniform, 'served as a lieutenant in the Guards, Vassily Ivanovitch Lutchinov, expired by the will of God in the year seventeen hundred and ninety. And this gentleman, to whom I have not the honour of being related, is a certain Pavel Afanasiitch Rogatchov, serving nowhere, as far as I'm aware.... Kindly take note of the hole in his breast, just on the spot where the heart should be. That hole, you see, a regular three-sided hole, would be hardly likely to have come there by chance.... Now, 'he went on in his usual voice, 'kindly seat yourselves, arm yourselves with patience, and listen.'

Gentlemen! (he began) I come of a rather old family. I am not proud of my descent, seeing that my ancestors were all fearful prodigals. Though that reproach cannot indeed be made against my great-grandfather, Ivan Andreevitch Lutchinov; on the contrary, he had the character of being excessively careful, even miserly--at any rate, in the latter years of his life. He spent his youth in Petersburg, and lived through the reign of Elizabeth. In Petersburg he married, and had by his wife, my great-grandmother, four children, three sons, Vassily, Ivan, and Pavel, my grandfather, and one daughter, Natalia. In addition, Ivan Andreevitch took into his family the daughter of a distant relation, a nameless and destitute orphan--Olga Ivanovna, of whom I spoke just now. My great-grandfather's serfs were probably aware of his existence, for they used (when nothing particularly unlucky occurred) to send him a trifling rent, but they had never seen his face. The village of Lutchinovka, deprived of the bodily presence of its lord, was flourishing exceedingly, when all of a sudden one fine morning a cumbrous old family coach drove into the village and stopped before the elder's hut. The peasants, alarmed at such an unheard-of occurrence, ran up and saw their master and mistress and all their young ones, except the eldest, Vassily, who was left behind in Petersburg. From that memorable day down to the very day of his death, Ivan Andreevitch never left Lutchinovka. He built himself a house, the very house in which I have the pleasure of conversing with you at this moment. He built a church too, and began living the life of a country gentleman. Ivan Andreevitch was a man of immense height, thin, silent, and very deliberate in all his movements. He never wore a dressing-gown, and no one but his valet had ever seen him without powder. Ivan Andreevitch usually walked with his hands clasped behind his back, turning his head at each step. Every day he used to walk in a long avenue of lime-trees, which he had planted with his own hand; and before his death he had the pleasure of enjoying the shade of those trees. Ivan Andreevitch was exceedingly sparing of his words; a proof of his taciturnity is to be found in the remarkable fact that in the course of twenty years he had not said a single word to his wife, Anna Pavlovna. His relations with Anna Pavlovna altogether were of a very curious sort. She directed the whole management of the household; at dinner she always sat beside her husband--he would mercilessly have chastised any one who had dared to say a disrespectful word to her--and yet he never spoke to her, never touched her hand. Anna Pavlovna was a pale, broken-spirited woman, completely crushed. She prayed every day on her knees in church, and she never smiled. There was a rumour that they had formerly, that is, before they came into the country, lived on very cordial terms with one another. They did say too that Anna Pavlovna had been untrue to her matrimonial vows; that her conduct had come to her husband's knowledge.... Be that as it may, any way Ivan Andreevitch, even when dying, was not reconciled to her. During his last illness, she never left him; but he seemed not to notice her. One night, Anna Pavlovna was sitting in Ivan Andreevitch's bedroom--he suffered from sleeplessness--a lamp was burning before the holy picture. My grandfather's servant, Yuditch, of whom I shall have to say a few words later, went out of the room. Anna Pavlovna got up, crossed the room, and sobbing flung herself on her knees at her husband's bedside, tried to say something--stretched out her hands... Ivan Andreevitch looked at her, and in a faint voice, but resolutely, called, 'Boy!' The servant went in; Anna Pavlovna hurriedly rose, and went back, tottering, to her place.

Ivan Andreevitch's children were exceedingly afraid of him. They grew up in the country, and were witnesses of Ivan Andreevitch's strange treatment of his wife. They all loved Anna Pavlovna passionately, but did not dare to show their love. She seemed of herself to hold aloof from them.... You remember my grandfather, gentlemen; to the day of his death he always walked on tiptoe, and spoke in a whisper... such is the force of habit! My grandfather and his brother, Ivan Ivanovitch, were simple, good-hearted people, quiet and depressed. My grand'tante Natalia married, as you are aware, a coarse, dull-witted man, and all her life she cherished an unutterable, slavish, sheep-like passion for him. But their brother Vassily was not of that sort. I believe I said that Ivan Andreevitch had left him in Petersburg. He was then twelve. His father confided him to the care of a distant kinsman, a man no longer young, a bachelor, and a terrible Voltairean.

Vassily grew up and went into the army. He was not tall, but was well-built and exceedingly elegant; he spoke French excellently, and was renowned for his skilful swordsmanship. He was considered one of the most brilliant young men of the beginning of the reign of Catherine. My father used often to tell me that he had known more than one old lady who could not refer to Vassily Ivanovitch Lutchinov without heartfelt emotion. Picture to yourselves a man endowed with exceptional strength of will, passionate and calculating, persevering and daring, reserved in the extreme, and--according to the testimony of all his contemporaries--fascinatingly, captivatingly attractive. He had no conscience, no heart, no principle, though no one could have called him positively a bad-hearted man. He was vain, but knew how to disguise his vanity, and passionately cherished his independence. When Vassily Ivanovitch would half close his black eyes, smiling affectionately, when he wanted to fascinate any one, they say it was impossible to resist him; and even people, thoroughly convinced of the coldness and hardness of his heart, were more than once vanquished by the bewitching power of his personal influence. He served his own interests devotedly, and made other people, too, work for his advantage; and he was always successful in everything, because he never lost his head, never disdained using flattery as a means, and well understood how to use it.

Ten years after Ivan Andreevitch had settled in the country, he came for a four months' visit to Lutchinovka, a brilliant officer of the Guards, and in that time succeeded positively in turning the head of the grim old man, his father. Strange to say, Ivan Andreevitch listened with enjoyment to his son's stories of some of his *conquests*. His brothers were speechless in his presence, and admired him as a being of a higher order. And Anna Pavlovna herself became almost fonder of him than any of her other children who were so sincerely devoted to her.

Vassily Ivanovitch had come down into the country primarily to visit his people, but also with the second object of getting as much money as possible from his father. He lived sumptuously in the glare of publicity in Petersburg, and had made a mass of debts. He had no easy task to get round his father's miserliness, and though Ivan Andreevitch gave him on this one visit probably far more money than he gave all his other children together during twenty years spent under his roof, Vassily followed the well-known Russian rule, 'Get what you can!'

Ivan Andreevitch had a servant called Yuditch, just such another tall, thin, taciturn person as his master. They say that this man Yuditch was partly responsible for Ivan Andreevitch's strange behaviour with Anna Pavlovna; they say he discovered my great-grandmother's guilty intrigue with one of my great-grandfather's dearest friends. Most likely Yuditch deeply regretted his ill-timed jealousy, for it would be difficult to conceive a more kind-hearted man. His memory is held in veneration by all my house-serfs to this day. My great-grandfather put unbounded confidence in Yuditch. In those days landowners used to have money, but did not put it into the keeping of banks, they kept it themselves in chests, under their floors, and so on. Ivan Andreevitch kept all his money in a great wrought-iron coffer, which stood under the head of his bed. The key of this coffer was intrusted to Yuditch. Every evening as he went to bed Ivan Andreevitch used to bid him open the coffer in his presence, used to tap in turn each of the tightly filled bags with a stick, and every Saturday he would untie the bags with Yuditch, and carefully count over the money. Vassily heard of all these doings, and burned with eagerness to overhaul the sacred coffer. In the course of five or six days he had *softened* Yuditch, that is, he had worked on the old man till, as they say, he worshipped the ground his young master trod on. Having thus duly prepared him, Vassily put on a careworn and gloomy air, for a long while refused to answer Yuditch's questions, and at last told him that he had lost at play, and should make an end of himself if he could not get money somehow. Yuditch broke into sobs, flung himself on his knees before him, begged him to think of God, not to be his own ruin. Vassily locked himself in his room without uttering a word. A little while after he heard some one cautiously knocking at his door; he opened it, and saw in the doorway Yuditch pale and trembling, with the key in his hand. Vassily took in the whole position at a glance. At first, for a long while, he refused to take it. With tears Yuditch repeated, 'Take it, your honour, graciously take it!'... Vassily at last agreed. This took place on Monday. The idea occurred to Vassily to replace the money taken out with broken bits of crockery. He reckoned on Ivan Andreevitch's tapping the bags with his stick, and not noticing the hardly perceptible difference in the sound, and by Saturday he hoped to obtain and to replace the sum in the coffer. As he planned, so he did. His father did not, in fact, notice anything. But by Saturday Vassily had not procured the money; he had hoped to win the sum from a rich neighbour at cards, and instead of that, he lost it all. Meantime, Saturday had come; it came at last to the turn of the bags filled with broken crocks. Picture, gentlemen, the amazement of Ivan Andreevitch!

'What does this mean?' he thundered. Yuditch was silent.

'You stole the money?'

'No, sir.'

'Then some one took the key from you?'

'I didn't give the key to any one.'

'Not to any one? Well then, you are the thief. Confess!'

'I am not a thief, Ivan Andreevitch.'

'Where the devil did these potsherds come from then? So you're deceiving me! For the last time I tell you--confess!' Yuditch bowed his head and folded his hands behind his back.

'Hi, lads!' shrieked Ivan Andreevitch in a voice of frenzy. 'A stick!'

'What, beat... me?' murmured Yuditch.

'Yes, indeed! Are you any better than the rest? You are a thief! O Yuditch! I never expected such dishonesty of you!'

'I have grown grey in your service, Ivan Andreevitch,' Yuditch articulated with effort.

'What have I to do with your grey hairs? Damn you and your service!'

The servants came in.

'Take him, do, and give it him thoroughly.' Ivan Andreevitch's lips were white and twitching. He walked up and down the room like a wild beast in a small cage.

The servants did not dare to carry out his orders.

'Why are you standing still, children of Ham? Am I to undertake him myself, eh?'

Yuditch was moving towards the door....

'Stay!' screamed Ivan Andreevitch. 'Yuditch, for the last time I tell you, I beg you, Yuditch, confess!'

'I can't!' moaned Yuditch.

'Then take him, the sly old fox! Flog him to death! His blood be on my head!' thundered the infuriated old man. The flogging began.... The door suddenly opened, and Vassily came in. He was almost paler than his father, his hands were shaking, his upper lip was lifted, and laid bare a row of even, white teeth.

'I am to blame,' he said in a thick but resolute voice. 'I took the money.'

The servants stopped.

'You! what? you, Vaska! without Yuditch's consent?'

'No!' said Yuditch, 'with my consent. I gave Vassily Ivanovitch the key of my own accord. Your honour, Vassily Ivanovitch! why does your honour trouble?'

'So this is the thief!' shrieked Ivan Andreevitch. 'Thanks, Vassily, thanks! But, Yuditch, I'm not going to forgive you anyway. Why didn't you tell me all about it directly? Hey, you there! why are you standing still? do you too resist my authority? Ah, I'll settle things with you, my pretty gentleman!' he added, turning to Vassily.

The servants were again laying hands on Yuditch....

'Don't touch him!' murmured Vassily through his teeth. The men did not heed him. 'Back!' he shrieked and rushed upon them.... They stepped back.

'Ah! mutiny!' moaned Ivan Andreevitch, and, raising his stick, he approached his son. Vassily leaped back, snatched at the handle of his sword, and bared it to half its length. Every one was trembling. Anna Pavlovna, attracted by the noise, showed herself at the door, pale and scared.

A terrible change passed over the face of Ivan Andreevitch. He tottered, dropped the stick, and sank heavily into an arm-chair, hiding his face in both hands. No one stirred, all stood rooted to the spot, Vassily like the rest. He clutched the steel sword-handle convulsively, and his eyes glittered with a weary, evil light....

'Go, all of you... all, out,' Ivan Andreevitch brought out in a low voice, not taking his hands from his face.

The whole crowd went out. Vassily stood still in the doorway, then suddenly tossed his head, embraced Yuditch, kissed his mother's hand... and two hours later he had left the place. He went back to Petersburg.

In the evening of the same day Yuditch was sitting on the steps of the house serfs' hut. The servants were all round him, sympathising with him and bitterly reproaching their young master.

'That's enough, lads,' he said to them at last, 'give over... why do you abuse him? He himself, the young master, I dare say is not very happy at his audacity....'

In consequence of this incident, Vassily never saw his father again. Ivan Andreevitch died without him, and died probably with such a load of sorrow on his heart as God grant none of us may ever know. Vassily Ivanovitch, meanwhile, went into the world, enjoyed himself in his own way, and squandered money recklessly. How he got hold of the money, I cannot tell for certain. He had obtained a French servant, a very smart and intelligent fellow, Bourcier, by name. This man was passionately attached to him and aided him in all his numerous manoeuvres. I do not intend to relate in detail all the exploits of my grand-uncle; he was possessed of such unbounded daring, such serpent-like resource, such inconceivable wiliness, such a fine and ready wit, that I must own I can understand the complete sway that unprincipled person exercised even over the noblest natures.

Soon after his father's death, in spite of his wiliness, Vassily Ivanovitch was challenged by an injured husband. He fought a duel, seriously wounded his opponent, and was forced to leave the capital; he was banished to his estate, and forbidden to leave it. Vassily Ivanovitch was thirty years old. You may easily imagine, gentlemen, with what feelings he left the brilliant life in the capital that he was used to, and came into the country. They say that he got out of the hooded cart several times on the road, flung himself face downwards in the snow and cried. No one in Lutchinovka would have known him as the gay and charming Vassily Ivanovitch they had seen before. He did not talk to any one; went out shooting from morning to night; endured his mother's timid caresses with undisguised impatience, and was merciless in his ridicule of his brothers, and of their wives (they were both married by that time)....

I have not so far, I think, told you anything about Olga Ivanovna. She had been brought as a tiny baby to Lutchinovka; she all but died on the road. Olga Iva-novna was brought up, as they say, in the fear of God and her betters. It must be admitted that Ivan Andreevitch and Anna Pavlovna both treated her as a daughter. But there lay hid in her soul a faint spark of that fire which burned so fiercely in Vassily Ivanovitch. While Ivan Andreevitch's own children did not dare even to wonder about the cause of the strange, dumb feud between their parents, Olga was from her earliest years disturbed and tormented by Anna Pavlovna's position. Like Vassily, she loved independence; any restriction fretted her. She was devoted with her whole soul to her benefactress; old Lutchinov she detested, and more than once, sitting at table, she shot such black looks at him, that even the servant handing the dishes felt uncomfortable. Ivan Andreevitch never noticed these glances, for he never took the slightest notice of his family.

At first Anna Pavlovna had tried to eradicate this hatred, but some bold questions of Olga's forced her to complete silence. The children of Ivan Andreevitch adored Olga, and the old lady too was fond of her, but not with a very ardent affection.

Long continued grieving had crushed all cheerfulness and every strong feeling in that poor woman; nothing is so clear a proof of Vassily's captivating charm as that he had made even his mother love him passionately. Demonstrations of tenderness on the part of children were not in the spirit of the age, and so it is not to be wondered at that Olga did not dare to express her devotion, though she always kissed Anna Pavlovna's hand with special reverence, when she said good-night to her. Twenty years later, Russian girls began to read romances of the class of *The Adventures of Marquis Glagol, Fanfan and Lolotta, Alexey or the Cottage in the Forest*; they began to play the clavichord and to sing songs in the style of the once very well-known:

'Men like butterflies in sunshine
Flutter round us opening blossoms,' etc.

But in the seventies of last century (Olga Ivanovna was born in 1757) our country beauties had no notion of such accomplishments. It is difficult for us now to form a clear conception of the Russian miss of those days. We can indeed judge from our grandmothers of the degree of culture of girls of noble family in the time of Catherine; but how is one to distinguish what they had gradually gained in the course of their long lives from what they were in the days of their youth?

Olga Ivanovna spoke French a little, but with a strong Russian accent: in her day there was as yet no talk of French emigrants. In fact, with all her fine qualities, she was still pretty much of a savage, and I dare say in the simplicity of her heart, she had more than once chastised some luckless servant girl with her own hands....

Some time before Vassily Ivanovitch's arrival, Olga Ivanovna had been betrothed to a neighbour, Pavel Afanasievitch Rogatchov, a very good-natured and straightforward fellow. Nature had forgotten to put any spice of ill-temper into his composition. His own serfs did not obey him, and would sometimes all go off, down to the least of them, and leave poor Rogatchov without any dinner... but nothing could trouble the peace of his soul. From his childhood he had been stout and indolent, had never been in the government service, and was fond of going to church and singing in the choir. Look, gentlemen, at this round, good-natured face; glance at this mild, beaming smile... don't you really feel it reassuring, yourselves? His father used at long intervals to drive over to Lutchinovka, and on holidays used to bring with him his Pavlusha, whom the little Lutchinovs teased in every possible way. Pavlusha grew up, began driving over to call on Ivan Andreevitch on his own account, fell in love with Olga Ivanovna, and offered her his hand and heart--not to her personally, but to her benefactors. Her benefactors gave their consent. They never even thought of asking Olga Ivanovna whether she liked Rogatchov. In those days, in the words of my grandmother, 'such refinements were not the thing.' Olga soon got used to her betrothed, however; it was impossible not to feel fond of such a gentle and amiable creature. Rogatchov had received no education whatever; his French consisted of the one word **bonjour**, and he secretly considered even that word improper. But some jocose person had taught him the following lines, as a

French song: 'Sonitchka, Sonitchka! Ke-voole-voo-de-mwa--I adore you--me-je-ne-pyoo-pa....' This supposed song he always used to hum to himself when he felt in good spirits. His father was also a man of incredible good-nature, always wore a long nankin coat, and whatever was said to him he responded with a smile. From the time of Pavel Afanasievitch's betrothal, both the Rogatchovs, father and son, had been tremendously busy. They had been having their house entirely transformed adding various 'galleries,' talking in a friendly way with the workmen, encouraging them with drinks. They had not yet completed all these additions by the winter; they put off the wedding till the summer. In the summer Ivan Andreevitch died; the wedding was deferred till the following spring. In the winter Vassily Ivanovitch arrived. Rogatchov was presented to him; he received him coldly and contemptuously, and as time went on, he, so alarmed him by his haughty behaviour that poor Rogatchov trembled like a leaf at the very sight of him, was tongue-tied and smiled nervously. Vassily once almost annihilated him altogether--by making him a bet, that he, Rogatchov, was not able to stop smiling. Poor Pavel Afanasievitch almost cried with, embarrassment, but--actually!--a smile, a stupid, nervous smile refused to leave his perspiring face! Vassily toyed deliberately with the ends of his neckerchief, and looked at him with supreme contempt. Pavel Afanasievitch's father heard too of Vassily's presence, and after an interval of a few days--'for the sake of greater formality'--he sallied off to Lutchinovka with the object of 'felicitating our honoured guest on his advent to the halls of his ancestors.' Afanasey Lukitch was famed all over the countryside for his eloquence--that is to say, for his capacity for enunciating without faltering a rather long and complicated speech, with a sprinkling of bookish phrases in it. Alas! on this occasion he did not sustain his reputation; he was even more disconcerted than his son, Pavel Afanasievitch; he mumbled something quite inarticulate, and though he had never been used to taking vodka, he at once drained a glass 'to carry things off'--he found Vassily at lunch,--tried at least to clear his throat with some dignity, and did not succeed in making the slightest sound. On their way home, Pavel Afanasievitch whispered to his parent, 'Well, father?' Afanasey Lukitch responded angrily also in a whisper, 'Don't speak of it!'

The Rogatchovs began to be less frequent visitors at Lutchinovka. Though indeed they were not the only people intimidated by Vassily; he awakened in his own brothers, in their wives, in Anna Pavlovna herself, an instinctive feeling of uneasiness and discomfort... they tried to avoid him in every way they could. Vassily must have noticed this, but apparently had no intention of altering his behaviour to them. Suddenly, at the beginning of the spring, he became once more the charming, attractive person they had known of old...

The first symptom of this sudden transformation was Vassily's unexpected visit to the Rogatchovs. Afanasey Lukitch, in particular, was fairly disconcerted at the sight of Lutchinov's carriage, but his dismay very quickly vanished. Never had Vassily been more courteous and delightful. He took young Rogatchov by the arm, went with him to look at the new buildings, talked to the carpenters, made some suggestions, with his own hands chopped a few chips off with the axe, asked to be shown Afanasey Lukitch's stud horses, himself trotted them out on a halter, and altogether so affected the good-hearted children of the steppes by his gracious affability that they both embraced him more than once. At home, too, Vassily managed, in the course of a few days, to turn every one's head just as before. He contrived all sorts of laughable games, got hold of musicians, invited the ladies and gentlemen of the neighbourhood, told the old ladies the scandals of the town in the most amusing way, flirted a little with the young ones, invented unheard-of diversions, fireworks and such things, in short, he put life into every thing and every one. The melancholy, gloomy house of the Lutchinovs was suddenly converted into a noisy, brilliant, enchanted palace of which the whole countryside was talking. This sudden transformation surprised many and delighted all. All sorts of rumours began to be whispered about. Sagacious persons opined that Vassily Ivanovitch had till then been crushed under the weight of some secret trouble, that he saw chances of returning to the capital... but the true cause of Vassily Ivanovitch's metamorphosis was guessed by no one.

Olga Ivanovna, gentlemen, was rather pretty; though her beauty consisted rather in the extraordinary softness and freshness of her shape, in the quiet grace of her movements than in the strict regularity of her features. Nature had bestowed on her a certain independence; her bringing up--she had grown up without father or mother--had developed in her reserve and determination. Olga did not belong to the class of quiet and tame-spirited young ladies; but only one feeling had reached its full possibilities in her as yet--hatred for her benefactor. Other more feminine passions might indeed flare up in Olga Ivanovna's heart with abnormal and painful violence... but she had not the cold pride, nor the intense strength of will, nor the self-centred egoism, without which any passion passes quickly away.

The first rush of feeling in such half-active, half-passive natures is sometimes extremely violent; but they give way very quickly, especially when it is a question of relentless conformity with accepted principles; they are afraid of consequences.... And yet, gentlemen, I will frankly confess, women of that sort always make the strongest impression on me. ... (At these words the speaker drank a glass of water. Rubbish! rubbish! thought I, looking at his round chin; nothing in the world makes a strong impression on you, my dear fellow!)

Piotr Fedoritch resumed: Gentlemen, I believe in blood, in race. Olga Ivanovna had more blood than, for instance, her foster sister, Natalia. How did this blood show itself, do you ask? Why, in everything; in the lines of her hands, in her lips, in the sound of her voice, in her glance, in her carriage, in her hair, in the very folds of her gown. In all these trifles there lay hid something special, though I am bound to admit that the--how can one express it?--*la distinction*, which had fallen to Olga Pavlovna's share would not have attracted Vassily's notice had he met her in Petersburg. But in the country, in the wilds, she not only caught his attention, she was positively the sole cause of the transformation of which I have just been speaking.

Consider the position. Vassily Ivanovitch liked to enjoy life; he could not but be bored in the country; his brothers were good-natured fellows, but extremely limited people: he had nothing in common with them. His sister, Natalia, with the assistance of her husband, had brought into the world in the course of three years no less than four babies; between her and Vassily was a perfect gulf.... Anna Pavlovna went to church, prayed, fasted, and was preparing herself for death. There remained only Olga--a fresh, shy, pretty girl.... Vassily did not notice her at first... indeed, who does notice a dependant, an orphan girl kept from charity in the house?... One day, at the very beginning of spring, Vassily was walking about the garden, and with his cane slashing off the heads of the dandelions, those stupid yellow flowers, which come out first in such numbers in the meadows, as soon as they begin to grow green. He was walking in the garden in front of the house; he lifted his head, and caught sight of Olga Ivanovna.

She was sitting sideways at the window, dreamily stroking a tabby kitten, who, purring and blinking, nestled on her lap, and with great satisfaction held up her little nose into the rather hot spring sunshine. Olga Ivanovna was wearing a white morning gown, with short sleeves; her bare, pale-pink, girlish shoulders and arms were a picture of freshness and health. A little red cap discreetly restrained her thick, soft, silky curls. Her face was a little flushed; she was only just awake. Her slender, flexible neck bent forward so charmingly; there was such seductive negligence, such modesty in the restful pose of her figure, free from corsets, that Vassily Ivanovitch (a great connoisseur!) halted involuntarily and peeped in. It suddenly occurred to him that Olga Ivanovna ought not to be left in her primitive ignorance; that she might with time be turned into a very sweet and charming woman. He stole up to the window, stretched up on tiptoe, and imprinted a silent kiss on Olga Ivanovna's smooth, white arm, a little below the elbow.

Olga shrieked and jumped up, the kitten put its tail in the air and leaped into the garden. Vassily Ivanovitch with a smile kept her by the arm.... Olga flushed all over, to her ears; he began to rally her on her alarm... invited her to come a walk with him. But Olga Ivanovna became suddenly conscious of the negligence of her attire, and 'swifter than the swift red deer' she slipped away into the next room.

The very same day Vassily set off to the Rogatchovs. He was suddenly happy and light-hearted. Vassily was not in love with Olga, no! the word 'love' is not to be used lightly.... He had found an occupation, had set himself a task, and rejoiced with the delight of a man of action. He did not even remember that she was his mother's ward, and another man's betrothed. He never for one instant deceived himself; he was fully aware that it was not for her to be his wife.... Possibly there was passion to excuse him--not a very elevated nor noble passion, truly, but still a fairly strong and tormenting passion. Of course he was not in love like a boy; he did not give way to vague ecstasies; he knew very well what he wanted and what he was striving for.

Vassily was a perfect master of the art of winning over, in the shortest time, any one however shy or prejudiced against him. Olga soon ceased to be shy with him. Vassily Ivanovitch led her into a new world. He ordered a clavichord for her, gave her music lessons (he himself played fairly well on the flute), read books aloud to her, had long conversations with her.... The poor child of the steppes soon had her head turned completely. Vassily dominated her entirely. He knew how to tell her of what had been till then unknown to her, and to tell her in a language she could understand. Olga little by little gained courage to express all her feelings to him: he came to her aid, helped her out with the words she could not find, did not alarm her, at one moment kept her back, at another encouraged her confidences.... Vassily busied himself with her education from no disinterested desire to awaken and develop her talents. He simply wanted to draw her a little closer to himself; and he knew too that an innocent, shy, but vain young girl is more easily seduced through the mind than the heart. Even if Olga had been an exceptional being, Vassily would never have perceived it, for he treated her like a child. But as you are aware, gentlemen, there was nothing specially remarkable in Olga. Vassily tried all he could to work on her imagination, and often in the evening she left his side with such a whirl of new images, phrases and ideas in her head that she could not sleep all night, but lay breathing uneasily and turning her burning cheeks from side to side on the cool pillows, or got up, went to the window and gazed fearfully and eagerly into the dark distance. Vassily filled every moment of her life; she could not think of any one else. As for Rogatchov, she soon positively ceased to notice his existence. Vassily had the tact and shrewdness not to talk to Olga in his presence; but he either made him laugh till he was ready to cry, or arranged some noisy entertainment, a riding expedition, a boating party by night with torches and music--he did not in fact let Pavel Afanasievitch have a chance to think clearly.

But in spite of all Vassily Ivanovitch's tact, Rogatchov dimly felt that he, Olga's betrothed and future husband, had somehow become as it were an outsider to her... but in the boundless goodness of his heart, he was afraid of wounding her by reproaches, though he sincerely loved her and prized her affection. When left alone with her, he did not know what to say, and only tried all he could to follow her wishes. Two months passed by. Every trace of self-reliance, of will, disappeared at last in Olga. Rogatchov, feeble and tongue-tied, could be no support to her. She had no wish even to resist the enchantment, and with a sinking heart she surrendered unconditionally to Vassily....

Olga Ivanovna may very likely then have known something of the bliss of love; but it was not for long. Though Vassily--for lack of other occupation--did not drop her, and even attached himself to her and looked after her fondly, Olga herself was so utterly distraught that she found no happiness even in love and yet could not tear herself away from Vassily. She began to be frightened at everything, did not dare to think, could talk of nothing, gave up reading, and was devoured by misery.

Sometimes Vassily succeeded in carrying her along with him and making her forget everything and every one. But the very next day he would find her pale, speechless, with icy hands, and a fixed smile on her lips.... There followed a time of some difficulty for Vassily; but no difficulties could dismay him. He concentrated himself like a skilled gambler. He could not in the least rely upon Olga Ivanovna; she was continually betraying herself, turning pale, blushing, weeping... her new part was utterly beyond her powers. Vassily toiled for two: in his restless and boisterous gaiety, only an experienced observer could have detected something strained and feverish. He played his brothers, sisters, the Rogatchovs, the neighbours, like pawns at chess. He was everlastingly on the alert. Not a single glance, a single movement, was lost on him, yet he appeared the most heedless of men. Every morning he faced the fray, and every evening he scored a victory. He was not the least oppressed by such a fearful strain of activity. He slept four hours out of the twenty-four, ate very little, and was healthy, fresh, and good-humoured.

Meantime the wedding-day was approaching. Vassily succeeded in persuading Pavel Afanasievitch himself of the necessity of delay. Then he despatched him to Moscow to make various purchases, while he was himself in correspondence with friends in Petersburg. He took all this trouble, not so much from sympathy for Olga Ivanovna, as from a natural bent and liking for bustle and agitation.... Besides, he was beginning to be sick of Olga Ivanovna, and more than once after a violent outbreak of passion for her, he would look at her, as he sometimes did at Rogatchov. Lutchinov always remained a riddle to every one. In the coldness of his relentless soul you felt the presence of a strange almost southern fire, and even in the wildest glow of passion a breath of icy chill seemed to come from the man.

Before other people he supported Olga Ivanovna as before. But when they were alone, he played with her like a cat with a mouse, or frightened her with sophistries, or was wearily, malignantly bored, or again flung himself at her feet, swept her away, like a straw in a hurricane... and there was no feigning at such moments in his passion... he really was moved himself.

One day, rather late in the evening, Vassily was sitting alone in his room, attentively reading over the last letters he had received from Petersburg, when suddenly he heard a faint creak at the door, and Olga Ivanovna's maid, Palashka, came in.

'What do you want?' Vassily asked her rather crossly.

'My mistress begs you to come to her.'

'I can't just now. Go along.... Well what are you standing there for?' he went on, seeing that Palashka did not go away.

'My mistress told me to say that she very particularly wants to see you,' she said.

'Why, what's the matter?'

'Would your honour please to see for yourself....'

Vassily got up, angrily flung the letters into a drawer, and went in to Olga Ivanovna. She was sitting alone in a corner, pale and passive.

'What do you want?' he asked her, not quite politely.

Olga looked at him and closed her eyes.

'What's the matter? what is it, Olga?'

He took her hand.... Olga Ivanovna's hand was cold as ice... She tried to speak... and her voice died away. The poor woman had no possible doubt of her condition left her.

Vassily was a little disconcerted. Olga Ivanovna's room was a couple of steps from Anna Pavlovna's bedroom. Vassily cautiously sat down by Olga, kissed and chafed her hands, comforted her in whispers. She listened to him, and silently, faintly, shuddered. In the doorway stood Palashka, stealthily wiping her eyes. In the next room they heard the heavy, even ticking of the clock, and the breathing of some one asleep. Olga Ivanovna's numbness dissolved at last into tears and stifled sobs. Tears are like a storm; after them one is always calmer. When Olga Ivanovna had quieted down a little, and only sobbed convulsively at intervals, like a child, Vassily knelt before her with caresses and tender promises, soothed her completely, gave her something to drink, put her to bed, and went away. He did not undress all night; wrote two or three letters, burnt two or three papers, took out a gold locket containing the portrait of a black-browed, black-eyed woman with a bold, voluptuous face, scrutinised her features slowly, and walked up and down the room pondering.

Next day, at breakfast, he saw with extreme displeasure poor Olga's red and swollen eyes and pale, agitated face. After breakfast he proposed a stroll in the garden to her. Olga followed Vassily, like a submissive sheep. When two hours afterwards she came in from the garden she quite broke down; she told Anna Pavlovna she was unwell, and went to lie down on her bed. During their walk Vassily had, with a suitable show of remorse, informed her that he was secretly married--he was really as much a bachelor as I am. Olga Ivanovna did not fall into a swoon--people don't fall into swoons except on the stage--but she turned all at once stony, though she herself was so far from hoping to marry Vassily Ivanovitch that she was even afraid to think about it. Vassily had begun to explain to her the inevitableness of her parting from him and marrying Rogatchov. Olga Ivanovna looked at him in dumb horror. Vassily talked in a cool, business-like, practical way, blamed himself, expressed his regret, but concluded all his remarks with the following words: 'There's no going back on the past; we've got to act.'

Olga was utterly overwhelmed; she was filled with terror and shame; a dull, heavy despair came upon her; she longed for death, and waited in agony for Vassily's decision.

'We must confess everything to my mother,' he said to her at last.

Olga turned deadly pale; her knees shook under her.

'Don't be afraid, don't be afraid,' repeated Vassily, 'trust to me, I won't desert you... I will make everything right... rely upon me.'

The poor woman looked at him with love... yes, with love, and deep, but hopeless devotion.

'I will arrange everything, everything,' Vassily said to her at parting... and for the last time he kissed her chilly hands....

Next morning--Olga Ivanovna had only just risen from her bed--her door opened... and Anna Pavlovna appeared in the doorway. She was supported by Vassily. In silence she got as far as an arm-chair, and in silence she sat down. Vassily stood at her side. He looked composed; his brows were knitted and his lips slightly parted. Anna Pavlovna, pale, indignant, angry, tried to speak, but her voice failed her. Olga Ivanovna glanced in horror from her benefactress to her lover, with a terrible sinking at her heart... she fell on her knees with a shriek in the middle of the room, and hid her face in her hands.

'Then it's true... is it true?' murmured Anna Pavlovna, and bent down to her.... 'Answer!' she went on harshly, clutching Olga by the arm.

'Mother!' rang out Vassily's brazen voice, 'you promised me not to be hard on her.'

'I want... confess... confess... is it true? is it true?'

'Mother... remember...' Vassily began deliberately.

This one word moved Anna Pavlovna greatly. She leaned back in her chair, and burst into sobs.

Olga Ivanovna softly raised her head, and would have flung herself at the old lady's feet, but Vassily kept her back, raised her from the ground, and led her to another arm-chair. Anna Pavlovna went on weeping and muttering disconnected words....

'Come, mother,' began Vassily, 'don't torment yourself, the trouble may yet be set right.... If Rogatchov...'

Olga Ivanovna shuddered, and drew herself up.

'If Rogatchov,' pursued Vassily, with a meaning glance at Olga Ivanovna, 'imagines that he can disgrace an honourable family with impunity...'

Olga Ivanovna was overcome with horror.

'In my house,' moaned Anna Pavlovna.

'Calm yourself, mother. He took advantage of her innocence, her youth, he--you wish to say something'--he broke off, seeing that Olga made a movement towards him....

Olga Ivanovna sank back in her chair.

'I will go at once to Rogatchov. I will make him marry her this very day. You may be sure I will not let him make a laughing-stock of us....'

'But... Vassily Ivanovitch... you...' whispered Olga.

He gave her a prolonged, cold stare. She sank into silence again.

'Mother, give me your word not to worry her before I return. Look, she is half dead. And you, too, must rest. Rely upon me; I answer for everything; in any case, wait till I return. I tell you again, don't torture her, or yourself, and trust to me.'

He went to the door and stopped. 'Mother,' said he, 'come with me, leave her alone, I beg of you.'

Anna Pavlovna got up, went up to the holy picture, bowed down to the ground, and slowly followed her son. Olga Ivanovna, without a word or a movement, looked after them.

Vassily turned back quickly, snatched her hand, whispered in her ear, 'Rely on me, and don't betray us,' and at once withdrew.... 'Bourcier!' he called, running swiftly down the stairs, 'Bourcier!'

A quarter of an hour later he was sitting in his carriage with his valet.

That day the elder Rogatchov was not at home. He had gone to the district town to buy cloth for the liveries of his servants. Pavel Afanasievitch was sitting in his own room, looking through a collection of faded butterflies. With lifted eyebrows and protruding lips, he was carefully, with a pin, turning over the fragile wings of a 'night sphinx' moth, when he was suddenly aware of a small but heavy hand on his shoulder. He looked round. Vassily stood before him.

'Good-morning, Vassily Ivanovitch,' he said in some amazement.

Vassily looked at him, and sat down on a chair facing him.

Pavel Afanasievitch was about to smile... but he glanced at Vassily, and subsided with his mouth open and his hands clasped.

'Tell me, Pavel Afanasievitch,' said Vassily suddenly, 'are you meaning to dance at your **wedding soon?**'

'I?... soon... of course... for my part... though as you and your sister ... I, for my part, am ready to-morrow even.'

'Very good, very good. You're a very impatient person, Pavel Afanasievitch.'

'How so?'

'Let me tell you,' pursued Vassily Ivanovitch, getting up, 'I know all; you understand me, and I order you without delay to-morrow to marry Olga.'

'Excuse me, excuse me,' objected Rogatchov, not rising from his seat; 'you order me. I sought Olga Ivanovna's hand of myself and there's no need to give me orders.... I confess, Vassily Ivanovitch, I don't quite understand you.'

'You don't understand me?'

'No, really, I don't understand you.'

'Do you give me your word to marry her to-morrow?'

'Why, mercy on us, Vassily Ivanovitch... haven't you yourself put off our wedding more than once? Except for you it would have taken place long ago. And now I have no idea of breaking it off. What is the meaning of your threats, your insistence?'

Pavel Afanasievitch wiped the sweat off his face.

'Do you give me your word? Say yes or no!' Vassily repeated emphatically.

'Excuse me... I will... but...'

'Very good. Remember then... She has confessed everything.'

'Who has confessed?'

'Olga Ivanovna.'

'Why, what has she confessed?'

'Why, what are you pretending to me for, Pavel Afanasievitch? I'm not a stranger to you.'

'What am I pretending? I don't understand you, I don't, I positively don't understand a word. What could Olga Ivanovna confess?'

'What? You are really too much! You know what.'

'May God slay me...'

'No, I'll slay you, if you don't marry her... do you understand?'

'What!...' Pavel Afanasievitch jumped up and stood facing Vassily. 'Olga Ivanovna... you tell me...'

'You're a clever fellow, you are, I must own'--Vassily with a smile patted him on the shoulder--'though you do look so innocent.'

'Good God!... You'll send me out of my mind.... What do you mean, explain, for God's sake!'

Vassily bent down and whispered something in his ear.

Rogatchov cried out, 'What!...!?'

Vassily stamped.

'Olga Ivanovna? Olga?...'

'Yes... your betrothed...'

'My betrothed... Vassily Ivanovitch... she... she... Why, I never wish to see her again,' cried Pavel Afanasievitch. 'Good-bye to her for ever! What do you take me for? I'm being duped... I'm being duped... Olga Ivanovna, how wrong of you, have you no shame?...' (Tears gushed from his eyes.) 'Thanks, Vassily Ivanovitch, thanks very much... I never wish to see her again now! no! no! don't speak of her.... Ah, merciful Heavens! to think I have lived to see this! Oh, very well, very well!'

'That's enough nonsense,' Vassily Ivanovitch observed coldly. 'Remember, you've given me your word: the wedding's to-morrow.'

'No, that it won't be! Enough of that, Vassily Ivanovitch. I say again, what do you take me for? You do me too much honour. I'm humbly obliged. Excuse me.'

'As you please!' retorted Vassily. 'Get your sword.'

'Sword... what for?'

'What for?... I'll show you what for.'

Vassily drew out his fine, flexible French sword and bent it a little against the floor.

'You want... to fight... me?'

'Precisely so.'

'But, Vassily Ivanovitch, put yourself in my place! How can I, only think, after what you have just told me.... I'm a man of honour, Vassily Ivanovitch, a nobleman.'

'You're a nobleman, you're a man of honour, so you'll be so good as to fight with me.'

'Vassily Ivanovitch!'

'You are frightened, I think, Mr. Rogatchov.'

'I'm not in the least frightened, Vassily Ivanovitch. You thought you would frighten me, Vassily Ivanovitch. I'll scare him, you thought, he's a coward, and he'll agree to anything directly... No, Vassily Ivanovitch, I am a nobleman as much as you are, though I've not had city breeding, and you won't succeed in frightening me into anything, excuse me.'

'Very good,' retorted Vassily; 'where is your sword then?'

'Eroshka!' shouted Pavel Afanasievitch. A servant came in.

'Get me the sword--there--you know, in the loft... make haste....'

Eroshka went out. Pavel Afanasievitch suddenly became exceedingly pale, hurriedly took off his dressing-gown, put on a reddish coat with big paste buttons... twisted a cravat round his neck... Vassily looked at him, and twiddled the fingers of his right hand.

'Well, are we to fight then, Pavel Afanasievitch?'

'Let's fight, if we must fight,' replied Rogatchov, and hurriedly buttoned up his shirt.

'Ay, Pavel Afanasievitch, you take my advice, marry her... what is it to you... And believe me, I'll...'

'No, Vassily Ivanovitch,' Rogatchov interrupted him. 'You'll kill me or maim me, I know, but I'm not going to lose my honour; if I'm to die then I must die.'

Eroshka came in, and trembling, gave Rogatchov a wretched old sword in a torn leather scabbard. In those days all noblemen wore swords with powder, but in the steppes they only put on powder twice a year. Eroshka moved away to the door and burst out crying. Pavel Afanasievitch pushed him out of the room.

'But, Vassily Ivanovitch,' he observed with some embarrassment, 'I can't fight with you on the spot: allow me to put off our duel till to-morrow. My father is not at home, and it would be as well for me to put my affairs in order to--to be ready for anything.'

'I see you're beginning to feel frightened again, sir.'

'No, no, Vassily Ivanovitch; but consider yourself...'

'Listen!' shouted Lutchinov, 'you drive me out of patience.... Either give me your word to marry her at once, or fight...or I'll thrash you with my cane like a coward,--do you understand?'

'Come into the garden,' Rogatchov answered through his teeth.

But all at once the door opened, and the old nurse, Efimovna, utterly distracted, broke into the room, fell on her knees before Rogatchov, and clasped his legs....

'My little master!' she wailed, 'my nursling... what is it you are about? Will you be the death of us poor wretches, your honour? Sure, he'll kill you, darling! Only you say the word, you say the word, and we'll make an end of him, the insolent fellow.... Pavel Afanasievitch, my baby-boy, for the love of God!'

A number of pale, excited faces showed in the door...there was even the red beard of the village elder...

'Let me go, Efimovna, let me go!' muttered Rogatchov.

'I won't, my own, I won't. What are you about, sir, what are you about? What'll Afanasey Lukitch say? Why, he'll drive us all out of the light of day.... Why are you fellows standing still? Take the uninvited guest in hand and show him out of the house, so that not a trace be left of him.'

'Rogatchov!' Vassily Ivanovitch shouted menacingly.

'You are crazy, Efimovna, you are shaming me, come, come...' said Pavel Afanasievitch. 'Go away, go away, in God's name, and you others, off with you, do you hear?...'

Vassily Ivanovitch moved swiftly to the open window, took out a small silver whistle, blew lightly... Bourcier answered from close by. Lutchinov turned at once to Pavel Afanasievitch.

'What's to be the end of this farce?'

'Vassily Ivanovitch, I will come to you to-morrow. What can I do with this crazy old woman?...'

'Oh, I see it's no good wasting words on you,' said Vassily, and he swiftly raised his cane...

Pavel Afanasievitch broke loose, pushed Efimovna away, snatched up the sword, and rushed through another door into the garden.

Vassily dashed after him. They ran into a wooden summerhouse, painted cunningly after the Chinese fashion, shut themselves in, and drew their swords. Rogatchov had once taken lessons in fencing, but now he was scarcely capable of drawing a sword properly. The blades crossed. Vassily was obviously playing with Rogatchov's sword. Pavel Afanasievitch was breathless and pale, and gazed in consternation into Lutchinov's face.

Meanwhile, screams were heard in the garden; a crowd of people were running to the summerhouse. Suddenly Rogatchov heard the heart-rending wail of old age... he recognised the voice of his father. Afanasey Lukitch, bare-headed, with dishevelled hair, was running in front of them all, frantically waving his hands....

With a violent and unexpected turn of the blade Vassily sent the sword flying out of Pavel Afanasievitch's hand.

'Marry her, my boy,' he said to him: 'give over this foolery!'

'I won't marry her,' whispered Rogatchov, and he shut his eyes, and shook all over.

Afanasey Lukitch began banging at the door of the summerhouse.

'You won't?' shouted Vassily.

Rogatchov shook his head.

'Well, damn you, then!'

Poor Pavel Afanasievitch fell dead: Lutchinov's sword stabbed him to the heart... The door gave way; old Rogatchov burst into the summerhouse, but Vassily had already jumped out of window...

Two hours later he went into Olga Ivanovna's room... She rushed in terror to meet him... He bowed to her in silence; took out his sword and pierced Pavel Afanasievitch's portrait in the place of the heart. Olga shrieked and fell unconscious on the floor... Vassily went in to Anna Pavlovna. He found her in the oratory. 'Mother,' said he, 'we are avenged.' The poor old woman shuddered and went on praying.

Within a week Vassily had returned to Petersburg, and two years later he came back stricken with paralysis--tongue-tied. He found neither Anna Pavlovna nor Olga living, and soon after died himself in the arms of Yuditch, who fed him like a child, and was the only one who could understand his incoherent stuttering.

1846.

ENOUGH

A FRAGMENT FROM THE NOTE-BOOK OF A DEAD ARTIST

I

II

III

'Enough,' I said to myself as I moved with lagging steps over the steep mountainside down to the quiet little brook. 'Enough,' I said again, as I drank in the resinous fragrance of the pinewood, strong and pungent in the freshness of falling evening. 'Enough,' I said once more, as I sat on the mossy mound above the little brook and gazed into its dark, lingering waters, over which the sturdy reeds thrust up their pale green blades.... 'Enough.'

No more struggle, no more strain, time to draw in, time to keep firm hold of the head and to bid the heart be silent. No more to brood over the voluptuous sweetness of vague, seductive ecstasy, no more to run after each fresh form of beauty, no more to hang over every tremour of her delicate, strong wings.

All has been felt, all has been gone through... I am weary. What to me now that at this moment, larger, fiercer than ever, the sunset floods the heavens as though aflame with some triumphant passion? What to me that, amid the soft peace and glow of evening, suddenly, two paces hence, hidden in a thick bush's dewy stillness, a nightingale has sung his heart out in notes magical as though no nightingale had been on earth before him, and he first sang the first song of first love? All this was, has been, has been again, and is a thousand times repeated--and to think that it will last on so to all eternity--as though decreed, ordained--it stirs one's wrath! Yes... wrath!

IV

Ah, I am grown old! Such thoughts would never have come to me once--in those happy days of old, when I too was aflame like the sunset and my heart sang like the nightingale.

There is no hiding it--everything has faded about me, all life has paled. The light that gives life's colours depth and meaning--the light that comes out of the heart of man--is dead within me.... No, not dead yet--it feebly smoulders on, giving no light, no warmth.

Once, late in the night in Moscow, I remember I went up to the grating window of an old church, and leaned against the faulty pane. It was dark under the low arched roof--a forgotten lamp shed a dull red light upon the ancient picture; dimly could be discerned the lips only of the sacred face--stern and sorrowful. The sullen darkness gathered about it, ready it seemed to crush under its dead weight the feeble ray of impotent light.... Such now in my heart is the light; and such the darkness.

V

And this I write to thee, to thee, my one never forgotten friend, to thee, my dear companion, whom I have left for ever, but shall not cease to love till my life's end.... Alas! thou knowest what parted us. But that I have no wish to speak of now. I have left thee... but even here, in these wilds, in this far-off exile, I am all filled through and through with thee; as of old I am in thy power, as of old I feel the sweet burden of thy hand on my bent head!

For the last time I drag myself from out the grave of silence in which I am lying now. I turn a brief and softened gaze on all my past... our past.... No hope and no return; but no bitterness is in my heart and no regret, and clearer than the blue of heaven, purer than the first snow on mountain tops, fair memories rise up before me like the forms of departed gods.... They come, not thronging in crowds, in slow procession they follow one another like those draped Athenian figures we admired so much--dost thou remember?--in the ancient bas-reliefs in the Vatican.

VI

I have spoken of the light that comes from the heart of man, and sheds brightness on all around him... I long to talk with thee of the time when in my heart too that light burned bright with blessing... Listen... and I will fancy thee sitting before me, gazing up at me with those eyes--so fond yet stern almost in their intentness. O eyes, never to be forgotten! On whom are they fastened now? Who folds in his heart thy glance--that glance that seems to flow from depths unknown even as mysterious springs--like ye, both clear and dark--that gush out into some narrow, deep ravine under the frowning cliffs.... Listen.

VII

It was at the end of March before Annunciation, soon after I had seen thee for the first time and--not yet dreaming of what thou wouldst be to me--already, silently, secretly, I bore thee in my heart. I chanced to cross one of the great rivers of Russia. The ice had not yet broken up, but looked swollen and dark; it was the fourth day of thaw. The snow was melting everywhere--steadily but slowly; there was the running of water on all sides; a noiseless wind strayed in the soft air. Earth and sky alike were steeped in one unvarying milky hue; there was not fog nor was there light; not one object stood out clear in the general whiteness, everything looked both close and indistinct. I left my cart far behind and walked swiftly over the ice of the river, and except the muffled thud of my own steps heard not a sound. I went on enfolded on all sides by the first breath, the first thrill, of early spring... and gradually gaining force with every step, with every movement forwards, a glad tremour sprang up and grew, all uncomprehended within me... it drew me on, it hastened me, and so strong was the flood of gladness within me, that I stood still at last and with questioning eyes looked round me, as I would seek some outer cause of my mood of rapture.... All was soft, white, slumbering, but I lifted my eyes; high in the heavens floated a flock of birds flying back to us.... 'Spring! welcome spring!' I shouted aloud: 'welcome, life and love and happiness!' And at that instance, with sweetly troubling shock, suddenly like a cactus flower thy image blossomed aflame within me, blossomed and grew, bewilderingly fair and radiant, and I knew that I love thee, thee only--that I am all filled full of thee....

VIII

I think of thee... and many other memories, other pictures float before me with thee everywhere, at every turn of my life I meet thee. Now an old Russian garden rises up before me on the slope of a hillside, lighted up by the last rays of the summer sun. Behind the silver poplars peeps out the wooden roof of the manor-house with a thin curl of reddish smoke above the white chimney, and in the fence a little gate stands just ajar, as though some one had drawn it to with faltering hand; and I stand and wait and gaze at that gate and the sand of the garden path--wonder and rapture in my heart. All that I behold seems new and different; over all a breath of some glad, brooding mystery, and already I catch the swift rustle of steps, and I stand intent and alert as a bird with wings folded ready to take flight anew, and my heart burns and shudders in joyous dread before the approaching, the alighting rapture....

IX

Then I see an ancient cathedral in a beautiful, far-off land. In rows kneel the close packed people; a breath of prayerful chill, of something grave and melancholy is wafted from the high, bare roof, from the huge, branching columns. Thou standest at my side, mute, apart, as though knowing me not. Each fold of thy dark cloak hangs motionless as carved in stone. Motionless, too, lie the bright patches cast by the stained windows at thy feet on the worn flags. And lo, violently thrilling the incense-clouded air, thrilling us within, rolled out the mighty flood of the organ's notes... and I saw thee paler, rigid--thy glance caressed me, glided higher and rose heavenwards--while to me it seemed none but an immortal soul could look so, with such eyes...

X

Another picture comes back to me.

No old-world temple subdues us with its stern magnificence; the low walls of a little snug room shut us off from the whole world. What am I saying? We are alone, alone in the whole world; except us two there is nothing living--outside these friendly walls darkness and death and emptiness... It is not the wind that howls without, not the rain streaming in floods; without, Chaos wails and moans, his sightless eyes are weeping. But with us all is peaceful and light and warm and welcoming; something droll, something of childish innocence, like a butterfly-- isn't it so?--flutters about us. We nestle close to one another, we lean our heads together and both read a favourite book. I feel the delicate vein beating in thy soft forehead; I hear that thou livest, thou hearest that I am living, thy smile is born on my face before it is on thine, thou makest mute answer to my mute question, thy thoughts, my thoughts are like the two wings of one bird, lost in the infinite blue... the last barriers have fallen--and so soothed, so deepened is our love, so utterly has all apartness vanished that we have no need for word or look to pass between us.... Only to breathe, to breathe together is all we want, to be together and scarcely to be conscious that we are together....

XI

Or last of all, there comes before me that bright September when we walked through the deserted, still flowering garden of a forsaken palace on the bank of a great river--not Russian--under the soft brilliance of the cloudless sky. Oh, how put into words what we felt! The endlessly flowing river, the solitude and peace and bliss, and a kind of voluptuous melancholy, and the thrill of rapture, the unfamiliar monotonous town, the autumn cries of the jackdaws in the high sun-lit treetops, and the tender words and smiles and looks, long, soft, piercing to the very in-most soul, and the beauty, beauty in our lives, about us, on all sides--it is above words. Oh, the bench on which we sat in silence with heads bowed down under the weight of feeling--I cannot forget it till the hour I die! How delicious were those few strangers passing us with brief greetings and kind faces, and the great quiet boats floating by (in one--dost thou remember?--stood a horse pensively gazing at the gliding water), the baby prattle of the tiny ripples by the bank, and the very bark of the distant dogs across the water, the very shouts of the fat officer drilling the red-faced recruits yonder, with outspread arms and knees crooked like grasshoppers!... We both felt that better than those moments nothing in the world had been or would be for us, that all else... But why compare? Enough... enough... Alas! yes: enough.

XII

For the last time I give myself up to those memories and bid them farewell for ever. So a miser gloating over his hoard, his gold, his bright treasure, covers it over in the damp, grey earth; so the wick of a smouldering lamp flickers up in a last bright flare and sinks into cold ash. The wild creature has peeped out from its hole for the last time at the velvet grass, the sweet sun, the blue, kindly waters, and has huddled back into the depths, curled up, and gone to sleep. Will he have glimpses even in sleep of the sweet sun and the grass and the blue kindly water?...

XIII

Sternly, remorselessly, fate leads each of us, and only at the first, absorbed in details of all sorts, in trifles, in ourselves, we are not aware of her harsh hand. While one can be deceived and has no shame in lying, one can live and there is no shame in hoping. Truth, not the full truth, of that, indeed, we cannot speak, but even that little we can reach locks up our lips at once, ties our hands, leads us to 'the No.' Then one way is left a man to keep his feet, not to fall to pieces, not to sink into the mire of self-forgetfulness... of self-contempt,--calmly to turn away from all, to say 'enough!' and folding impotent arms upon the empty breast, to save the last, the sole honour he can attain to, the dignity of knowing his own nothingness; that dignity at which Pascal hints when calling man a thinking reed he says that if the whole universe crushed him, he, that reed, would be higher than the universe, because he would know it was crushing him, and it would know it not. A poor dignity! A sorry consolation! Try your utmost to be penetrated by it, to have faith in it, you, whoever you may be, my poor brother, and there's no refuting those words of menace:

'Life's but a walking shadow, a poor player,
That struts and frets his hour upon the stage
And then is heard no more: it is a tale
Told by an idiot, full of sound and fury
Signifying nothing.'

I quoted these lines from **Macbeth**, and there came back to my mind the witches, phantoms, apparitions.... Alas! no ghosts, no fantastic, unearthly powers are terrible; there are no terrors in the Hoffmann world, in whatever form it appears.... What is terrible is that there is nothing terrible, that the very essence of life is petty, uninteresting and degradingly inane. Once one is soaked through and through with that knowledge, once one has tasted of that bitter, no honey more seems sweet, and even the highest, sweetest bliss, the bliss of love, of perfect nearness, of complete devotion--even that loses all its magic; all its dignity is destroyed by its own pettiness, its brevity. Yes; a man loved, glowed with passion, murmured of eternal bliss, of undying raptures, and lo, no trace is left of the very worm that devoured the last relic of his withered tongue. So, on a frosty day in late autumn, when all is lifeless and dumb in the bleached grey grass, on the bare forest edge, if the sun but come out for an instant from the fog and turn one steady glance on the frozen earth, at once the gnats swarm up on all sides; they sport in the warm rays, bustle, flutter up and down, circle round one another... The sun is hidden--the gnats fall in a feeble shower, and there is the end of their momentary life.

XIV

But are there no great conceptions, no great words of consolation: patriotism, right, freedom, humanity, art? Yes; those words there are, and many men live by them and for them. And yet it seems to me that if Shakespeare could be born again he would have no cause to retract his Hamlet, his Lear. His searching glance would discover nothing new in human life: still the same motley picture--in reality so little complex--would unroll before him in its terrifying sameness. The same credulity and the same cruelty, the same lust of blood, of gold, of filth, the same vulgar pleasures, the same senseless sufferings in the name... why, in the name of the very same shams that Aristophanes jeered at two thousand years ago, the same coarse snares in which the many-headed beast, the multitude, is caught so easily, the same workings of power, the same traditions of slavishness, the same innateness of falsehood--in a word, the same busy squirrel's turning in the same old unchanged wheel.... Again Shakespeare would set Lear repeating his cruel: 'None doth offend,' which in other words means: 'None is without offence.' and he too would say 'enough!' he too would turn away. One thing perhaps, may be: in contrast to the gloomy tragic tyrant Richard, the great poet's ironic genius would want to paint a newer type, the tyrant of to-day, who is almost ready to believe in his own virtue, and sleeps well of nights, or finds fault with too sumptuous a dinner at the very time when his half-crushed victims try to find comfort in picturing him, like Richard, haunted by the phantoms of those he has ruined...

But to what end?

Why prove--picking out, too, and weighing words, smoothing and rounding off phrases--why prove to gnats that they are really gnats?

XV

But art?... beauty?... Yes, these are words of power; they are more powerful, may be, than those I have spoken before. Venus of Milo is, may be, more real than Roman law or the principles of 1789. It may be objected--how many times has the retort been heard!--that beauty itself is relative; that by the Chinese it is conceived as quite other than the European's ideal.... But it is not the relativity of art confounds me; its transitoriness, again its brevity, its dust and ashes--that is what robs me of faith and courage. Art at a given moment is more powerful, may be, than nature; for in nature is no symphony of Beethoven, no picture of Ruysdael, no poem of Goethe, and only dull-witted pedants or disingenuous chatterers can yet maintain that art is the imitation of nature. But at the end of all, nature is inexorable; she has no need to hurry, and sooner or later she takes her own. Unconsciously and inflexibly obedient to laws, she knows not art, as she knows not freedom, as she knows not good; from all ages moving, from all ages changing, she suffers nothing immortal, nothing unchanging.... Man is her child; but man's work--art--is hostile to her, just because it strives to be unchanging and immortal. Man is the child of nature; but she is the universal mother, and she has no preferences; all that exists in her lap has arisen only at the cost of something else, and must in its time yield its place to something else. She creates destroying, and she cares not whether she creates or she destroys--so long as life be not exterminated, so long as death fall not short of his dues.... And so just as serenely she hides in mould the god-like shape of Phidias's Zeus as the simplest pebble, and gives the vile worm for food the priceless verse of Sophokles. Mankind, 'tis true, jealously aid her in her work of of slaughter; but is it not the same elemental force, the force of nature, that finds vent in the fist of the barbarian recklessly smashing the radiant brow of Apollo, in the savage yells with which he casts in the fire the picture of Apelles? How are we, poor folks, poor artists to be a match for this deaf, dumb, blind force who triumphs not even in her conquests, but goes onward, onward, devouring all things? How stand against those coarse and mighty waves, endlessly, unceasingly moving upward? How have faith in the value and dignity of the fleeting images, that in the dark, on the edge of the abyss, we shape out of dust for an instant?

XVI

All this is true,... but only the transient is beautiful, said Schiller; and nature in the incessant play of her rising, vanishing forms is not averse to beauty. Does not she carefully deck the most fleeting of her children--the petals of the flowers, the wings of the butterfly--in the fairest hues, does she not give them the most exquisite lines? Beauty needs not to live for ever to be eternal--one instant is enough for her. Yes; that may be is true--but only there where personality is not, where man is not, where freedom is not; the butterfly's wing spoiled appears again and again for a thousand years as the same wing of the same butterfly; there sternly, fairly, impersonally necessity completes her circle... but man is not repeated like the butterfly, and the work of his hands, his art, his spontaneous creation once destroyed is lost for ever.... To him alone is it vouchsafed to create... but strange and dreadful it is to pronounce: we are creators... for one hour--as there was, in the tale, a caliph for an hour. In this is our pre-eminence--and our curse; each of those 'creators' himself, even he and no other, even this *I* is, as it were, constructed with certain aim, on lines laid down beforehand; each more or less dimly is aware of his significance, is aware that he is innately something noble, eternal--and lives, and must live in the moment and for the moment.[2] Sit in the mud, my friend, and aspire to the skies! The greatest among us are just those who more deeply than all others have felt this rooted contradiction; though if so, it may be asked, can such words be used as greatest, great?

---

2   One cannot help recalling here Mephistopheles's words to Faust:--
     'Er (Gott) findet sich in einem ewgen Glanze,
     Uns hat er in die Finsterniss gebracht--
     Und euch taugt einzig Tag und Nacht.'
     --AUTHOR'S NOTE.

XVII

What is to be said of those to whom, with all goodwill, one cannot apply such terms, even in the sense given them by the feeble tongue of man? What can one say of the ordinary, common, second-rate, third-rate toilers--whatsoever they may be--statesmen, men of science, artists--above all, artists? How conjure them to shake off their numb indolence, their weary stupor, how draw them back to the field of battle, if once the conception has stolen into their brains of the nullity of everything human, of every sort of effort that sets before itself a higher aim than the mere winning of bread? By what crowns can they be lured for whom laurels and thorns alike are valueless? For what end will they again face the laughter of 'the unfeeling crowd' or 'the judgment of the fool'--of the old fool who cannot forgive them from turning away from the old bogies--of the young fool who would force them to kneel with him, to grovel with him before the new, lately discovered idols? Why should they go back again into that jostling crowd of phantoms, to that marketplace where seller and buyer cheat each other alike, where is noise and clamour, and all is paltry and worthless? Why 'with impotence in their bones' should they struggle back into that world where the peoples, like peasant boys on a holiday, are tussling in the mire for handfuls of empty nutshells, or gape in open-mouthed adoration before sorry tinsel-decked pictures, into that world where only that is living which has no right to live, and each, stifling self with his own shouting, hurries feverishly to an unknown, uncomprehended goal? No... no.... Enough... enough... enough!

XVIII

...The rest is silence.[3]

1864.

---

3   English in the original.--TRANSLATOR'S NOTE.

The Codes Of Hammurabi And Moses
W. W. Davies

QTY

The discovery of the Hammurabi Code is one of the greatest achievements of archaeology, and is of paramount interest, not only to the student of the Bible, but also to all those interested in ancient history...

Religion   **ISBN:** *1-59462-338-4*   Pages:132
MSRP $12.95

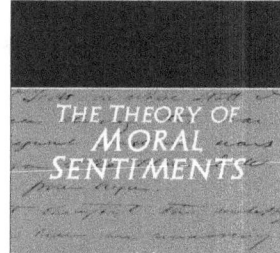

The Theory of Moral Sentiments
Adam Smith

QTY

This work from 1749. contains original theories of conscience amd moral judgment and it is the foundation for systemof morals.

Philosophy ISBN: *1-59462-777-0*   Pages:536
MSRP $19.95

Jessica's First Prayer
Hesba Stretton

QTY

In a screened and secluded corner of one of the many railway-bridges which span the streets of London there could be seen a few years ago, from five o'clock every morning until half past eight, a tidily set-out coffee-stall, consisting of a trestle and board, upon which stood two large tin cans, with a small fire of charcoal burning under each so as to keep the coffee boiling during the early hours of the morning when the work-people were thronging into the city on their way to their daily toil...

Childrens   ISBN: *1-59462-373-2*   Pages:84
MSRP $9.95

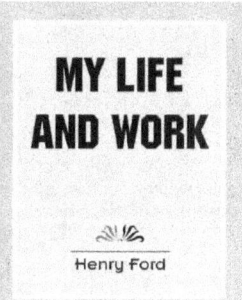

My Life and Work
Henry Ford

QTY

Henry Ford revolutionized the world with his implementation of mass production for the Model T automobile. Gain valuable business insight into his life and work with his own auto-biography... "We have only started on our development of our country we have not as yet, with all our talk of wonderful progress, done more than scratch the surface. The progress has been wonderful enough but..."

Biographies/   ISBN: *1-59462-198-5*   Pages:300
MSRP $21.95

www.bookjungle.com *email: sales@bookjungle.com fax: 630-214-0564 mail: Book Jungle PO Box 2226 Champaign, IL 61825*

The Art of Cross-Examination
Francis Wellman

QTY

I presume it is the experience of every author, after his first book is published upon an important subject, to be almost overwhelmed with a wealth of ideas and illustrations which could readily have been included in his book, and which to his own mind, at least, seem to make a second edition inevitable. Such certainly was the case with me; and when the first edition had reached its sixth impression in five months, I rejoiced to learn that it seemed to my publishers that the book had met with a sufficiently favorable reception to justify a second and considerably enlarged edition. ..

Reference   **ISBN: *1-59462-647-2***   **Pages:412**

MSRP $19.95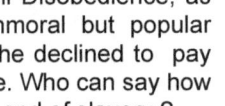

On the Duty of Civil Disobedience
Henry David Thoreau

QTY

Thoreau wrote his famous essay, On the Duty of Civil Disobedience, as a protest against an unjust but popular war and the immoral but popular institution of slave-owning. He did more than write—he declined to pay his taxes, and was hauled off to gaol in consequence. Who can say how much this refusal of his hastened the end of the war and of slavery ?

Law   **ISBN: *1-59462-747-9***   **Pages:48**

MSRP $7.45

Dream Psychology Psychoanalysis for Beginners
Sigmund Freud

QTY

Sigmund Freud, born Sigismund Schlomo Freud (May 6, 1856 - September 23, 1939), was a Jewish-Austrian neurologist and psychiatrist who co-founded the psychoanalytic school of psychology. Freud is best known for his theories of the unconscious mind, especially involving the mechanism of repression; his redefinition of sexual desire as mobile and directed towards a wide variety of objects; and his therapeutic techniques, especially his understanding of transference in the therapeutic relationship and the presumed value of dreams as sources of insight into unconscious desires.

Psychology   **ISBN: *1-59462-905-6***   **Pages:196**

MSRP $15.45

The Miracle of Right Thought
Orison Swett Marden

QTY

Believe with all of your heart that you will do what you were made to do. When the mind has once formed the habit of holding cheerful, happy, prosperous pictures, it will not be easy to form the opposite habit. It does not matter how improbable or how far away this realization may see, or how dark the prospects may be, if we visualize them as best we can, as vividly as possible, hold tenaciously to them and vigorously struggle to attain them, they will gradually become actualized, realized in the life. But a desire, a longing without endeavor, a yearning abandoned or held indifferently will vanish without realization.

Self Help   **ISBN: *1-59462-644-8***   **Pages:360**

MSRP $25.45

www.bookjungle.com *email: sales@bookjungle.com fax: 630-214-0564 mail: Book Jungle PO Box 2226 Champaign, IL 61825*

QTY

☐ **The Rosicrucian Cosmo-Conception Mystic Christianity** *by Max Heindel*   ISBN: *1-59462-188-8*   **$38.95**
The Rosicrucian Cosmo-conception is not dogmatic, neither does it appeal to any other authority than the reason of the student. It is; not controversial, but is; sent forth in the, hope that it may help to clear...   New Age/Religion Pages 646

☐ **Abandonment To Divine Providence** *by Jean-Pierre de Caussade*   ISBN: *1-59462-228-0*   **$25.95**
"The Rev. Jean Pierre de Caussade was one of the most remarkable spiritual writers of the Society of Jesus in France in the 18th Century. His death took place at Toulouse in 1751. His works have gone through many editions and have been republished...   Inspirational/Religion Pages 400

☐ **Mental Chemistry** *by Charles Haanel*   ISBN: *1-59462-192-6*   **$23.95**
Mental Chemistry allows the change of material conditions by combining and appropriately utilizing the power of the mind. Much like applied chemistry creates something new and unique out of careful combinations of chemicals the mastery of mental chemistry...   New Age Pages 354

☐ **The Letters of Robert Browning and Elizabeth Barret Barrett 1845-1846 vol II**   ISBN: *1-59462-193-4*   **$35.95**
by Robert Browning and Elizabeth Barrett   Biographies Pages 596

☐ **Gleanings In Genesis (volume I)** *by Arthur W. Pink*   ISBN: *1-59462-130-6*   **$27.45**
Appropriately has Genesis been termed "the seed plot of the Bible" for in it we have, in germ form, almost all of the great doctrines which are afterwards fully developed in the books of Scripture which follow...   Religion/Inspirational Pages 420

☐ **The Master Key** *by L. W. de Laurence*   ISBN: *1-59462-001-6*   **$30.95**
In no branch of human knowledge has there been a more lively increase of the spirit of research during the past few years than in the study of Psychology, Concentration and Mental Discipline. The requests for authentic lessons in Thought Control, Mental Discipline and...   New Age/Business Pages 422

☐ **The Lesser Key Of Solomon Goetia** *by L. W. de Laurence*   ISBN: *1-59462-092-X*   **$9.95**
This translation of the first book of the "Lemegton" which is now for the first time made accessible to students of Talismanic Magic was done, after careful collation and edition, from numerous Ancient Manuscripts in Hebrew, Latin, and French...   New Age/Occult Pages 92

☐ **Rubaiyat Of Omar Khayyam** *by Edward Fitzgerald*   ISBN:*1-59462-332-5*   **$13.95**
Edward Fitzgerald, whom the world has already learned, in spite of his own efforts to remain within the shadow of anonymity, to look upon as one of the rarest poets of the century, was born at Bredfield, in Suffolk, on the 31st of March, 1809. He was the third son of John Purcell...   Music Pages 172

☐ **Ancient Law** *by Henry Maine*   ISBN: *1-59462-128-4*   **$29.95**
The chief object of the following pages is to indicate some of the earliest ideas of mankind, as they are reflected in Ancient Law, and to point out the relation of those ideas to modern thought.   Religiom/History Pages 452

☐ **Far-Away Stories** *by William J. Locke*   ISBN: *1-59462-129-2*   **$19.45**
"Good wine needs no bush, but a collection of mixed vintages does. And this book is just such a collection. Some of the stories I do not want to remain buried for ever in the museum files of dead magazine-numbers an author's not unpardonable vanity..."   Fiction Pages 272

☐ **Life of David Crockett** *by David Crockett*   ISBN: *1-59462-250-7*   **$27.45**
"Colonel David Crockett was one of the most remarkable men of the times in which he lived. Born in humble life, but gifted with a strong will, an indomitable courage, and unremitting perseverance...   Biographies/New Age Pages 424

☐ **Lip-Reading** *by Edward Nitchie*   ISBN: *1-59462-206-X*   **$25.95**
Edward B. Nitchie, founder of the New York School for the Hard of Hearing, now the Nitchie School of Lip-Reading, Inc, wrote "LIP-READING Principles and Practice". The development and perfecting of this meritorious work on lip-reading was an undertaking...   How-to Pages 400

☐ **A Handbook of Suggestive Therapeutics, Applied Hypnotism, Psychic Science**   ISBN: *1-59462-214-0*   **$24.95**
by Henry Munro   Health/New Age/Health/Self-help Pages 376

☐ **A Doll's House: and Two Other Plays** *by Henrik Ibsen*   ISBN: *1-59462-112-8*   **$19.95**
Henrik Ibsen created this classic when in revolutionary 1848 Rome. Introducing some striking concepts in playwriting for the realist genre, this play has been studied the world over.   Fiction/Classics/Plays 308

☐ **The Light of Asia** *by sir Edwin Arnold*   ISBN: *1-59462-204-3*   **$13.95**
In this poetic masterpiece, Edwin Arnold describes the life and teachings of Buddha. The man who was to become known as Buddha to the world was born as Prince Gautama of India but he rejected the worldly riches and abandoned the reigns of power when...   Religion/History/Biographies Pages 170

☐ **The Complete Works of Guy de Maupassant** *by Guy de Maupassant*   ISBN: *1-59462-157-8*   **$16.95**
"For days and days, nights and nights, I had dreamed of that first kiss which was to consecrate our engagement, and I knew not on what spot I should put my lips..."   Fiction/Classics Pages 240

☐ **The Art of Cross-Examination** *by Francis L. Wellman*   ISBN: *1-59462-309-0*   **$26.95**
Written by a renowned trial lawyer, Wellman imparts his experience and uses case studies to explain how to use psychology to extract desired information through questioning.   How-to/Science/Reference Pages 408

☐ **Answered or Unanswered?** *by Louisa Vaughan*   ISBN: *1-59462-248-5*   **$10.95**
Miracles of Faith in China   Religion Pages 112

☐ **The Edinburgh Lectures on Mental Science (1909)** *by Thomas*   ISBN: *1-59462-008-3*   **$11.95**
This book contains the substance of a course of lectures recently given by the writer in the Queen Street Hail, Edinburgh. Its purpose is to indicate the Natural Principles governing the relation between Mental Action and Material Conditions...   New Age/Psychology Pages 148

☐ **Ayesha** *by H. Rider Haggard*   ISBN: *1-59462-301-5*   **$24.95**
Verily and indeed it is the unexpected that happens! Probably if there was one person upon the earth from whom the Editor of this, and of a certain previous history, did not expect to hear again...   Classics Pages 380

☐ **Ayala's Angel** *by Anthony Trollope*   ISBN: *1-59462-352-X*   **$29.95**
The two girls were both pretty, but Lucy who was twenty-one who supposed to be simple and comparatively unattractive, whereas Ayala was credited, as her Bombwhat romantic name might show, with poetic charm and a taste for romance. Ayala when her father died was nineteen...   Fiction Pages 484

☐ **The American Commonwealth** *by James Bryce*   ISBN: *1-59462-286-8*   **$34.45**
An interpretation of American democratic political theory. It examines political mechanics and society from the perspective of Scotsman James Bryce   Politics Pages 572

☐ **Stories of the Pilgrims** *by Margaret P. Pumphrey*   ISBN: *1-59462-116-0*   **$17.95**
This book explores pilgrims religious oppression in England as well as their escape to Holland and eventual crossing to America on the Mayflower, and their early days in New England...   History Pages 268

QTY

The Fasting Cure by *Sinclair Upton* ISBN: *1-59462-222-1* **$13.95**
In the Cosmopolitan Magazine for May, 1910, and in the Contemporary Review (London) for April, 1910, I published an article dealing with my experiences in fasting. I have written a great many magazine articles, but never one which attracted so much attention... New Age/Self Help/Health Pages 164

Hebrew Astrology by *Sepharial* ISBN: *1-59462-308-2* **$13.45**
In these days of advanced thinking it is a matter of common observation that we have left many of the old landmarks behind and that we are now pressing forward to greater heights and to a wider horizon than that which represented the mind-content of our progenitors... Astrology Pages 144

Thought Vibration or The Law of Attraction in the Thought World ISBN: *1-59462-127-6* **$12.95**
by *William Walker Atkinson* *Psychology/Religion Pages 144*

Optimism by *Helen Keller* ISBN: *1-59462-108-X* **$15.95**
Helen Keller was blind, deaf, and mute since 19 months old, yet famously learned how to overcome these handicaps, communicate with the world, and spread her lectures promoting optimism. An inspiring read for everyone... Biographies/Inspirational Pages 84

Sara Crewe by *Frances Burnett* ISBN: *1-59462-360-0* **$9.45**
In the first place, Miss Minchin lived in London. Her home was a large, dull, tall one, in a large, dull square, where all the houses were alike, and all the sparrows were alike, and where all the door-knockers made the same heavy sound... Childrens/Classic Pages 88

The Autobiography of Benjamin Franklin by *Benjamin Franklin* ISBN: *1-59462-135-7* **$24.95**
The Autobiography of Benjamin Franklin has probably been more extensively read than any other American historical work, and no other book of its kind has had such ups and downs of fortune. Franklin lived for many years in England, where he was agent... Biographies/History Pages 332

Name	
Email	
Telephone	
Address	
City, State ZIP	

☐ **Credit Card**   ☐ **Check / Money Order**

Credit Card Number	
Expiration Date	
Signature	

Please Mail to: Book Jungle
PO Box 2226
Champaign, IL 61825
or Fax to: 630-214-0564

www.ingramcontent.com/pod-product-compliance
Lightning Source LLC
Chambersburg PA
CBHW080729020726
47503CB00010B/2849